The Best Wild Idea

ALSO BY LILY PARKER

OFF-LIMITS SERIES
Book 1: The Best Wrong Move
Book 2: The Best Worst Mistake
Book 3: The Best Wild Idea

The Best Wild Idea

LILY PARKER

Choc Lit, London
A Joffe Books company
www.choc-lit.com

First published in Great Britain in 2025

© Lily Parker

This book is a work of fiction. Names, characters, businesses, organizations, places and events are either the product of the author's imagination or are used fictitiously. Any resemblance to actual persons, living or dead, events or locales is entirely coincidental. The spelling used is American English except where fidelity to the author's rendering of accent or dialect supersedes this. The right of Lily Parker to be identified as author of this work has been asserted in accordance with the Copyright, Designs and Patents Act 1988.

No part of this book may be used or reproduced in any manner for the purpose of training artificial intelligence technologies or systems. In accordance with Article 4(3) of the Digital Single Market Directive 2019/790, Joffe Books expressly reserves this work from the text and data mining exception.

Cover art by Rachel Lawston at Lawston Design

ISBN: 978-1781898581

*To my husband,
for never failing to love the journey.
This one's for you, babe.*

PROLOGUE

Juliet

I'm panting by the time I trudge over the last sand-covered dune, emerging from a different spot than where I walked a few moments ago. It's our last night here, and I was the one who forgot the champagne back at the rental. But now that I've retrieved it, the chilled bubbly will go perfectly with the heat of our bonfire — if I can figure out which direction I left the two guys I'm here with.

I look both ways, finally spotting the familiar broad-shouldered silhouettes. They're sitting in a pair of Adirondack chairs, nearly hidden behind long strands of beach grass waving in the breeze.

They look like a postcard, their backs to me, facing out toward the water, and I grin, letting my feet sink into the sand while I watch them.

Grant and Silas stare out to the waves as they talk, bathed in a canvas of orange and rose gold hues. The warmth of the day is slowly disappearing above us as light bounces and churns off the Atlantic surf. Likely still frigid from the colder-than-usual spring we've had this year without a chance to warm yet beneath a summer sun.

Silas' laugh carries with the breeze to me, followed by Grant's. It's the soundtrack of our last four years at Harvard together, and one I can't imagine ending quite yet. But that's why we're here: to bookmark the end of one thing and the beginning of another.

It's our first and probably only time staying at this Cape Cod bungalow. Grant's parents had surprised the three of us with the reservation before we collected our diplomas in Cambridge outside Boston a few days ago.

I bite back a wave of nostalgia and absorb the moment I'm in now like a sponge. It'll be our last time the three of us will be together for a while and I already miss everything about it, even though I'm still standing right here. Bottle in hand.

Silas says something I can't hear in the wind while Grant nods and chuckles beside him. Then he reaches over to pat Grant on the shoulder. Grant returns the gesture so their arms stretch across the sand between them for a moment. They smile at each other, the wind whipping their hair.

My grin widens and I wonder when they'll notice that I'm only a few yards behind them.

Both drop their arms and gaze at the sea, settling into the comfortable silence that comes with a friendship nearly as old as they are.

What will Grant do without his best friend after we all part ways? I already promised myself I wouldn't cry again this weekend. But it feels like the end of an era before the final push of adulthood rushes in like the tide first thing tomorrow.

When we get back to Boston, Silas will use his father's jet to take him to Amsterdam, where he'll begin a solo backpacking trip through Europe. He'll start in Switzerland, then go wherever the wind blows him after that, I suppose. He's the only one of us who doesn't have to worry about starting his career right after graduation. I know his father would prefer that he take a different path, one that looks very similar to his own. But much to Silas' surprise, his dad hasn't insisted on him starting work yet and has given Si at least a year to do what he wants. Maybe more, we'll see.

Speaking of, Silas must feel me watching them because he suddenly turns around. His face lights up when he sees me and we grin at each other. I hold up the bottle I've just grabbed from the fridge at the house.

He nudges Grant's shoulder, and Grant turns around then stands to move the third chair in the group closer to his side before I reach them.

The sand is deep and I kick off my sandals when I get there. It's cold but soft and damp between my toes. I curl up in the chair and tuck my feet beneath me.

"A sight for sore eyes," Si says, pointing at the champagne bottle. He stands to take it from me while I settle in next to Grant. "I was ready to send out a search party."

Grant squeezes my knee and laughs. "I told him you were probably just enjoying some alone time — without this goon around to bother you." He points at Silas.

I laugh and Silas smirks while unwrapping the neck of the bottle.

"Hardly," he mumbles, but his voice carries off in the breeze. He's about to start working the cork out when he turns to me. "Glasses?"

I gasp and cover my eyes. "Shit."

They both chuckle.

"You forgot the glasses," Grant confirms, already knowing my answer.

I lean over to kiss him. "You're more than welcome to go grab some if you'd like, my love. I just got my cardio in for the day by running back there, thanks." My hair flies around my head and a long strand catches between our lips.

When we break apart, Silas is facing the ocean, poised to push the cork out of the bottle with the neck pointed up toward the sky. He glances over his shoulder.

"Fuck it, Jules," he says. "We don't need glasses. You're fine. Thanks for grabbing this. We'll manage without."

I smile then raise my brows at Grant as if to say, *See? We don't need 'em.*

I'm on the verge of giving Grant a victory peck when the cork shoots out and we each give a little cheer. A decent volcano of fizz erupts but settles quickly enough, thank God. I'm not about to make the trek back to fetch another if this one spills any more.

Si hands the bottle to me without taking any for himself.

"You put the work in so you get the first sip," he tells me. "But there's a catch."

I take the bottle from him and roll my eyes. "Isn't there always a catch with you?"

Grant laughs in agreement. "Always."

But Silas isn't deterred. "This will be our last time together for a while, so—"

"A while? Just how long do you plan to be in Europe?" Grant interrupts. He's been trying to get an answer out of him for a few weeks. The two have been attached at the hip since long before I met them in our freshman year. The stretch of time starting tomorrow might be the longest they've ever been apart.

"Not sure. Six months? A year?" Si puts a hand on his hip. "You're welcome to join me, you know."

Grant's face falls. He and I are driving back to Boston to get our careers started as soon as we leave. Grant's taken a small amount of seed money from his parents to fund the non-profit he's hell-bent on starting, and my parents don't have the means to support a single month of me not working. They're supportive, but nowhere near as wealthy as Grant's and Si's families, so my new job in HR starts on Monday.

"What's the catch?" I ask, hoping whatever game Silas wants to play will keep our spirits high.

"The catch is, you have to say your favorite memory that involves all three of us, and then follow it up with where you see yourself in five years *before* taking a drink."

I groan but secretly enjoy the idea. I love when Silas gets a little sappy since it happens so rarely.

Grant nods, and I know he's game because he's always up for anything. It's one of the many things I love about him.

"Do I have to go first?" I ask, searching my mind for the perfect memory out of the dozens that surface.

"No, I'll go," Grant offers, reaching toward my lap for the bottle. "I already know mine."

I hand him the champagne while Silas and I go silent, waiting for Grant to woo us with his words. Grant holds the bottle out in front of him like he's about to give a toast.

Silas subtly winks at me, grinning. We both adore Grant's inner sap, never the one to shy away from a nostalgic moment like this.

"My favorite memory has to be meeting you," he says, tipping the neck of the bottle in my direction. I smile, remembering the day I met both of them. Si shifts his gaze out toward the water. "And in five years, I see myself getting engaged," Grant adds. My cheeks flush hot above my collar. I already know that's our plan, but my stomach still does a little flip to hear him say it. "I'll also be running my nonprofit if I can get it off the ground."

"No worries on that, bro." Silas turns to assure him. "It'll be a success."

"It'll be *more* than a success by then," I add. I squeeze Grant's arm before tucking my hand back inside my sweater sleeve, trying not to shiver since the sun is well on its way to disappearing now.

Silas must notice because he kneels to grab some of the dry firewood we brought with us from the porch and begins arranging it inside the metal fire pit at our feet.

Grant takes a careful pull from the bottle, keeping the fizzy liquid from spilling over the top. Then he holds it out to Silas.

"Jules next," Si directs, then lights one of the long matches before holding it at the base of the wood pyramid he's just built. The kindling catches and a tiny flame appears inside the splintered pile. "Give it another minute and we'll all be backing up from this thing."

"I hope so," I mumble, willing the flame to grow.

I take the bottle from Grant. It's still cold from the fridge and a slight shiver races up my spine, but I'm not sure if it's from the early evening air or the moment we're here sharing.

"Okay." I sigh, glancing between them. My eyes suddenly disobey the little pep talk I gave them earlier and I blink a few times, trying not to let any more emotion spring to the surface right now. "Ugh, why'd you have to pick this type of game, Si?"

I laugh through a frown, blinking a few more times in an effort to clear my nostalgia all the way out.

He grins before grabbing a stick to tend the flame. "Because I love to keep you guessing, Jules."

"Always," I assure him.

I force the rest of the emotional upheaval away, while using my toe to smush a rock deeper into the sand, thinking of what to say.

"Whenever you're ready," Grant encourages.

Silas tosses another bit of kindling into the metal pit.

I hold the bottle out in front of me, just like Grant did. The fire's flame is already big enough to feel some warmth beneath it.

"Okay, my favorite memory has to be when the two of you showed up in the middle of the night, freshman year, throwing rocks at my window. I still have no idea why you didn't just call my phone to ask me to come down for that meteor shower you were so hell-bent on watching."

"Because throwing rocks is so much more romantic," Si jokes, grinning slyly at Grant.

Grant joins in, amused. "More like, we didn't want to wake Molly up."

"Trust me, the rocks you threw at our window did not stop you from waking her up. She was so annoyed."

"Whatever," Silas snickers. "Your roommate loved it."

"Only because she loved *you*," I remind him. Every one of my friends had a crush on Silas during college, but none of them managed to hang on to him for long, including my freshman year roommate, Molly.

"Okay, so getting woken up with rocks was the best time of your life at Harvard. Noted," Si says, sarcastically. "Christ, we should have had more fun."

"No, we had the *most* fun," I insist. "I just loved that it was so random that night. Plus, I'd just met you guys so it seemed all wild and dangerous, sneaking out like that." And it had. It felt like something out of a movie when I went to the window — getting woken up by the two cute guys I'd just befriended in class. We'd sat on the riverbank, watching a meteor shower rain over the Charles until dawn.

"Your turn," I say, offering the bottle to Silas next.

He shakes his head. "You forgot to add where you're going to be in five years."

"Right." I bring it back to my chest. "In five years, I see myself—" I pause to smile at Grant — "living in Boston with you. We have more than one bedroom now because we're a hugely successful couple and are considering a dog but settle on a baby instead." Grant laughs. He knows I can't wait to have a family one day. "And you—" I say, turning to Silas — "you like to come over for Sunday dinners. You're there so much the neighbors think you must be Grant's brother since the two of you are always doing something ridiculous. And we're all happy." I smile at them both. "Like really, really happy. That's all I want."

I tip the bottle up to take a drink but do it too fast and the carbonation erupts straight out the top, splashing across my face.

I jump out of my chair and hold the bottle away, but not before spilling more down the front of my sweater. I begin laughing, using the back of my sleeve to wipe the champagne from my face, half-blinded by the mess.

Both Silas and Grant jump up. Grant looks around for a towel or napkin, even though we all know there aren't any, while Silas takes his jacket off and bends an arm around the fire to hand it to me.

I take it from him.

"Now it's a party," he adds, grinning.

"Do you want to go back to the house to change?" Grant asks, looking around. "I don't have a coat otherwise I'd—"

"I'm fine," I insist, wiping the last bit off my chin. "I hate when I do that with champagne. I swear I forget it's going to happen every single time."

Grant laughs, knowing it's true. He's seen me do that before. "You sure you don't want to go back to the house to change?" he asks, then uses Silas' coat to wipe a stray drop above my eye. "I can run back with you."

"I don't want to make that hike again, plus we'll miss the last bit of the sun." I point toward the sky. It's already turned a deep shade of plum with orange and gray tiger stripes shooting out in all directions. "This coat is great, thanks."

I hand the bottle out to Silas so I can wrap the jacket around myself with both hands. It's still warm from him wearing it and it heats me up immediately when Grant and I sit back down.

Silas stays standing and holds the bottle out in front of him like he's about to make a full-blown speech.

Grant takes my hand and the warmth of it feels perfect right now. I wish we had a double Adirondack couch so I could snuggle into him beside the fire until the stars come out later.

Silas clears his throat.

"Now, I'm going to get real nostalgic here for a minute," he starts. I groan, but my eyes twinkle up at him. "And don't pretend like you don't love it, Jules," he adds, smirking back at me.

Grant snorts and squeezes my hand.

I'm going to miss this. Grant's love and Silas' ridiculous friendship. I'll still have them, of course, but it'll never be the same as it's been with all three of us on the same campus.

Si raises the champagne an inch higher to begin again. "My favorite memory of college was the whole damn thing. You guys know my family is kind of nonexistent to me so you all became my family over the last four years." He clears his throat. "Even longer for you, Grant." He tilts the bottle up to take a pull, I think to distract us from the emotion welling up in his eyes.

"Ah—" I exclaim, pointing at the bottle, and Grant does the same, adding, "Not yet!"

Si takes his time with a long drink, then adds a second, somehow without it all shooting back up at his face when he's done.

"Sorry, kids, my game, my rules." His eyes shine.

"And where on God's green earth do you plan to be in five years?" Grant asks, watching him finish the game.

Silas stares past us and out to the water for a beat, lost in his own thoughts before answering.

"That's a great question." He speaks slowly. "With any luck, I'll be as far away from an office or a desk as I can possibly be. As long as my father hasn't nailed me to one yet."

We each fall silent, knowing the weight of what he'll eventually have on his shoulders one day. How he's watched his own father devote his entire life to eighteen-hour workdays behind a desk. Imagining Silas with a company — an empire, really — of that size under his sole responsibility seems impossible.

He snaps out of it and grins back down at us, shoving the reminder of his inevitable future to the side. "And until then, I'll probably be shacked up in that spare bedroom of yours, unless a couple little ankle-biters kick me out of it. In which case, I'll religiously show up to your Sunday dinners, no matter where I am in the world. Bringing a healthy dose of chaos to your lives whenever Uncle Si comes to town." His eyes shine brighter. "But until then . . ." He holds the bottle up in a silent toast as he trails off, then takes another pull of champagne.

He hands it back to Grant.

"Until then," Grant repeats solemnly, taking the next sip.

He passes it to me next, and I hold it out, nervous to try this for a second time.

"To us," I tell them, rounding out our toast with the real reason why we're all gathered here, adding silently to myself, *To friendship. To love. To the two people I'll never want to live without.* But instead of saying all that out loud, which I know will only bring more emotion than I can handle without welling up again, I say, "And to a lifetime of even better memories ahead."

Then I close my eyes and take the final sip — leaving nothing left to spill out the top when I'm done.

CHAPTER 1

Silas
Seven years later

My body feels like it's vibrating as everything in me screams to turn around.

Just jump off the porch and run before Jules opens the door.

Sure, her doorstep would be empty if I ran now, but a doorbell ditch is probably a more welcome prank than me showing up here unannounced. I'm not exactly on the short list of people she'd like to see right now.

I stare at the little Ring camera mounted on her doorbell.

Fucking hell.

It's too late. She already knows I'm here.

I shift back and forth. One foot to the next. Shocked I'm still standing upright after today. Everything about this feels unreal and wrong, right down to my fingertips that are just as numb as my mind.

I nearly called Grant on my way here, purely out of habit.

Flexing my fist beneath her porch light, I zero in on my right index finger, the one that had hovered over his name in my phone while Patrick drove me here. I'm still wondering how my own hand hasn't caught up to the fact that he's gone, and how long it'll take until the urge to call him disappears.

Never, most likely.

It feels just as surreal now as the day I got the call. Stepping off my plane to get here, to talk through his last wild idea face-to-face, before it was too late. That was the worst day of my life, and I have quite a few to choose from.

Quite a few now, including today.

And today's not over yet.

Not by a long shot.

I stare at the little camera, wondering if she's somewhere inside right now, staring back.

Probably still wearing that black dress she was in earlier today . . .

I look over my shoulder at the idling SUV where my driver Patrick is sitting behind the wheel. His face is illuminated by the exterior lights lining her house. He's already starting to fall asleep. I'm not surprised. It's late and I told him this might take a while.

Or, knowing Jules, this might take all of thirteen seconds. Maybe seven. Probably long enough for her to get a glimpse of me followed by the guy sitting half-asleep behind the wheel, signaling that someone else drove me here. Yeah, I give her about seven seconds before she's shoving me back out toward the car and the driver I *should* have had park around the corner so she couldn't see him. She hates that shit. She hates everything about me now.

I turn to jog off the porch, ready to tell Patrick to park it further down the road, but I stop in my tracks when I hit the last step.

There's a slow creak behind me.

Old wood on metal hinge.

Shit.

I turn around, and freeze.

It's Jules standing in the doorway.

Her silhouette is outlined by the warm yellow glow behind her.

Our eyes meet and her face softens, then instantly morphs into stone. She stands up straighter, wrapping her arms around herself in a hug. She doesn't have to say a word for me to know she's not happy to see me here.

Fucking great.

I'm not happy to be here either, Jules.

I blink, and in the split second it takes to close my eyes, I realize this is the first time in years that I've been alone with just her and not him, too. The unshakable link between us now buried.

I was right about one more thing. She's still wearing that black dress she had on at the funeral today.

His funeral.

My stomach twists like a knife. He was the last of my family, even if it was friendship that bonded us instead of blood.

"Hey, Si," Jules says, blinking her eyes with a sniff, like the light on the porch is too harsh for her mood right now. Her lips and nose are flushed red against the alabaster of her skin. She was crying before I got here. *Of course she's been crying, you asshole.* "What are you doing here?" she asks. There's a bite to her voice.

"Jules." My voice cracks on the *u* as if I'm twelve years old again. A fitting sign of how this is going to go.

More words drain into the back of my throat.

I can't say what I came here to say.

Not when she's looking at me like that.

And not after today.

Before, she would have welcomed me in with a tight hug and a drink, ready to collapse on the couch. Talking for as long as it took for us to unwind everything that happened and all the words that still need to be said. But we both know those days are gone. *Long* gone, if you ask her.

"What is it, Si?" She swallows, like even that's a struggle right now. "Can't it wait until . . . until it's not *today*?"

"Can I come in?"

She doesn't answer. Her arms squeeze tighter across her chest.

I fucking hate this but I press on gently. "For just a few minutes maybe?"

Her jaw clenches, but she swings the door open, stepping to the side so I can pass her on my way in.

She doesn't close the door behind me.

I stand in the foyer, unsure of how to say what I need to say. This all could — *and should* — have waited.

She runs a hand through her hair, and I catch sight of a small crescent of dirt still stuck beneath one of her fingernails. *Jesus Christ.* It's from that handful she tossed onto Grant's grave earlier. Some type of honor or symbol as his fiancée, although watching her do it nearly broke something in me. Probably broke something in everyone who was there. The sound of it hitting that thick wooden box echoes between my ears.

"How are you?" I ask, immediately feeling like an idiot. "Sorry. That was a dumb . . . I mean . . . obviously you're exhausted."

She clears her throat to stop a sarcastic snort, but fails, and we both look down awkwardly. The black heels she was wearing earlier have been swapped out for a pair of fuzzy white slippers with *Bride To Be* spelled out across the toes.

Christ. I swallow a lump in my throat.

"Yeah, but I don't know if *exhausted* is the right word," she admits, then all but adds the word *idiot* at the end with a brow raise. Then she pulls at the neckline of her dress like it's suddenly too tight. "Why are you here, Si?"

Because I seem to be a glutton for self-punishment, I nearly say. *Because even after all the water under the bridge between us, you and I are all that's left, and that has to mean something right now.*

Instead, I take a harsh inhale and mutter, "Fuck it," under my breath. "I know this is probably the worst timing but before I leave town I wanted you to know that I'd be happy to give you, uh, *whatever* you want or need to get through the next year or so. Longer if that's what it takes. Seriously, take as long as necessary to get back on your feet, I won't care. There's more than enough, um . . ." I pause, silently screaming *fuck everything about this moment,* but somehow manage to go on. "Um, there's more than enough. I know we haven't really been in touch much recently, but I just want you to be able to take your time without having to worry about—"

"Are you kidding me right now?" she interrupts. The words fire from her mouth like a cannon — one that was already loaded and ready to take aim. "I don't fucking need your money, Silas, but you never change, do you? Not even . . ." She trails off, shaking her head like my offer revolts her. "You know, when I saw you out there, before I opened the door, I actually thought that maybe, just maybe, the *old* you was showing up. Especially after losing him." She points through the open door to the driveway. "And is that a *fucking driver* out there? Did you take a fucking *driver* to my house tonight?"

I follow her finger to Patrick, who appears to be drooling now behind the wheel.

Shit.

"Jules, you know I didn't come here to offer you money. There's more I have to—"

"Do I know that? Really? Because it sure as shit sounds like that's exactly what you just did."

"Okay, not *only* that."

I take a step toward her, but she matches it with a quicker one back.

Then she tightens her jaw, glaring up at me like she's not afraid to take me on. Jules is a solid twelve inches shorter than me, probably a hundred and twenty pounds soaking wet, and from what I remember, she's pretty damn scrappy.

I stare back, hands splayed by my sides, a white flag on the battlefield.

"Come on," I plead gently, angry with myself for not using my better judgment and getting back in the car when I still had the chance. But that's not what he would have wanted.

I shift back and forth then slip my hands into my pockets, darting my eyes around her foyer for a distraction.

A long table against the wall is covered in a collection of stark white flower arrangements and cards. Roses, daisies, gardenias, and tulips. Some I don't even recognize. Like the whole damn flower shop was ordered to send every variety to her in the same stone-cold hue.

I hadn't sent her any.

It's a shitty trade, if you ask me. A show of support, but a glaring reminder of what — and who — was lost just sitting there, waiting to greet you each morning until they, too, wither up and die.

I would know.

"They forgot the lilies," I tell her, gesturing to the table, rocking back on my heels, wishing I had the good sense to shut up.

"What?" She narrows her eyes at the table of flowers.

"Lilies. They brought every other kind of flower but it looks like . . . they . . ." My mouth goes dry.

She closes her eyes and inhales sharply, tucking her teeth behind her lips as if she's ready to drag me back out to the curb.

"Silas, I really can't do small talk right now."

"Look, I *know* you don't need anything from me, but I would feel like a real ass if I—"

"Got it." She stands taller and crosses her arms the other way, nodding like her head's attached to a spring. "You've done your due diligence now, thank you. Thank you *so, so much*. You've offered me the one thing you have to give. The only thing you've ever had to give, turns out. But, if that's all you came here for, then you can head back out to your *driver*. Poor guy looks like he needs sleep nearly as much as I do. So . . ."

She holds her breath and stares at the wall behind my head. Dismissing me with silence.

I blink, my feet nailed to the floor. I didn't want to come here, but now I don't want to leave.

"I'm selling the building, by the way," she declares suddenly, still avoiding my eyes. "The Smithfield. Unless you want it back. I've already decided."

For the last three years, Grant has been running his nonprofit out of the Smithfield building that I gave him soon after my father died. The Starlight Foundation was in a rough patch at the time, and the building alleviated some of his overhead, allowing him to keep going.

"No, I don't want it back. Sell it if you want. Keep whatever you can get for it."

"I don't *need* the money." She glares at me.

"We don't need to talk business right now, Jules. Just call me in a few days or months, hell, years, if you want to talk about it then."

"I don't need a reason to get in touch unless there's a *reason* you don't want it back?" She tilts her head, studying me.

"It was a gift. I'm not taking it back. It's yours. Do whatever you want with it. I'll help with the sale though, if you need. Dax can take care of it for you."

Her breath picks up, the rise and fall of her chest bordering on panic like she wants to say something else, but her eyes find that empty spot on the wall again. She bites her lip to stop tears from forming.

"Jules," I try again, but she's quick to stop me.

"It's been a fucking long day, Si. Surely you, of all people, can understand how burying the dead just doesn't really put one in the mood to talk *finances*. But you know the worst part of this?" She circles the heavy air between us with her hand. "I thought that maybe you coming here—" Her voice wavers, then her eyes flood.

Fuck.

Just as I'm about to fill the silence — apologize for coming *again*, apologize for more if she'll let me — she beats me to it.

"But no." She throws her hands up. "Here I was, stupid enough to think that my heart couldn't break any more than it already had. And then here you come offering me some cold hard cash tonight — the day I buried him — you arrogant asshole prick of a man."

The day we buried him, Jules. I want to correct her, but I don't.

Her eyes sear mine like she sees straight through me, and I wish she could because then she'd know that none of this was ill-willed between us.

A lone tear slides down her cheek. I pray to God it's the only one, but another one comes.

And another.

Without thinking, I close the gap between us and grab her arms, pulling her into a hug before tucking her head under my chin. Completely aware that I shouldn't be the one hugging her right now, but no one should cry alone. Especially while someone else just stands there watching. Even more so when it's just Jules and me.

For one quick moment, the air dissolves into something more calm and familiar.

Me hugging Jules.

Jules almost hugging me.

Until she starts shoving me.

Hard.

"Silas, I'm fine. Really. I—" She pushes against my chest with fists balled up like battering rams positioned to bring a heavy blow.

I instantly let her go and hold both my palms up in front of me again. We stare at each other, chests heaving from whatever the hell that was.

When did we turn into this? Where I can't even hug her after losing someone?

She shakes her head and runs the dirt-stained fingernails through her hair.

"You've been a real prick, you know? Even before . . ." She pauses, looking startled at the words that should come next. I don't want her to finish that sentence.

"I know," I interrupt. "I wish I could take it all back."

"Plus, just seeing you here reminds me of *us*. The three of us. It's too weird to be standing here with you but not him, too."

"Yeah, I keep wondering when Grant's going to come walking around that corner." I point my thumb down the nearest hallway. Her eyes follow my thumb into the dark, as if my saying it might actually bring him back. "I'm sorry, Jules. I shouldn't have—"

She shrugs, and a shade of anger drains from her face when her shoulders fall.

"I keep feeling the exact same way. Normally, after spending an entire day with a bunch of people, I'd come back to the house and unload the day's worth of gossip to him. Who was arguing with who. Who made a questionable comment about Aunt Rory's dress length. You know, all that family drama that you just store up in your head to come back home to tell your person about. But when I got back to the house today—" Her voice cracks and she stops to collect herself. "When I got back from the funeral, I felt like a dam about to burst because there was no one to talk to. No one to tell how awful it was. This whole stupid house just feels so fucking empty now, you know?"

"Yeah, I do know," I tell her, quietly. Then add, "You can tell *me* about Aunt Rory's dress length and the stupid fights your relatives were getting into if you want. Patrick is already sleeping out there. I can just stay. As long as you want. We can order some takeout if you're hungry, although you're probably not. God, neither am I but—"

I stop talking when the waterworks start streaming down her face. I take the smallest step toward her, not wanting her to shove me away again.

"Can I—" I start to ask if it would be okay to hug her, but she closes the gap this time. Crumbling into my chest. Big, heavy sobs work their way out while her forehead presses into my shoulder.

I close my eyes, wishing more than anything that I could replace my chest with his right now.

Fucking hell.

I wrap an arm around her, testing it out, then the other, more slowly this time, until I've enveloped her frame against me. She leans in more, like she needs me to hold her up, to stop her knees from buckling beneath her. Releasing whatever she's pent up all at once, probably losing sight of the fact that *I'm* the one holding her up at all.

We stand like that until she's ready for me to let her go.

Then she slides out of my arms looking bewildered and spent.

Embarrassed.

Unkempt.

"No," she says, firmly, "I'm going to be fine."

"I know." I start to tell her to just forget what I said earlier. "Unless you really do need anything and then I'm—"

"Oh my God, no!" She throws her hands up. "I'm sorry, I don't think you should be here right now." Then her face twists, dissolving back into anger. "Just go. If Grant knew you were here, offering me your fucking money right now, he'd die."

No, he wouldn't, Jules.

She sniffs, looking painfully aware of the irony tucked inside her words.

But I don't have it in me to argue. "You're right," I say, instead. "Forget it. I'll go. Call me if you change your mind."

She moves toward the door, finding that spot on the wall to focus on again without having to look directly at me, then she pulls the door wider not saying a word.

I step outside before turning back. "One more thing."

Her eyes flick to mine, hope pooling inside them.

I open my mouth, but instead of telling her about everything she has barreling toward her at the end of this year, I don't. Not yet. And not right now.

"Take care of yourself," I say, stepping all the way off the porch.

Her chin quivers and she bites her lip to stop it. "I will."

We both have more to say, clearly, but now is not the time. The door closes with a soft thud.

Slipping my hands into my pockets, I walk to the car still idling in the dark, back to my life that annoys her to no end, and back to a life without him. Knowing damn well that the only thing worse than leaving her to crawl back into that empty house and bed all alone tonight is knowing that I have to come back here one year from now to blow her whole world apart.

All over again.

CHAPTER 2

Juliet
One year later

I debate how harshly to phrase this next tidbit of advice for the man sitting across from me. He keeps glancing over the starchy tablecloth, stretched between us, like he can tell something is off. However, he doesn't stop doing the one thing that's making me want to jump across the table at him — and definitely not in a good way.

I set my fork down beside my plate before narrowing my eyes in his direction.

The sound of his jaw hacking away at that poor wilted salad the waiter set down a few moments ago is damn-near murdering my soul.

Pete has been fairly receptive as far as my coaching clients go, but some habits are nearly impossible to break without a little tough love shoved somewhere in the middle of a coaching session. And, as I love to remind myself before handing a client some prickly advice, it's my job to serve it up in spades. I'm *paid* to improve their dating life, hone their seduction skills for whatever love interest they have at the moment, and, given the fact that he's already a few weeks past the *How to Get (and Keep!) a Second Date* phase of my coaching program, it's time to give it to him straight.

No holding back.

"Pete," I begin.

Pete's soft brown eyes shoot to mine, and for one teensy moment, I'm reminded of the scared look in an antelope's eyes shortly before the lion springs from the bushes in that Animal Planet special. Like the prey somehow sensed the danger coming.

Someone should have taught this poor man how to chew properly.

Today's the day, Pete. Carpe diem.

I take a steady breath to settle the nerves coursing through me, none of which have anything to do with poor Pete here. I shouldn't have scheduled this particular client for today, with all his habitual shark-like mashing of food, but it's too late for that. We're already here. And besides, the torched edges of my nervous system have more to do with today's date on my wall calendar back home and less to do with Pete's chewing.

Today's date.

Ugh.

The memory hits me like an ice bath and my eyes fling open.

"Stop chewing," I suddenly snap. Then I feel bad and throw a bleak smile out to him like a tattered life raft to grab on to before taking him down. He's going to need it, and I'm going to get out of here before I strangle him.

His forkful of lettuce piled with greasy bits of bacon hovers between his elbows. A chunk of it falls to the tablecloth, pooling where it lands.

His jaw halts mid-chew.

I force a tight smile until the urge to mutter *good boy* is gone. Then I use the corner of my napkin to dab at an imaginary spot of dressing on my upper lip, carefully sealing off the valve before all my high-strung annoyance comes spewing out at this poor man.

It's May 17th.

The May 17th.

And after this coaching session is over, I plan to go home, twist the cap off that big red Sharpie sitting on my kitchen counter like I've done every night over this past year, and make one last, final X. Two deep red slashes across today's calendar date.

It'll be the last one before the whole thing goes into the trash. Completing a collection of three hundred and sixty-five identical red Xs.

Then, I'll hang up the new one I bought last week to replace it. A new calendar that won't be covered in a steady pattern of blood-red slashes through each aggravating little box because tomorrow marks the beginning of a clean slate for me — one I both want and hate so much that it hurts. One that is both clean and empty, painful and freeing.

I've earned every one of those red X's by getting through my waking hours with great precision and determination. The strength of which I didn't know I had in me one full year ago. This little ritual started out of survival but turned into a one-dimensional trophy room, showcasing hard-earned victories: days I've spent living without him.

Make it one whole year, I'd told myself after standing beside Grant's graveside, tossing that first handful of dirt onto my fiancé's final resting place. *Keep going through the motions, and when one year has passed, promise yourself to begin again.*

Or, at the very least, *try*.

And now, that day is here.

May 17th.

One horrible year later.

What started out as a crawl has turned into a sprint. A blank page hovering over a new story that I so badly need to read. To know that the pages that follow this year aren't blank at all, but are full of something other than missing him.

I'm in the homestretch.

I force a more gentle smile at Pete before speaking again. "Go ahead and swallow that bite you have in there, and then we'll talk."

Pete's cheeks puff out on either side, smiling as though I've done him a great favor by granting permission to digest the half-chewed mush sitting in the pocket of his jaw. His lips smack a few more times and he swallows the lettuce loudly enough for me to hear it hit the back of his throat before it descends.

Okay.

"Pete. As your dating coach, I'm going to be wildly honest with you here." I lean in closer. He sits taller, and I lower my voice to a dangerous level. "If you chew like that on your upcoming date with Amber, you're not going to get a second chance to impress her. In fact, she might even excuse herself to the restroom after you take your first bite, pretend like she's coming back, then climb out the window above the toilet just to vacate the premises so there's no chance she'll have to listen to you smack your lips for one more tiny, little millisecond. It'll all be over before it can properly begin. Is that what you want?"

Pete's shoulders slump. Even more than usual. Any semblance of excitement that he'd just been expressing to me only a moment ago about his upcoming date with a woman he's been chatting with online drains out of him. Poor, gross-eating Pete suddenly resembles a wounded animal — all dressed in tweed and plaid.

I bite down hard on my lip. That was harsh. Even for me.

"I'm sorry, but we've talked about how eating habits can be a real deal-breaker on a date. Especially on a *first* date. You get caught up in talking and sharing your stories, fine, but you only get *one* first impression. You need to be able to chew *and* converse without repulsing the woman sitting across from you. Wouldn't you agree?"

His eyes drop to the tablecloth and I hope he notices it's splattered with grease only on *his* side of the table.

"Repulsing?" he repeats.

"You've literally paid me to tell you that," I remind him.

He leans back against the booth, then finally cracks a smile. It's sheepish and small, but it's there.

"I didn't even realize I was doing it again," he admits, shrugging, then he drops his fork. Little bits of dressing scatter.

I make eye contact with the waiter when he stoops to refill our waters and gesture a scribbling motion with my hand, signaling that we're ready for the check.

Then I throw back a fresh swig, fantasizing that it's a shot of vodka instead of water from the tap.

Almost there.

"You're right. You're always right, Juuules." He draws my name out like he's just been scolded. Then he chuckles to himself. *Thank God.* The last thing I need right now is a mini tantrum from my last client of the day.

"That's why you hired a dating coach though, right? Smart of you to do that for yourself." I pat his paw-like hand resting beside the half-eaten salad, then flash him a reassuring smile. "You haven't had a second date in two years, ever since Britta broke up with you. Little changes like this are going to help you be more successful in getting that *elusive* second date to prove yourself. Promise."

"That's fair," he answers and we both break into an amused grin. "Thanks for being honest."

"Wouldn't dream of being anything less," I tell him. I pull my hand away, glad he isn't upset, and even more glad that we've finally reached the appropriate time for me to excuse myself from our table.

Not that I'm even remotely interested in Pete — he's nearly twice my age, and after a lifetime of teaching high school math, he's probably more comfortable dining in a sticky cafeteria filled with rowdy teens than a beautifully set table with a woman — but there's nothing more attractive than a man who can make light of his own mistakes. I'm proud of him for being humble enough to take the feedback.

Our waiter drops the check between us, and I quickly snatch it from the table. My coaching fees are inclusive of the bill.

"When's your upcoming date with Amber?" I ask.

"Tomorrow night. I booked us a wine tasting at Telaya."

I avoid his eyes while I focus on signing the receipt. This poor guy's manners won't be ready to woo anyone by then.

"I suggest you spend the rest of your evening practicing in front of a mirror, just in case. Stick to the wine. Save a full meal for next time. Amber looks lovely, by the way." *And out of your league*, I want to add, but I don't. Pete showed me a photo of her off his dating app when we first sat down. She has fiery red hair and sharp green eyes while Pete is sweet if not a little frumpy and rough around the edges.

"I'll arrive fifteen minutes early to secure the table in case she's early." He repeats the advice I've given him at least half a dozen times.

I nod at him.

Bravo, Pete.

"Perfect. Your date will want to see you've been thinking of her," I remind him, "and that little extra bit of care lies in the details like that."

His eyes shine. "You should teach a master class in this stuff."

I laugh. "Coaching one-on-one seems a bit more my speed." I push back my chair. "And you better let me know how it goes afterward. Keep practicing here with the rest of that salad, but I've got to run."

I purposefully packed today with more coaching appointments than usual and have been running between them with less time than I prefer. I didn't want one empty moment to dwell on today's anniversary. And now that this last session is over, I can feel the angst of getting through the rest of my evening drawing out like a choppy river I'd rather not sail down.

But what choice do I have?

I plan to shut myself in, open that bottle of wine I bought a few days ago for this exact purpose, and have a good cry while flipping through old photographs of Grant and me before placing them all in the box I have ready to shove under my mattress for safekeeping. All before passing out cold.

Tomorrow, I'll wake up to day number three hundred and sixty-six with a clean calendar hung on my wall, void of any red X's. No more painful reminders of how far I've come staring me in the face every morning.

It'll be a fresh start.

My fresh start.

That's the plan anyway. I just have to walk three blocks back to the townhouse we shared — the one I live in all by myself now — before I can totally fall apart while basking in the comfort of a good sob behind a closed door.

I say goodbye and set off down the sidewalk for my short trek home.

Weaving between women meandering while they hold their toddler's hand or passing businessmen in tailored suits talking too loud into their AirPods, I walk with a purpose. I've spent the last year deliberately putting one foot in front of the other and now it feels like I'm in the final sprint toward home to cap off the race.

No celebratory champagne waiting, and no selfies to brag with online about how my perseverance has really paid off.

Just me, a bottle of red, and a box of what reminds me of what I lost.

In the beginning, when I'd initially resumed my coaching schedule to make ends meet and pay all the bills that had started piling up after he died, I could barely make it through a single coaching session. All the fake dates I had to take my clients on reminded me of him. The way one would carefully lay their napkin across their lap. Or the time a man next to me ordered Grant's favorite ale on tap. I'd had to excuse myself from the table to have a good cry in the ladies' room before slathering on a fresh coat of under-eye concealer and carrying on back at the table afterward as if nothing had happened. Even chuckling halfheartedly at a client's joke somehow felt wrong in those early days, like I shouldn't have been allowed to laugh when my heart had just been buried six feet under. Laughing somehow meant that I'd forgotten what had happened, if only for a moment, and forgetting wasn't allowed. Not to me. I nearly gave up, but something in me kept going.

And lately, against all odds, I've felt that unmistakable nudge to live again.

I pick up my pace.

The late spring evening feels warm. I pull my hair up into a makeshift bun, tossing it off my collar before opening up the first two buttons of my emerald-colored cardigan — the one with the buttery yellow buttons that I love. After an unusually cold, wet winter, warmer weather is finally knocking — nearly ready to break through Boston's bleak winter skies. A few birds chirp above, perched in the branches of the tree-lined street while tulips and azalea blossoms jut out of wooden garden boxes painted white, all strung together in a pattern that lead me toward home. We're all bursting out of hibernation together, ready to get moving again it seems.

I rush around the final corner onto my street, but immediately slow my pace when I notice a man I've never seen before.

He's probably around nineteen or twenty, standing on my front porch. His hair is rumpled, longer than average, and so dark that it's nearly black — exactly like Grant's was when he was still alive. For one gut-wrenching moment, my brain tricks me into thinking that it's him, turned up here and back from the dead somehow.

I walk closer. *No, Grant will never stand there again*, I remind myself.

No matter how much I want to hear him greet me or fill our home with laughter instead of nerve-bending silence, it's not possible. It'll never be possible.

My stomach sinks when I see his doppelganger is holding a white envelope.

"Not more legal work," I mutter to myself. "Not today."

I, with the help of Grant's parents, finally wrapped up everything having to do with his will a few months ago, and I don't think I could handle any more of that type of paperwork right now. Possibly not ever again. His parents were sweet the whole time, but I could tell that I slowly became one more reminder of the son they lost. I haven't heard from them since the final documents were filed, and the sale of the Smithfield building was complete soon after. Probably too painful for them to see me, I imagine, but I find it hard to believe they'd spring something new on me like this. Especially today.

"Juliet Hart?" the man asks, turning around when I walk up the steps.

"Yes?" I ask wearily, praying that he's just a roaming door-to-door solicitor who somehow knows my name. "What can I do for you?"

"I'm here to drop this off." He holds the envelope out to me but I don't take it. Instead, I eye him suspiciously. "I was hired by Monica Braverman to deliver this to your address. Does that name ring a bell?"

"No." I frown. Then I study the envelope between us, still not reaching for it, but looking for a clue of what it might be. He shakes it a bit in my direction as if that might entice me enough to grab it. It doesn't. "Are you serving me court papers or something?"

He shakes his head, amused.

I cross my arms, waiting for a stronger answer than that. I don't normally take random envelopes from strangers, especially without recognizing the name of who they're from and *Monica Braverman* is not a name that I recognize.

"I'm not serving you papers," he promises. He looks friendly, I'll give him that, then again I've never encountered a process server. "I have no idea what this is. Honest. I'm just supposed to deliver it. Monica is my boss. She's a travel agent."

"This isn't one of those *you've won a trip* scams, is it? Where you show up with some papers, claiming I've won a fancy trip, just to get me to call a number and give you all my personal info. Because if it is, I'm so *not* interested."

"I've never hand-delivered anything to one of her clients, and this is not a scam. Which tells me this is something seriously important."

He rustles the envelope at me.

I reluctantly take it, but when I flip it over for a closer look, my heart skips a beat. My name is handwritten in what looks eerily similar to Grant's handwriting.

Your imagination is on fire today, I scold myself, burying any traces of false hope.

The anniversary of his death must be making my brain misfire all the tiny synapses that miss him to my core, making me see things that aren't there. Whoever this Monica Braverman is, she probably has similar penmanship to Grant. That's all.

"Thank you," I say, squeezing the envelope between my fingers for any indication of what might be inside. But it's papery and flat, not giving anything away. "Is she—?" I start to ask, but he's already skipping down the front steps of my porch, looking relieved to have fulfilled his duty.

He waves over his shoulder.

"Have a good day!" he calls before disappearing around the corner.

"The best day," I mutter, turning to push my key into the door.

I cross the threshold and shut myself inside. Silence embraces my nervous system like a warm hug while I study my name on the envelope. The way the J loops around is enormously exaggerated while the rest of the letters are scribbled so tiny beside it. Exactly the way Grant used to write my name. An absurd little spark of anticipation bubbles up in my stomach before I can shove it back down again.

If only. I close my eyes, willing the thought to be real.
But no.

This is from someone named Monica. Not Grant.

I beeline to the kitchen, envelope in hand, tossing my keys and purse onto the counter so I can rip it open, slowly making my way toward the recycling bin under the sink. I'm expecting to see a few colorful sales flyers boasting travel services by whoever she is while I pull out the papers from inside.

But my hands begin trembling when I see the delicate stationery is covered with the impossibly familiar script — one I never thought I'd see again.

CHAPTER 3

By the time I reach the end of the second line, I have to set everything down on the counter and collect myself before going on.

I rub my eyes with balled fists, blinking fiercely, as if my lids are windshield wipers attempting to clear the view in the midst of a downpour.

My mind *has* to be playing the most wild tricks on me today.

This is impossible.

He's dead.

Jules, he's dead.

So how am I holding a letter that I've never seen before that was so clearly written by him?

And who the hell is Monica Braverman?

Again, I start at the top, my mind a jumbled collection of explanations for what I'm about to read, though none of it makes any sense.

My dearest Jules,
 Don't hate me for doing this.

What the hell? I can't help it. I flip to the last page, and sure enough, it has *his* name there at the end. Written just like he would write it.

Grant

I flip back to the top and strain my eyes to keep reading through a fresh set of tears that quickly pool up along the rims.
This just can't be.
"How the hell?" I mumble to no one in particular and look around for someone to jump out and yell *surprise!* like I'm caught up in some sick joke, but my house is empty. It's always empty. I race to the little window by my front door and look out toward the street, needing to know if that guy is still standing out there, ready to slink back in to claim ownership over this poorly timed prank that someone thought might be funny. To deliver a letter on the anniversary of his death. One that looks eerily similar to something that might be written by him.
But no one is outside, and no one is hiding in my house either.
"He wrote this," I say out loud as if I'm reciting a spell. Somehow making it real.
I don't know whether to read it or hold it, savoring the knowledge that it exists in the world, looking forward to reading it for just a little while longer.
"Read it now," I whisper to myself. *It's the last you'll ever hear from him.*
But why now?
Why today?
And why did I have to wait one whole year to read whatever this is?
With every conceivable, crazy notion running through my head, I start again from the top.
And this time, I don't stop.

CHAPTER 4

Grant
One year ago

My dearest Jules,
Don't hate me for doing this.
But here it goes.
My love. My heart. My everything. You have no idea how much I wish you were holding me right now instead of this stupid piece of paper.
First off, I'm going to start by saying it again, and then once more at the end, and possibly in every letter forthcoming from now on until it sinks in and I am sure that you can't possibly: Please don't hate me.
Don't hate me because what I'm about to ~~suggest~~ ~~demand~~ suggest sounds utterly ridiculous.
So just hear me out.
Because right now, I'm watching you quietly snore in that horrid blue fold-out chair thing that the hospital has given you to sleep on in this stupid white room, void of anything remotely cheerful. And while everything in here screams medical! Sterile! — you are the most pure form of oxygen

there is. My breath, my life. Like a daisy springing up in the dark. The way your sunny blonde hair spills out across that craggy, old plastic bed, your always-red lips parted, just so. Your lashes curled up at the ends, even when you haven't showered in three days since you've basically refused to leave my side for weeks at this point. Sweetheart, you are the sun in a room that lacks windows. The best of everything I've ever loved — and everything I'll never get the chance to love again.

You passing out in that chair is the only thing that's given me the chance to write you this letter in secret without you catching me. And what I'm about to say is something I've thought a lot about ever since Dr. Solano, well, you know. Ever since my future was cut short from yours.

So, let me get to the point of all this before you wake up.

I've planned a trip for you.

Not just any trip.

That trip.

Yes, that one. The one we've always talked about taking, to do things we've both always talked about doing, ever since you told me that you'd never actually been out of the country. That day our World Civ professor put up a slide of the Colosseum, and you leaned over and whispered, "Do you have a pen?" Then, while you waited for either Silas or I to hand you one, you added, "You know, I've never been there. To Italy." And I frantically shoved everything around in my backpack to find you a pen before Silas could, when all I could think was — how has the most beautiful girl in the world never been to Italy?

That was the moment I fell in love with you, by the way. I know I've always played it cool by insisting that I didn't actually fall head over heels for you until two solid months later because thirty seconds of knowing someone isn't a socially acceptable time frame in which to fall in love.

But for me it was. It was because you were always breaking the mold of what I thought I knew to be true.

Now, a decade-ish later, here you are. Still clinging to me, to our future, and looking all tiny and beautiful curled up on a blue plastic chair thing, knowing damn well that we won't be able to watch each other's hair turn gray together anymore. Which — if I can stop blabbing on about how beautiful you are for just one minute — is the reason why I'm writing: The trip.

Our trip. The one I'd like you to take without me now.

I've set the entire thing in motion, starting with a travel agent named Monica Braverman, who you'll need to contact after you're done reading this.

Brace yourself for this next bit because it's a doozy: I've also selected a travel partner for you.

(This is the part where I'm going to remind you, again, to not hate me.)

Your travel partner is going to be Silas. Silas Davenport. As if there was any other Silas in our world, but, given the history between you and him, I feel like I have to specify his full name due to the intensity of your hatred and how that might prevent you from believing or accepting that Silas is, in fact, your travel buddy. Surprise! (I'm sorry) Effective immediately, starting first thing tomorrow morning.

His jet will be waiting. His crew will be ready.

Before you argue, you need to know that he's already agreed. In fact, taking you on this trip was my final request of him, and now I'm asking the same from you.

(In an effort to refrain from repeating myself, please refer back to Line Two.)

By this point, and if all the pieces of the puzzle have come together correctly to get you this letter on the right day, it has been one whole year. Enough time for you to grieve. Enough minutes for you to spend angry. For you to hate me for leaving you. And hopefully, for you to forgive me for leaving you too soon, because forgiveness will only help you heal.

My hope is that, if luck would have it, you're now at the point of grief where you're able to look ahead again, ready to craft a beautiful life and live to be one hundred and two with every sort of laugh line etched deeply into that gorgeous face of yours.

I hope that this letter finds you just as you're remembering what it feels like to wake up without a knife stuck in the middle of your chest every day because it's time to look forward, sweetheart. Look only ahead.

As much as it pains me to say, I want the best days of your life to happen now, like that old Frank Sinatra song we were going to dance to at our wedding: "The Best Is Yet to Come." Like a field of a thousand wildflowers, and you can't possibly pick just one perfect moment or memory-yet-to-be-had, stretched out before you.

That said, why am I sending you on a trip with the one person in the world that you despise?

It's because I know Silas better than anyone, and, although we were three peas in a pod once, I still know him better than you ever did. Which means that I know he'll be good for you — for this particular journey — as long as you're open and as long as you suspend your feelings about the past.

Just go and pack your bag. Don't argue in your head about why you can't possibly do this because you leave in the morning. If you had time to brood and spend your energy picking this trip apart, I know that you would.

Make it simple for yourself.

Go.

Go and don't look back.

Go, and do everything I've set out for you to do without reserve or regret.

Just live, sweetheart. It's all I've ever wanted for you, and me dying isn't going to change that.

Please don't hate me for planning this.

And thank you, always, for letting me love you,

Grant

PS If you're still not convinced to board a plane with Silas in the morning, then know that I've dangled four carrots for you to chase at each location around the world. Every time you reach a new place, another letter will be there waiting for you.

PPS You and Silas are the only people allowed to pick up the letters. Short of Silas' death certificate in hand (<u>don't even think about it</u>), both of you will need to be present to retrieve the letters from me along the way.

PPPS Monica's business card is in the envelope. She's waiting for your call. I love you.

CHAPTER 5

Juliet

In a daze, I set Grant's letter down on the counter and pull Monica's card out of the envelope. I feel dizzy knowing that Grant placed that card inside this very envelope himself while imagining me reading it one whole year later.

I set her card down on the counter next before taking a step back, staring at the collection of papers, feeling like I've just seen a ghost.

My body breaks out in a cold sweat while my heart pounds in my ears. How did he set all this up? Especially without me knowing? Did Silas know this whole time? Did he know when he came over that night?

My eyes land on the business card.

Monica Braverman, Luxury Travel Agent

The swooping cobalt blue M of Monica's name looks too cheerful for the way I feel right now. Too cheerful and too real.

She's written, *Looking forward to your call!* with a smiley face just below her signature line, along with what I imagine to be her personal phone number. I'll bet she's never received a call quite like the one I'm supposed to make right now, and maybe she never will again.

I push my hands against the cold, stone countertop and drop my head, exhaling slowly while trying to catch my breath.

This is not what I had planned for tonight, and certainly not what I'd planned for the next few weeks of my life.

Reading Grant's words feels like a balm laced with salt, poured right into my broken heart, slicing through a wound that had only just begun to heal — somehow both soothing and extraordinarily painful at the same time.

Getting the slightest taste of him without being able to fully indulge doesn't feel fair, but I also wouldn't trade it. Not for the world. And knowing that at least four more letters like this are waiting for me in different locations around the world makes me want to drop everything and sprint straight to the airport.

Which means? I have to go.

Even if Silas is my travel partner.

Of all the people . . .

Why would Grant do that? Why would he ensure that each letter will only be released to me if Silas is there? Why wouldn't he just send me on my own?

I mean, he's right. At one point, the three of us were an inseparable trio. Silas was the brother Grant never had, and in turn, he was my best friend, too. At one point, he was one of the best people I ever knew.

Long before college and before I ever met Grant and Silas that day in World Civ class, those two were a package deal. Best friends. Bros for life. Coming from two incredibly connected families, both of them had attended the same prestigious boarding school just outside of Boston. They graduated side by side at the top of their class, then roomed together at Harvard, while I was there on scholarship. Most of Grant's boyhood stories involved tales of Silas and him doing outrageous things together, sometimes with the other kids they befriended along the way, usually Dax or Ryeson, but always with each other.

I'd seen Si and Grant gallivanting around campus together early on in my freshman year. Noticing how cute they both were, if not completely opposite of one another. Grant with his serious nature and classic prep school good looks. A mop of thick black hair giving way to wide-rimmed glasses and dark blue eyes you could get lost in forever if you weren't careful. And then there was Silas: a Ralph Lauren model in another lifetime. Unnaturally attractive, if not overly cocky and charismatic on top of it all, making him extremely popular with girls on campus. His dark brown hair naturally held on to traces of the sun, with streaks of amber tones bringing out the flecks of gold in his forest green eyes. You could hear his laugh around campus before you saw him, usually up to something loud and generally obnoxious with Grant. But in the best way.

When in World Civ I'd asked the pair of them for a pen, knowing full well that I had at least two spares in my backpack, I'd simply wanted to get to know them. Grant asked me out soon after, and the rest was our history. I might have fallen in love with both of them, if I hadn't grown so attached to Grant shortly after he took me out. I told myself that Grant was the safer of the two. The mellow, down-to-earth one between them that made me feel secure and cared for. But they complemented each other, and I felt lucky to have them *both* in my corner.

I'd set Silas up with a few of my girlfriends over the years who were always batting their eyes at him and asking me if he was single, but I stopped doing that after realizing he was never one to settle down into anything serious. Which meant he was always with Grant and I, hanging out between his own hookups and dates, entertaining us with his playboy antics.

I loved them. One as a friend, and the other as my everything.

But that was before.

And I'll never forget the week everything changed.

Grant and I got engaged. Then less than one week after that, Silas' father died.

His entire world changed in one loss of a heartbeat. Si inherited his father's multi-billion-dollar business portfolio. So if he'd been a bit brash and cocky before his inheritance was signed for, the instant media attention as one of the world's most wealthy — and arguably most handsome — young bachelors did a huge number on his ego.

Right here is where it happened. Silas disappeared. Not physically, but in every way that someone can disappear while standing right in front of you. He went from being someone I loved and admired to someone who oozed the uglier sides of wealth and privilege, acting like money could solve anything he said or did that hurt. The loss of who Si was broke my heart, and within months he was a man I could barely stand to be around.

The immediate shouldering of immense responsibility might have been too much for any twenty-six-year-old to handle gracefully, but it took him to a place that was so different and so dark that I rarely saw him outside the sleaziest tabloid photos — usually with a few women draped around him as he stumbled out of a nightclub in some random location around the world.

And whenever I did see him in person? He'd grown so bitter toward me — toward everyone that had someone left to love — that all I ever received were sarcastic jabs thrown my way, usually at the expense of being Grant's ol' ball and chain.

The transition gave me whiplash and felt as bad as if he'd slapped me across the face himself. It hurt losing him. And that was before I lost Grant, too.

Over the last year, I haven't heard a single peep from Silas since he walked off my porch the day of Grant's funeral. Not even after I sold the building he gave us. I'd heard through their friend, our mutual attorney, Dax, that Silas had asked him about the sale, but that he didn't look into it any further.

I think it's because Silas already knew the role the building had played in the end.

I've never allowed myself to question Silas about the building. Afraid of what I might uncover if I do. Afraid that if I say the words out loud and notice any hesitation in his response — or see any look in his eye that might suggest Silas already knew — the knowledge of that would break me for good.

I like to think Silas meant well that night he showed up to offer me money, but the conversation was tone-deaf and cold.

We were so stiff and awkward that night, shifting on our feet inside the home that Grant and I had shared and made memories in without him.

Me, with my swollen red eyes, pulling miserably at my thick black dress that had grown too tight while Silas stood quietly in my foyer.

Him, dressed in a crisp charcoal suit, looking fresh off a designer runway in Milan. Like he was more ready to jet set or spend all night getting bottle service at a swanky nightclub nearby than having just attended his best friend's funeral a few hours before.

The house was so quiet when he came. I could hear him breathing over the floorboards creaking beneath his feet as he shifted around, unsure of what to say.

Just seeing him had sent a flood of nostalgia that felt more like a desperate need for something of the past to still exist between us. Threatening to make me forget how horrible things were between us. When really, I just wanted more than anything to spend ten minutes living in the past, where Silas and I could laugh with each other, and Grant was just another room away.

But everything about it was uncomfortable.

He'd stood too close.

Studied me too intently.

Spoken too gently.

The familiarity and softness in his eyes while he watched me squirm had nearly ended me. The old Si was still in there and I could see it.

I could tell he was hurting, too. Of course he was. But seeing him again that night, with no one else around to ease the mood, was like seeing a second ghost. One I wanted to turn back time for.

I knew, in my gut, it was the old him standing at my door. His words and his offer didn't match his demeanor, as if someone else had put him up to the task, asking him to make me feel small. He'd squirmed so uncomfortably, like he hated himself just for saying it all out loud.

But I didn't know what else to do. So instead of saying anything meaningful, I'd glared too harshly, forcing myself to ignore the sickening wave of missing him that I'd felt when I'd first seen him, the old him, standing outside.

Without Grant to buffer things, everything we said felt charged and electric and wrong. Like I couldn't get away from him fast enough but also like I never wanted him to leave. Never wanted that part of me that was alive with both Silas and Grant to walk out the door with him forever.

But it did. And I'd practically pushed him out.

I knew I wouldn't reach out to him after that, but he hadn't either. And now, a whole year has gone by.

I glare down at Monica's card wondering whether I can just retrieve the travel itinerary from her and fly solo to these places. Opting to convince whatever hotel staff is holding Grant's letters hostage to give them to me without Silas there.

But I toss the card back on the counter and exhale stiffly.

Years ago, I would have hopped on a plane with Silas without a second thought. Especially if Grant was coming along, too. But those days, those carefree moments, feel impossible now.

"Why would you put me in this position, Grant?" I whisper.

After everything I've already gone through?

I check the clock above the stove.

Seeing it's almost five o'clock makes my head spin.

The letter mentioned that our plane takes off first thing tomorrow morning, which means I need to get in touch with

Monica now if I'm going to keep this absolutely asinine ball rolling forward.

I could spend hours debating whether or not to go, torturing myself over the decision I have to make, but it would only be a waste of time.

I already know that if there's a plane taking off tomorrow that'll bring me closer to another letter, another lost piece of Grant, then I'm going to be on it.

Even if Silas is right there beside me.

CHAPTER 6

Silas

I laid in bed all morning, staring up at the ceiling, recovering from yet another dream where Jules was pushing me out the open door of my own plane. I've been having the same reoccurring nightmare nearly every night leading up to today. Each time I wake up unable to shake the sound of her screaming my name as I fall, before jolting awake from my own voice.

It's fucking awful.

And I hope it's not a sign of the way this trip is going to go.

Or *not* go, depending on whether she agrees to board my plane with me tomorrow.

Exhausted by the wait, I twist the cap off a fresh bottle. I had this one shipped in for Dax's visit from LA. It's a little game we like to play where I attempt to woo him with the best bottles money can buy. Not because Dax gives a shit about the price tag, but because I know the man enjoys a memorable scotch or bourbon.

I drag a couple of glasses across the bar before splashing a bit into each, then give the bourbon time to breathe.

My mother had this custom lounge area added to my father's office as an anniversary gift to him over twenty-five years ago. It's been *my* office now for over three years, but it's still hard to think of it as my own. Some days I can practically feel the ghost of my father breathing down my neck when I start to slack off. Which rarely happens now.

I glance at my watch. It's half past five. I should have heard from her by now.

My anxiety is interrupted by a twanging metal sound. The dart Dax just threw has bounced off the target and slid to a stop near my shoe.

I eye the dart then him.

He smirks, his hand frozen above his shoulder from taking poor aim, and I half wonder if he did that on purpose just to pull me out of my head.

We're playing another little game we like to play called *Dax Pretends He Can Beat Me at Darts*.

"What do you mean Raven broke things off with you because of a dream?" he asks, like he can't believe that would actually happen.

I ignore the question and hand him one of the glasses I've just poured, waiting for him to take a sip so I can see if he likes it.

"1982 Buffalo Trace," I tell him. "I may have found the Holy Grail with this one."

Dax takes a sip then whistles like he's just had a little taste of heaven, and I make a mental note to send the bottle back home to LA with him tomorrow, then ship the only case left in existence to his house after he gets there.

"That's amazing," he says, picking up the bottle to inspect it. "There's no bite."

"It's yours," I tell him. "Abby will love it." I add that last part just to see him smile the way he does whenever Abby's name comes up in conversation. It doesn't disappoint. Dax's whole face softens at the mere mention of her.

"I can't take that home with me." He shakes his head. "I'm guessing it cost more than I make in a year?"

I scoff. "Hardly. I'd never let you make so little."

He chuckles and sets the bottle down. He's not only the managing partner who handles all my mergers and acquisitions, he's been one of my best friends since Grant and I met him back at Fox Glenn. Dax and Ryeson were roommates across the hall from us that very first year of boarding school but the four of us were inseparable every year after.

"So, what's this dream that Raven was suspicious of?" he asks. "I find it hard to believe that anyone would break up with the infamous Silas Davenport over a stupid dream." He eyeballs me like there's more to the story than I'm telling him. "Unless there was a deeper meaning behind it."

"Wrong again. No deep meaning behind it, and Raven was not your typical girl. Although, I suppose it might shake any woman's confidence to have your boyfriend waking up almost every morning in a cold sweat while babbling on about the girl he's going to travel with, right?"

Dax lets another dart fly. It's a near bullseye. "That still doesn't seem like a good reason to break up with you."

I smile, happy to be distracted from the fact that my phone still isn't fucking ringing.

"You didn't know Raven very well," I tell him. "The idea of any woman's name but hers coming out of my mouth was reason enough to break up with me."

"Was she aware of how estranged you and Jules have become?" he asks, and I nod. "I still can't figure out why Grant was hell-bent on putting the two of you in a plane together. Seems like a recipe for disaster." He grimaces. "No offense."

I can't bring myself to tell him *why* Grant insisted on sending Jules and I on this trip together.

The first time I had the dream was the night I held Jules following Grant's funeral. Since then, I've had variations of the same dream dozens and dozens of times, each one ending with her shoving me out the plane door while I call her name to stop.

But, Raven was right.

It's gotten to the point of happening almost nightly. And a few weeks back, she finally had enough.

"I don't care if she was your best friend's fiancée and you swear she's untouchable. You're now dreaming about her almost every night and I'm not going to stand by while you travel alone with her. It's either her or me. Stay home or go. I won't be waiting for you like an idiot if you choose to go."

I'd promised nothing was going on between us, and reminded her that the trip was my best friend's final request.

"What am I supposed to do?" I'd asked. "Cancel everything and disappoint Grant over a stupid dream that I have no control over? Don't be ridiculous."

"You can't disappoint someone who's already dead, Si," she said, her eyes finally filling with defeat. "Only the living can have their heart broken."

And that was it.

It was over between us.

I drain my glass and set it back down on the bar top.

"Disaster or not," I remind Dax, "I don't even know if Jules is planning on showing up tomorrow."

"She's been through a lot, Si." His voice is low. As if I need the reminder.

"I'm well aware." I'm trying not to lose my cool. I didn't plan for any of this to happen. I've found myself smack dab in the middle of Grant's plan, just like Jules has by now.

Monica's courier dropped the letter off to her nearly an hour ago. What if she thought it was a solicitation and didn't open it? Or she did read it and is choosing to ignore what it said? Maybe she's still so angry with me that she'd rather lose Grant's four other letters than get on the same plane?

Every time I think about what she's going to read in that letter, I get a rancid tightness in my chest. The same one that sneaks up on me every time I've thought about her since I showed up at her house that night.

The anger in her eyes is burned into my memory.

We're supposed to board my jet in the morning and I still don't have a damn clue whether or not she's agreed to go. It's nearly six o'clock. Monica should have called me by now.

Something's wrong.

I glare at my phone, fighting the urge to throw it against the wall while Dax watches me try not to fume.

I walk to my desk and hit the intercom button. It immediately turns red.

"Ryan!" I bark.

"Sir?" he replies into the speaker, sounding chipper if not a bit hesitant.

"No calls yet?"

"I'll let you know the moment she calls. *If* she calls." His quick correction grows my annoyance. "But Monica's been instructed to call your phone so I think—"

"I know," I interrupt, cutting the intercom feed without saying another word.

Ryan's been with me a long time, and I want to keep it that way, but the anxiety of today has twisted me into a righteous double knot. Imagining Jules' reaction to the news that we're supposed to go on this trip together has haunted me all year. I've run through every conceivable response she could have upon finding out that I'm her travel partner, except for one: her smiling. Because that's not actually conceivable.

When Grant called me from the hospital to tell me his plan, that he wanted *me* to take his fiancée on the kind of trip they'd only dreamed of together, I put up quite the fight. It wouldn't be right. Having me, of all people, join her was simply too much to expect of Jules who was already going through hell and back.

"I need it to be you because I can't trust anyone else with her," Grant insisted before having a coughing fit that threatened to break me in half, even through the shoddy cell service with me in another country. "And because I know you've always loved her," he added so quietly that I almost didn't catch it.

My blood had turned to ice.

I tried to protest, arguing with him that I wasn't in love with his fiancée, the woman he'd been with for nearly a decade. He'd laughed ironically, the sound of it straddling the line between anger and defeat.

"Anyone who meets her falls in love with her, man," Grant said above the whirring of machines beeping off and on in the background. "It's impossible not to. Listen, I don't blame you, but I also don't want to have a big conversation about it. Just do me a favor and make this simple. Agree to take care of her. Agree to all of it. I need to know that she'll have someone I trust watching out for her. Doing whatever it takes, even if she has no idea that it's you behind the curtain. I'd only trust you."

"She can hardly stand to be in the same city as me, or have you forgotten that?" I reminded him. "Let alone a trip like this."

"I'm well aware there's a pile of shit under the bridge between you two. But I also know that losing your dad turned you into a real dick. And once you get around to pulling your head out of your ass, I know that it's still you in there." His voice softened. "Just say yes. If you don't, I'll haunt the fuck out of you."

I managed to laugh at that, but the whole thing was killing me.

"Whatever you need," I quietly promised, feeling the air escape my lungs as I said it loud enough to make it real. "I can promise that Juliet will want for nothing as long as I'm alive, and after I'm gone, too. If that's how you want it."

He thanked me then, the relief in his voice utterly gut-wrenching.

"And be nice to her, Si," he warned. "I mean it. I want you to bring her back to life, not bury whatever's left of her by then. You'll have a year to get yourself right. Don't let this—"

"I won't," I interrupted before I had to hear him say it. *Don't let this fuck you up even worse than losing your dad did.*

Some things shouldn't have to be said out loud.

We'd talked a bit more, but mostly left it at that. I was supposed to take care of the woman he loved when he no longer could. The request, I imagine, was excruciating for him.

"I'll be there Tuesday," I promised. "As soon as this merger is done. We'll talk details when I'm back. I'll get my PA in touch with Monica to sort it all out."

He let the silence linger before his voice came strained from the other end, "Sure, man, yeah. Monica's got the details. Thank you, Si. For everything."

"Just thank me when I get there Tuesday. Better yet, don't thank me at all."

I know now that he probably knew he wasn't going to make it until Tuesday.

His words and the promise I made that day have echoed in my mind ever since.

Even now, I don't like knowing that my best friend could see right through me all those years the three of us hung out together. Roomed together. Did everything together. Wondering which moment he'd realized that we were both in love with the same girl.

I'd fought hard to hide it, dating anyone who sparked my interest, then became someone even I hardly recognized following my father's death — the week they got engaged — just to prove to Grant that I didn't have the slightest romantic feelings toward her. Every woman I was photographed with after that was in stark contrast to the type of woman Jules is. Beautiful, yes, but opposite in everything else. She'd tried to salvage our friendship at first, but I'd pushed against her and pretty soon she'd pushed back. We started butting heads over everything after that. It was the beginning of the end for us.

I sit down and rest my elbows on my desk, rubbing my jaw.

"Do you want to order dinner while we wait?" Dax asks, settling into the chair across from me. "Or head out to that new place you wanted to try over on Avery? A little distraction while you wait to get the news? Either way, I'm good."

"It's fine," I tell him. "I'm sorry. I've had a whole year to build this up in my mind, and I really don't want to let Grant down when she refuses to go because of my stupid past mistakes. You go on with the rest of the legal team." Dax came out to supervise a handful of junior associates handling a merger for me at his firm. They've just completed the deal here today. "Enjoy your night. You guys have plenty to celebrate. I'll let you know what she says."

After he heads out, reluctantly, I sit back down, watching the clock tick on the corner of my desk, growing more and more frustrated with every passing minute that I don't hear the damn phone ring.

I grab my phone to call Monica but it starts ringing before I can punch in her name.

"Monica," I say instead of hello, my chest constricting so hard I can hardly breathe. "What'd she say?"

"Well, I just got off the phone with her." Her voice is hesitant.

"And?" I ask, impatiently. "How mad is she?" I grab a pen from my drawer and start tapping it nervously against the edge of the desk.

"A good amount," she says, adding a nervous laugh. "Ms. Hart was pretty shocked about everything, which is to be expected, you know, *considering*."

"And the part about taking the trip? Specifically with me? What'd she say? Is she asking for a fake death certificate with my name on it to be faxed over so she can do it alone?" I'm only half kidding.

She chuckles. "Yeah, she wasn't too thrilled about any of it."

I sigh and recline my chair to stare up at the ceiling, then set the pen down in favor of rubbing my temples, right where a vicious headache is about to set in. I can feel it.

"She didn't ask for a fake death certificate, but she did ask for her own flights," she admits. "Separate from yours."

I sit up straighter, then rise to my feet and begin pacing the room, turning the phone to speaker mode.

"The entire trip?" I knew it was going to be bad, but not *that* bad. I can hear Ryan's footsteps rummaging around outside my office door. I take my voice down a notch before continuing. "That wasn't what Grant wanted though. I'm supposed to *escort* her. Ensure her safety. Keep an eye on her. I can't do that if she's—"

"I know," Monica interrupts. "I let her know the arrangements couldn't be changed this late. You're confirmed to fly out first thing in the morning."

"Together?"

"Together."

There's a long pause on my end of the line as it all sinks in.

A whole year of holding my breath is coming to an end.

"She's agreed to go," Monica confirms again through what sounds like a smile. "But first, she asked for the itinerary so she could just call these hotels herself to claim that you died and couldn't go with her so she can get the letters without you. I only let her know which countries and hotels you're heading to, but you'll have to break the news of the activities once you get there. She might not board the first flight if she knows what's waiting at the other end of it."

My relief turns into a full-blown laugh. Leave it to Jules to push the envelope, headstrong forever.

"Any changes to the plan?"

"No. You'll pick her up at seven tomorrow morning with your driver. The flight crew will be waiting when you arrive. Wheels off the tarmac at eight. First stop is Bern where a car will be waiting at the airport to take you to the helicopter. From there, you'll fly to Interlaken. It'll be a long travel day, but your crew is ready for it, and now so is she."

"Thank you," I say, now ready to hang up. "You've done an impeccable job, Monica. We'll be in touch along the way."

"I'll keep things running smoothly on my end. You just enjoy the trip. Take care, Silas. It's been a pleasure."

Once we hang up, I type another name into my phone. One I haven't had a reason to call in well over a year. Realizing how odd it is that someone so important to me — someone I used to talk to on a daily basis — now seems impossible to call.

I stare at the photo attached to Jules' contact info on my screen.

Striking blue eyes — so light that they're nearly white around the center ring. Thick blonde hair trailing down to her waist. And a smile so wide that, nine times out of ten, I nearly forget my own name when I see it.

I want to call her.

I *should* call her.

To ask if there's anything else I can do to help her get ready for the trip that she never wanted to take with me at all.

My thumb hovers over the green call button and I wag it back and forth while I imagine how the conversation might go.

She could change her mind about going if I say the wrong thing, or if just hearing my voice repulses her, like it did a year ago when we last saw each other.

I can't risk it. I toss the phone out of my reach to save myself *from* myself for the rest of the night. Deciding, for my own good as well as hers, that it'll be better to let her digest what lies ahead of us without me interrupting her any more than this plan unfolding tonight already has.

Besides, she's about to get another surprise that she also wasn't expecting tonight.

I hit my intercom button to get the next phase rolling.

"Sir?" Ryan's voice fills my office.

"Time to take it over," I tell him.

CHAPTER 7

Juliet

Thirty minutes after I get off the phone with Monica, there's another knock on my door. Normally, I'd ignore it, but since this evening is going everywhere but according to plan, I decide that I'd better check to make sure it's not another letter or bomb or something else I'd never expect waiting for me on the other side.

A second guy I've never seen is standing on my porch when I crack the door open, leaving the thick security chain pulled tight across the gap. I've about had it with surprises today, but there are eight enormous roller bags lined up behind him, all matching cream with tan leather trim and the letters LV scattered across the surface of each one.

My eyes wander over the dreamy set before it dawns on me who's behind it.

"Are you Juliet Hart?" the man asks.

"Yes, but I definitely did not order those," I tell him, secretly wishing that I could have. The bags are gorgeous. However, I don't need to hear another word to know that Silas is behind this ridiculous pile of them on my porch.

"Delivery from Silas Davenport," the man confirms, holding out a clipboard. "Please sign here to confirm receipt."

Instead of giving in to the temptation, I shake my head.

"Nope. I already have perfectly adequate suitcases, thank you." I silently say goodbye to the luggage before pushing the door shut, then pull it open to add, "Please let him know that I don't need these or need *anything else*. Mmm k?"

"These aren't just suitcases, Ms. Hart." The man smiles, raising his brows while motioning for me to keep the door open. It feels a bit awkward that he's addressed me as *Ms.* Hart. "And I'm not really supposed to let you refuse them. Sorry."

He twists a toe into the vinyl doormat, like he was hoping that I wasn't going to be difficult. I close the door to slide off the chain then swing it wide open.

"Not supposed to *let me* refuse them?" I ask, fully aware that I'm taking the bait. "Oh, is that right? Is that what Silas told you?"

His neck grows a few red splotches.

"Sorry. I just have to deliver them. Don't shoot the messenger, and all that." He smiles weakly.

I remind myself that I'm annoyed at Silas, but not at this innocent young man standing here on my porch. The second one of the evening, as it turns out.

"If they're not *just* suitcases, then what are they?" I ask, pressing him gently.

"Oh shit — *shoot* — here, there's a note." He digs into his back pocket, looking even more apologetic, then holds out a small white envelope. "Sorry, I should have just started with this but I forgot."

My stomach jumps at the sight of another envelope and I grab it immediately, ripping it open, praying it's another letter from Grant.

Instead, the handwriting is totally different from Grant's letter, but it's still vaguely recognizable.

Silas.

My heart constricts. This is the first concrete evidence I've gotten today that he's orchestrating all this, besides the phone call earlier with Monica in which she insisted we have to travel together instead of apart.

My brows nearly touch while I force myself to read it.

Jules,

> *Grant asked that I take care of this since you wouldn't be prepared to take off on a trip like this tomorrow otherwise. There are three sets of identical clothing in various sizes that I've had picked out for you. I haven't seen you in a while, so we had to guess on sizes. I've included a packing list of what you'll need.*
>
> *Take whatever fits.*
>
> *Leave the rest, and I'll have Ryan pick it up tomorrow after we head to the airport.*
>
> *Looking forward to catching up.*
>
> *See you in the morning,*
>
> *Si*

I roll my eyes and hand the note back to the poor guy.

"You can keep the note," I tell him. "I don't want it. And I wish you could keep all these too, but I get it. It's your job to deliver them to me, which now you have. Fabulous."

I look at the bags, wondering if I even have enough room in my living room for this many.

"I'll help you carry them inside," he tells me, looking like he'd rather bolt as far away from here as he can instead of following me anywhere. "Silas told me not to leave them outside."

"Well, doesn't he just think of everything!" I murmur sarcastically, then remind myself again that this guy has nothing to do with our beef. "I mean, thank you," I tell him, grabbing the bag nearest to me. It has to weigh at least fifty pounds. "Dear Lord, what did he put in here?"

"Not totally sure. He had Katie pick it all out," he adds, like I should know who Katie is, before grabbing another bag to follow me in. Of course, Silas wouldn't spend time doing a lowly task that someone else could do for him, like pack eight bags of women's clothing.

"Who's Katie?" I ask, heaving another bag over the threshold, wondering if it's his current woman-of-the-week. Or, let's face it, his current woman-of-the-*hour*.

"The stylist," he answers, grabbing two bags at a time and pushing them over the doorway. I turn to drag them further into my tiny living room which is filling up fast. "Katie is Silas' stylist. She's actually pretty cool."

"Wonderful," I murmur, picturing some poor girl making it her life's goal to dress Silas, and now me. I try to imagine the guy I knew in college having a stylist named Katie dress him up daily, but I just can't. He was way too immature, too goofy, too likable back then to care about such things. Oh, how time has changed him. This is going to be torture.

"He didn't need to do this. I'm sure I have some swimsuits and whatever else I need in my closet somewhere." I search my memory for the last time I put a swimsuit on though, and I can't quite recall. "Sorry you got suckered into delivering these tonight."

"I'm not," he says, smiling warmly before lifting another bag inside. "I'm just glad you decided to accept them. Silas has been obsessed with preparing for this trip for months. I'm glad it's finally here."

I pause, watching him lift another bag over the small step that leads into my home.

"Obsessed for *months*?" I repeat, feeling slightly shocked that he's spent any attention on this trip at all. Especially if he can't even be bothered to dress himself, and apparently, now me. "Was it actually him obsessing? Or does he have more people to obsess on his behalf?"

He chuckles.

"I've actually never seen him take this much interest in any of his travel. He usually wings it when traveling for leisure, or depends on the rest of his team to plan work trip details. But he really cares about this one."

Silas must have taken Grant's request to heart. It makes me feel a bit pink in the ears, followed by a tinge of longing that feels dangerously close to nostalgia hitting me square in the chest.

I push it away.

"This is the only trip I've seen him give a damn — *darn* — about," he continues.

I smile at the guy. He can't seem to rein in his intermittent swearing habit in front of me, which I find a bit endearing. I wonder if his boss minds.

"What do you do for him?" I ask.

"Anything he needs. I'm Silas' PA. I've worked with him for years. You two are going to have a blast, I think. No one in the world does life like that guy."

I roll my eyes again. *That's what I'm afraid of.*

"I tried to get out of it," I admit, walking back toward the door to grab another bag.

"You wanted to cancel? I can't even imagine . . ." He trails off, rubbing his forehead. "He would have been fucking pissed. Sorry. *Freaking* pissed, I mean."

I laugh, but focus my attention on getting what's possibly the heaviest bag into the house, unsure of what to say. Silas' PA is less formal than I'd imagine him being. And it feels a little odd that even this total stranger in my foyer knows more about what I'll be doing for the next couple weeks than I do. I know we're heading to Switzerland first, but I have no clue what's on the agenda once we get there. I suppose that's where Katie's handy packing list comes in.

"That's all of them," he says after double-checking my empty porch.

I study the eight bags now filling my living room, imagining the type of clothing and gear Silas' assistant picked out for me.

"Thank you," I tell him. "What's your name by the way?"

"Ryan." He smiles brightly. "And no need to thank me. I should be thanking you for helping me keep my job." He gives me a sideways grin. "Silas might have killed me if I came back with them."

I swallow hard as he turns to go. If Silas would have killed him for failing to deliver a few bags, I wonder what type of fury he'd release on me if I refused the whole trip. Memories of hearing Si ream out his dad's assistant over funeral details in the days after his father's death flood my mind.

"Any last-minute advice on how to handle him?" I ask, prodding the loose-lipped assistant. "We were friends a long time ago. Until . . . until we weren't." I'm not sure how else to describe what happened between us. After his father died, our friendship just slowly dissolved. More like death by a thousand pinpricks.

"*Deal* with him?" he repeats, looking amused. He stares past me for a beat before shifting his eyes back to focus on mine. "Silas is many things. But I can tell that you mean a great deal to him. So, the best way to *handle* Silas is to just enjoy yourself. Let him see that all this made you happy. I think that's the only thing he cares about at the end of the day. He just wants to see people happy."

"Happy?" I repeat, confused. My happiness on this trip will have absolutely nothing to do with Silas. "The only thing I can imagine making me happy on this trip is the moment I have all four letters safely in my hands and we're heading back home."

He smiles at the floor, nodding, like he's not surprised to hear me say that. Then he turns to go but veers back suddenly.

"Don't mind me asking, but, when did you last spend time with him?" he asks, cocking his head to the side.

"For about twenty minutes following a funeral last May."

"And before that?"

I search my memory, trying to recall the last time I spent any significant time in Silas' presence.

"I guess it's been about three years before that. He gave us the building for Grant's nonprofit, but he and I never really saw eye-to-eye on much of anything else recently." His smile widens, like he knows something I don't, which definitely annoys me.

"So not much time at all in the last few years," he confirms.

"Why?" I've never been able to hide what I'm thinking, so I can imagine my annoyance is written all over my face right now.

"Well, I've worked with Silas for a few years now, since right after his father passed. I've seen him at his worst. But if there's one bit of advice I could give you, it's that people change." Ryan raises his eyes to the ceiling as if trying to find the right words. "They *evolve*."

Then he opens the door, turning back to give me one last smile.

"Evolve," I repeat with a snort. *Right*.

"Safe travels, Ms. Hart. Just let him show you the time of your life."

Fat chance, I want to say.

Instead, I thank him and close the door, then peek out the window, wondering if I should just camp out right here to wait for the next unexpected delivery. But my street finally looks quiet and dark.

Sinking into the couch, I push my hair back, feeling exhausted. If I had my way, I'd be tucked in bed with my bottle of wine and the box of old photos, having a good cry or snoring by now with my red marker in hand after closing out the last day of this rollercoaster.

Truthfully, a trip like this is probably what I need to kick off my next year. To get away from everything familiar, and live a little as myself again, instead of as the sad near-widow who lost her fiancé.

In fact, I can totally see myself enjoying the mountains of Switzerland, or walking along the ancient rock walls of Italy with a smile on my face, happy to soak up the sun. It sounds cleansing and necessary.

Just not with Silas there watching me do it.

CHAPTER 8

Silas

Where the hell is she? Patrick and I have been waiting in front of Jules' house for the last thirty-five minutes and she still hasn't come out of the front door.

I look over my driver's shoulder at the clock on the dashboard. The flight crew is supposed to have wheels up in the next ten minutes. There's no way we're going to get to the airport and loaded onto the jet in that amount of time.

I study the stillness of her door, wondering if I should just go in there to retrieve her myself.

When we first pulled up, I felt the thrill of adrenaline from the idea of seeing her for the first time in a year. Now, after waiting for what feels like forever, I'm left with a sour feeling in the pit of my stomach. She must be in there changing her mind at the last minute. What else would be taking her this long?

"Sir?" Patrick asks, glancing at me through the rearview mirror. He senses my annoyance. "Would you like me to—?" He points toward the door.

"Yes, please go check on her again," I answer, impatiently. "Just go ask if she needs any help getting — I don't know — whatever it is that she might need help with. If I go up there she'll never come out."

Patrick e[...] the driver door and makes his way up to Juliet's house [wh]ile I watch from the back seat. I could have just sent a car to deliver her to the airport separately, but I wanted to make sure she didn't need anything on the way. Plus, if I'm being totally honest, I wanted to be here to talk her out of bailing if she tried to ditch at the last minute. Good thing, too, because it appears that's exactly what's happening.

I pick up the coffee I planted in her cup holder about forty minutes ago, gauging the temperature through its thick, cardboard sleeve. It feels cold now but there's no time to stop for another. I'll have Andy make her an espresso or whatever else she'd like once we get on board.

I look at my watch, then her door. I hate being late to anything, even if I'm the one paying everyone's salaries to wait for me, or in this case, to wait for Jules.

Patrick rocks on his heels like he's about to head back to the car just as Juliet flings her front door open. She has three roller bags behind her, instead of the eight I had dropped off late last night. They exchange a few words before she attempts to juggle three bag handles herself, fending Patrick off from taking them from her by holding up her palm.

I break into a smile as I watch her try to figure out how to get all three bags to the car at once without his help. Patrick stands nearby, hands clasped at his waist, side-eyeing her. I can tell she's flustered and probably significantly sleep deprived, even from here.

I chuckle, resting my chin on my fist while I watch out the window.

There you are, Jules.

Stubborn as ever. Present as ever.

Beautiful as ever.

After a bit more talking, she gives up with a huff. Patrick grabs two of the bag handles before they briskly make their way toward the blacked-out Escalade idling in her driveway with me inside. She's wearing dark sunglasses, though it's not very light out yet, which, I realize, is not a good sign.

Patrick leaves her bags at the tail end of the SUV, then follows her to the opposite side to open her car door for her. Without looking over, she climbs into the captain's chair next to mine and sits back against the thick leather seat.

"Thank you," she mumbles to Patrick before he shuts the door and heads to the back.

It's only two words, but it's the first time I've heard her speak since I left her sobbing in her foyer last year. The sound of her voice hits me like a ton of bricks. I've thought about her quite a bit since I left her all alone to pick up the pieces of her life, but I knew that me staying away was what she wanted. That and I knew we had this trip together at the end of it.

I exhale a year's worth of waiting and settle back into my own captain's chair, smiling to myself.

She's here.

She's packed.

And we're headed to the airport.

A light, floral scent of shampoo and probably some perfume she spritzed on at some point wafts over to my side of the car.

Patrick loads her luggage into the trunk with a few thuds. The car dips beneath the weight each time another heavy bag lands in the trunk.

Meanwhile, we awkwardly hold our breath through the silence that follows. I keep my face forward, but side-eye her as much as I can without making it obvious that I'm watching. She sniffs and shifts her body away from me to look out the window, resting her elbow in the nook of the door.

"Fancy meeting you here," I say deeply, trying to sound casual but it comes out as horribly stiff instead.

"Morning," she replies, not bothering to face me.

Her blonde hair is piled high in a messy bun with wavy tendrils spilling out the sides. Like she was frazzled upon waking up this morning and it was the best she could do.

Exhaustion and annoyance roll off her, so thick that it might actually be contagious. She grabs one side of her tan sweater and pulls it tightly around her torso, shifting her whole body toward the window side of her seat. She can't get far enough away from me.

"I had this made for you, but—" I hold the cold coffee cup out to her — "you might want a new one once we board. It's probably cold by now."

"Sorry I made you wait," she says, not sounding sorry at all. But she takes the cup from me, careful not to let our fingers touch in the exchange.

"That's not what I meant—" I start to say, but she glances down at the to-go cup before taking a big swig, wincing as she forces herself to swallow.

I make a face, imagining how badly she must need caffeine if she's willing to drink that.

"Cold?" I ask.

"Very."

I try to take the cup back but she pulls it closer to her body, claiming it as hers. Then she looks out the window again.

"I don't care if it's cold," she says, stubbornly. "I still need the caffeine."

She grips the paper cup tightly, like it's a valued possession, running her thumb up and down the thick seam.

"Tired?" I ask.

"One might say."

"You can take a nap on the way to the airport if you'd like. Although there's a—"

"Thanks to your unexpected delivery, and, really, this whole unexpected trip, I was up half the night trying to decide what to bring," she interrupts before I can tell her about the bed on the plane that she's welcome to use. She sighs angrily then glances across the aisle, as if this whole thing was my idea.

I press my lips together and raise a brow at her.

"You know I didn't plan this, right?" I remind her, gently. "I was just trying to help by sending over the bags of clothes to choose from. You didn't have to take anything from them if you already had what you needed. No pressure."

She thumbs the seam of the cup even faster.

"Right. *No pressure.* Totally. Got it."

She takes another mouthful of coffee, wincing bitterly as it goes down.

I try to stop a smile from creeping over my face but fail.

"You really don't have to drink that. I can ask the crew to make you whatever you'd like once we get on the plane. Cappuccino, macchiato, Americano . . . do you still drink those triple shot—"

"Of course you can," she shoots back firmly, "but no thank you." She chokes down another disgusting swig for good measure.

I purse my lips, fighting the urge to respond too quickly or let my unsettled nerves get the best of me.

"I was only offering some hot form of caffeine that wouldn't make you gag over there. But, hey, that's fine. You're welcome to choke it down, if you can't make it all the way to the plane for a fresh cup."

After a year's worth of imagining how this trip might go, I have my answer loud and clear. It's going to go terribly.

She relents, though still clearly aggravated. "I mean, sure, Si, I'll have some coffee on the plane." She places the cup back in the cupholder. "I know you didn't plan this. I just didn't sleep very well. I can pay you back for whatever I kept of the clothes. I made a list on my phone to keep it fair. I'll email it so you can tally up the cost. Or maybe I can send it straight to Katie?"

"No need," I tell her, throwing a tight smile over the aisle. She has no idea that any one of the mere T-shirts Katie picked out cost no less than a few hundred dollars each. And then there was everything else.

"No. I don't want to owe you for anything, Si. I can pay for my half of the trip, too."

This time, I can't hold back a laugh. It erupts from somewhere deep inside before I can stop it.

She cranes her neck in what must be a glare. I can't be completely sure, since her glasses are so dark, but it would certainly fit the mood.

I clear my throat, trying to stifle the laugh and what I'm sure is an obnoxious smile taking over my face.

"No. The trip is all taken care of. And you definitely don't have to pay me back for an unexpected delivery of clothing and luggage that you never even asked for. I was happy to help get you ready for this trip, even if delivering every item in three different sizes turned out to be a nuisance to you last night instead of helpful. I knew you wouldn't have time to shop, and I didn't want you to be stuck with something three sizes too big if we estimated your sizing all wrong. It's been a while since I've — since we've — well, since I've seen you. Katie did all the work anyway, so, no worries. She's on payroll. It's not a big deal."

If I had to guess, I'd say she just rolled her eyes at me.

I look down, trying not to smile too hard.

God, I've missed her.

"Ah, yes, you have someone to handle *all the things*. Please thank *Katie on payroll* for me then," she replies, sounding sarcastic as hell. "I already owned most of what I packed, but I hadn't worn a few things in a while, so some of it no longer fit. Like a swimsuit. Can't remember the last time I went swimming, so I appreciated having the options, even if *Katie* thought I should wear a couple cuts of dental floss pretending to be a bikini on this little adventure."

I break into a wider grin without even trying to hide it. Truthfully, I had no part in that, although I'm happy to hear Katie's taste in clothing options will suit Jules well. All I did was show Katie her Instagram page to show her what Jules is like, and then I gave her creative freedom to style some options for the trip. No doubt she must have taken note and shopped accordingly. Can't argue with that.

"Grant really didn't give me much of a heads-up to get ready for all this though, did he? Or to budget for this type of trip, like, at all. But just tell me what I owe you and I'll send it over Venmo or something."

"No need," I say, wanting to change the subject away from money.

"Let me pay for my half," she says firmly, turning to me.

"No."

"I insist."

"Nope."

"Tell me what I owe you or I'll be forced to guess and send it over Venmo. And I wouldn't want to hurt your man pride by guessing too low."

I scoff.

"Jules, just the jet fuel and crew for the first leg of the flights costs more than what most people make in a year," I say, coolly. There's no way I'm letting her touch her bank account again for anything until we're back on US soil, officially parting ways. It's just not happening.

She angles her body back toward the window, sulking, staring blankly toward the rising sun.

"Doesn't matter. My coaching business does fine, and I still have the money from the sale of the—" She pauses before finishing that sentence. "I can pay my half," she adds defiantly.

"I know. You do very well for yourself. But just let this be my treat so we can move on."

She grumbles something under her breath that sounds a bit like *asshole*.

"I'm really proud of you, by the way. Growing that business yourself from scratch," I tell her, trying to shift our conversation in a new direction.

A choking sound sputters out of her and she turns to face me again. "Proud? Gee, thanks, Daddy."

I almost forgot how feisty she can be. This might be more fun than I thought.

"Okay, I'm *happy* for you then." I correct my wording. "I know you're killing it. I know you don't need anything from me."

"Correct."

"But just let this trip be my gift to you. And to Grant. For old time's sake."

A blanket of silence fills the car.

There, I've said it out loud. *Grant's name.* Successfully ripped the bandage off. Seated the elephant right here in the middle of the car. The one thing still holding us together, even though we've obviously drifted apart.

Finally, she nods solemnly and turns back toward the window.

"Fine," she whispers a moment later. "You can do it for Grant."

We ride the rest of the way to the airport, following our little truce, in silence, minus the light piano music Patrick has playing over the speakers to keep the mood cheery when it feels anything but.

While planning this trip, I took every minuscule detail into consideration, from what she might like to drink on the way to the airport to what thread count sheets she might find the most comfortable while sleeping in the bed during long flights abroad. But, the one thing I couldn't adequately plan for was how to hedge off a broken heart. How she might show up to the car this morning with dark sunglasses on, probably from crying all night since I'm the man taking her on this trip instead of the love of her life. I could never have planned for how she clearly doesn't want to look at me, even as a friend.

I've taken care of everything I could think of to keep her comfortable and safe, but I don't know how to take care of *that*.

So, instead of pushing her more or filling the car ride with aimless chatter that'll probably do more harm than good, we race toward the runway without saying another word.

Meanwhile, I silently apologize for having to put her through any of this.

The torture of having to travel with *me*, to ride with *me* instead of Grant, doing things they talked about doing together. I get it. She hates me. I did that. But I promised my best friend that I would look after her for the next few weeks.

So that's exactly what I'm going to do.

Whether she actually wants me to or not.

CHAPTER 9

We park on the private tarmac. Patrick quickly starts to unload our suitcases from the trunk, handing them off to one of the crew members who will roll them on a cart to be stored in the underbelly of the plane. I know my crew well, and I know they like to be as punctual as I do. So even though it's half past eight o'clock now, they'll try and get us up in the air as soon as possible, making up for lost time on the flight as well.

"Do you have anything you'd like to keep onboard with you?" I ask, turning to Jules.

She hasn't made any motion to get out of the car yet, even though Patrick is nearly done unloading the luggage. She looks lost in thought, staring across the red carpet they've rolled out between the Escalade and the sleek gunmetal jet waiting for us a few yards away.

"Just my purse is fine," she says, still hugging it to her chest.

Patrick slams the trunk shut, leaving us in muted silence. Our first time truly alone together in one year and a day. I wait another moment, hoping she makes the first move to get out of the SUV, wondering what she's waiting for.

"Are you ready?" I prod, hoping this isn't the moment she decides to bail.

She turns to me then and pulls the sunglasses off her face. Beneath the lenses, her eyes are gaunt, like she didn't sleep a wink last night between an onslaught of tears and mentally fighting against this plan. The pale blue-green shade of her irises looks translucent in the light of the morning sun streaming in through the car window.

"Are you?" she asks. Her tone makes it sound like a loaded question.

I want to say that I've never been more ready for anything in my entire life. That I know how quickly life can flash before your eyes, or the eyes of the person that you love. And that I wake up ready for anything, every single day, including this. But I know she wouldn't want me to say any of that.

So, I don't.

Instead, I force my voice into more gentle territory. "Yes, Jules, I woke up ready for today, but I've had longer to anticipate this than you. Take as long as you want. That plane is ours."

"That plane is *yours*," she corrects.

"*Ours*," I say, more firmly. "We're in this together. For better or worse, we can sit right here — all day if you need — until you're ready to hop out and get this thing off the ground. We waited all morning, and we can keep waiting."

We stare across the tiny aisle at each other.

"You know, I really didn't see this happening today," she says, narrowing her eyes. "You've had a whole year to wrap your head around this trip, while I . . ." She trails off, gazing out at the plane. "Right now, I'm just a dog on a leash getting pulled in a direction I don't want to go, in order to get my treat."

A low chuckle escapes my lips, but I manage to rein it in before it turns into full-blown laughter. This woman is anything but a dog on a leash.

She scowls at me.

"I'm so glad you find this amusing, Si," she growls. "I'm just trying to be honest with you. This isn't easy, but, isn't that why I'm here? To get my treats? To get those four letters? I don't know why Grant planted them all over the world like a pile of bait to make me go through this worldwide scavenger hunt with *you*."

She suddenly jerks the handle back and pushes the door open, hopping onto the sprawling piece of concrete outside. Andy, one of the flight attendants, steps out from inside the plane and waves at her from the top of the steps leading up to the door.

I watch her walk away and feel a sigh of relief escape my lips. Not just because Jules finally exited the car and is actually on her way into the jet, but because I know there's one crew member who can put a smile on anyone's face. No matter how pissy they feel upon arrival. I know, because I've been more than pissy myself several times while boarding my flights, but by the end of it, Andy has me in stitches. Works like a charm.

I pull my steel aviators off to watch her make her way toward the bottom of the stairs. She gives a halfhearted wave up to Andy when they appear to make eye contact.

I hold my breath, waiting until she takes her first true step up the stairs, officially leaving Boston behind.

She's on.

Grant's plan is working. His letter got her this far, and now it's up to me to carry her the rest of the way.

"Alright, buddy," I mutter to myself, shaking my head in disbelief that we're here. As if Grant can actually hear me right now. "Let's go get your girl through this."

Then I pull my door open and slowly make my way across the tarmac, just in time to see her disappear inside.

CHAPTER 10

Juliet

"Honey, you look like shit," the man standing at the top of the plane says to me with a deep southern drawl. This must be one of Silas' flight attendants.

I widen my eyes at him, then look around, certain he can't be addressing me like that. Sure enough, though, his eyes are sparkling right at me. We've never met, but I'm the only one climbing up these stairs right now, and Silas is at least twenty yards behind me, just now exiting the SUV. Plus, Si is definitely not looking like shit this morning. Quite the opposite, actually. So that leaves only me. And since everything about my last twenty-four hours has featured one ridiculous event after another, why not add this sassy attendant to the list?

I huff, looking up at him, ready to let him know *why* I look like shit, but when our eyes meet, I can't help but break into an unexpected grin. He's smiling right at me with one arm outstretched, his eyes dancing, like we're already friends.

I give up. Everything about my life is completely absurd right now.

I shrug and keep climbing.

"You're not wrong," I announce when I reach the top, pushing tufts of hair back up toward my messy bun. "I really do look like shit."

He puts his arm around my shoulders, wrapping me in an intimate side-hug, then starts leading me into the sleek charcoal tube that's about to go hurtling down the runway.

"Well, who can blame you? And besides, that was just a little white lie to get you to smile. Break the ice. We've got a lot of ground to cover, you and I. Figuratively and literally."

He nudges me a little closer to him, then bumps me away with his hip. I feel my smile widen and give up any preconceived notion about how this flight was going to go, letting him lead me into the plane's bougie interior.

He goes on as we walk. "Ninety-nine-point-nine percent of the world would kill to look as beautiful as you, even on a bad day, and the other point-one percent would just be lyin' to themselves. Besides, this type of trip here just doesn't happen every day, honey! So, we can't be wastin' any more time. I saw you debating whether or not to even hop in here for the last ten minutes, sitting in that car out there like that."

My ears redden.

"There's a reason for that," I start to tell him, but he interrupts as we pass the plane's sleek galley kitchen.

"It's because you didn't know whether we'd be packin' the good stuff here on this bird or not, am I right?" He winks at me. "Well, I can assure you we have everything on board you could possibly need. Including that tall drink of water I see coming up the steps behind you."

The flight attendant has to stoop as we go through another doorway, but the aisle is wide enough for us to glide down together side by side.

I've never seen the inside of a private jet to be able to compare this to anything else, but this one seems particularly striking. Everything inside is chiseled and sleek, similar to its owner and exterior. The cupboards and floors are outlined in thick, polished wood accents. Dim lighting and coffee-colored leather make the jet's interior feel like a broody nightclub or whiskey bar, which doesn't surprise me. It's all a little over the top, but undeniably masculine, kind of like Silas himself.

I reach out to touch one of the plushy seat's headrests as we pass, wondering if it's lined in cashmere.

"We're gonna sit you right here, honey," he tells me, patting my shoulder. I slink down into an overstuffed chair that feels more like a cushy La-Z-Boy than an airplane seat. If this whole thing wasn't owned by Silas, I might never leave. "My name is Andy. Now what can I get you? A shot of vodka? A chardonnay? All the above plus an Ambien?"

I laugh for the second time since meeting Andy. Of course, Silas would have a crew expecting to serve hard alcohol or sleeping pills with the rising sun.

"At eight thirty in the morning?" I ask, turning my cheek.

"Oh, excuse me, Miss, but I didn't ask you the time!" he trills, winking at me. "I asked you how stiff you want your drink! Mimosa? Straight champagne? We have enough liquor to kill a horse back here and I'll keep you hydrated so it won't hurt tomorrow. Just tell me what you typically like and I'll bring you somethin' that suits. Sweet? Savory? Did you want to remember the flight? Or should we just get to work on making it as unmemorable as possible?"

His smile widens.

Andy resembles a Ken doll, all muscles and taut tan skin, with a wide smile full of teeth as white as the snow. His short frosted hair stands up perfectly on the top of his head, thanks to a heavy helping of stiff hair gel.

I'm just about to tell him my order when Silas comes on board. Seeing him move toward me down the long aisle makes me feel on edge all over again, as if all the oxygen got sucked right out the door behind him. If only I could convince him to stay here in Boston while Andy and I travel to get the letters instead, I might actually enjoy myself.

"I'll have a mimosa," I say, eyeballing Silas while praying he chooses a seat further up the row. "If you have those."

"Of course," he says, beaming at me. Then he follows my narrowed eyes over to Silas and back to rest on my face again. "Anything else to make your flight more comfortable? A blanket? A noose?" He raises a brow.

"That's it," I tell him with a laugh. "Thank you."

"My pleasure. I'll be right back with that. And what can I get for you, sir?"

Andy turns to Silas as he reaches the seat right across the aisle from mine.

Ugh.

"Just black coffee, Andy, thank you," Silas says.

I'm a little jealous since I drained the nasty cup on the drive over, just to prove a point. But a mimosa sounds better right now anyway.

"How did things go in Tampa last week with your mom?" Silas asks.

Andy straddles the aisle, resting both forearms across one of the seat's backs in front of us.

"Mama pulled through just fine. Thank you again for insisting that I take ol' Gloria down there to be with her. Appendicitis waits for no one, just like her doctor told me. I wouldn't have been down there in time to be with her when she woke up from surgery if you hadn't insisted on it. Thank you again."

"It was nothing," Silas tells him, while pulling the seatbelt across his lap. "Glad she's recovering alright."

"Gloria?" I ask, confused. "Who's ol' Gloria?"

"That's just what the crew has nicknamed this jet," Silas says, smiling over at me before buckling his seatbelt.

Andy smiles at me warmly before adding, "After Gloria Estefan. This ol' bird was just begging to be addressed properly." He grazes my shoulder with a squeeze before making his way down the aisle toward the service kitchenette at the front of the plane. "And if you think ol' Gloria is pretty, you should see the Queen B!" he calls over his shoulder. "She's *gorgeous*!"

"Queen B?" I ask Silas, grinning as Andy disappears into a kitchenette. "Do you name all your jets after music icons?"

"If it helps the crew get us from point A to point B safe and sound, then I don't care what they call them," he says, smirking. "This flight is only around seven hours so we're taking this one. We'll take Queen B on anything over that."

"Oh," I say, feeling surprised. I didn't picture Silas having jets named after female pop stars, but I'm not totally surprised. The Si I knew back in college was always up for a good time, which I suppose hasn't changed. "Seven hours to Switzerland?" I frown.

"Long enough to take a shower and a long nap, if you'd like."

"Why, you think I need a shower?" I ask, preparing to be insulted, before realizing that he's actually offering me a shower *on an airplane*. "Wait, there's a shower on this thing?" I dart my eyes around the jet, trying to picture it. Of course he would have a shower on a plane. "And you use it? Isn't that dangerous? Like some mile-high shower club? That has to be slick."

He laughs.

"Yes, I do use it, and you're welcome to as well. There's a full bathroom in the back. No tub, sorry. But I had it stocked with the same toiletries you're used to, or at least . . ." He trails off, looking like he wants to kick himself for speaking out of turn. Then he clears his throat while I wait for him to finish explaining how he knows what type of shampoo I use. "Or at least the same brands you used a year ago, back when . . ." He gives me a sad sort of half-smile, balling his fists on his thighs before flattening his palms against them again.

"How would you know what type of toiletries I used a year ago?" I ask, feeling a bit unnerved. Sure, we were practically roommates when Grant and I were dating so he would have maybe seen what my toiletries were at one point, but not recently.

"Grant left quite a few notes on things like that for me while planning," he says, quietly. "To make sure you'd be comfortable."

I close my eyes when it sinks in. *Grant.*

"Never mind. Forget I asked. I showered this morning, thanks. I know it probably doesn't look like it anymore, but I'm good."

Andy returns down the aisle with a coffee mug and a mimosa balanced on a little tray. From how light in color it is, I can tell he filled the glass mostly with champagne, adding the tiniest little splash of orange juice, just to fulfill the promise of a mimosa.

"Thank you," I tell him when he hands me the champagne flute. I've never even flown first class, let alone had a whole private jet and staff almost entirely to myself.

"You let me know if that needs more juice," Andy says before handing the steaming mug to Silas next. "Though I basically only spritzed the fizz with OJ. You don't really need it when you're drinking Dom."

I nearly spill my glass.

"This is Dom Pérignon?" I stutter, gaping at Andy. I hold my glass up to take a closer look — as if Dom Pérignon has a different look than regular old bottom-shelf André. "Oh shoot, I wish I hadn't added any juice to it at all. I've always wondered what this tastes like. Though you really shouldn't have opened a whole bottle for me. I honestly won't even be able to taste the difference, I bet. I'm pretty low-maintenance, unlike Princess Silas over there."

I eyeball Si, annoyed that he's already waving his money around, stocking his plane with champagne that costs at least five hundred dollars a bottle. He just can't help himself.

"I'll get you a fresh glass to go with that one, then. Sans the juice," Andy says with a sweet smile before making his way back up the aisle. "The bottle is already open, so don't you dare say no or I'll be forced to finish it all myself!"

"No!" I call after him. "That's fine! I don't need another! You feel free to have it!"

But Andy doesn't turn around.

"It's fine." Silas holds a hand over the aisle, as if to reassure me, when all it does is annoy me. "There's always a couple of bottles of that on the plane, and the crew will stock it back up after we land. You could drink every bottle on this flight and every one after that too if you want. It really wouldn't matter to me."

"Andy can have it," I insist. "This is fine." I take a sip of the mimosa, then stare at the delicate bubbles rising to the surface.

Oh my God. It's more than fine.

"My crew doesn't drink while working." Silas smiles like I should already know that.

"Right. However, I still don't need two thousand dollars' worth of Dom Pérignon on the flight," I murmur toward the window. "Some of us don't drink *excessively*." I can feel Silas side-eyeing me after emphasizing the word. "And besides, I wouldn't have had him break the seal on anything if I'd have known it was so expensive."

Andy comes back a moment later with a second flute, which he places on my tray. This one doesn't have any orange juice added. Silas thanks him before he disappears into the galley of the plane again.

I make sure Si isn't watching before I sniff the straight champagne, then take a little sip.

"Oh wow, that's delicious," I admit quietly. "Tastes like a dry brut alright. Though I thought it might taste like twenty-four karat gold or a pile of money or something."

"Nah, you're thinking of the gold-infused champagne I have specially made back in Boston. That one tastes like gold-plated dollar bills."

I immediately shoot him a look, half-wondering if he's serious.

He remains deadpan until our eyes meet; then a hearty laugh bursts out of him. A sound, I admit, I've missed.

"Insufferable," I mutter, turning away before stealing another small sip.

"I suppose you've crossed off your first bucket list item then," he tells me. "Trying a champagne you've always wanted to try. Glad to see the trip is finally off to the right start."

I return a stiff smile, instantly remembering the reason behind our adventure.

The pilot's voice comes over the loudspeaker, commanding the crew to prepare for departure. Then the plane starts vibrating as the jet engines fire up and we ease toward the runway. My stomach begins hammering one warning shot after another. I don't know if I've ever *not* felt anxious during takeoff.

I feel Silas' eyes on me. When I turn, he looks as cool and calm as ever, giving me a faint, familiar smile as the plane's pace picks up speed. I soften, realizing for the first time that this trip we're starting might mean something to him, too.

"To Grant," I say, lifting my champagne up across the aisle between us. *May he keep us safe somehow*, I add silently.

Silas clinks his coffee mug against my champagne, and we both take a sip. I drain the rest of the glass before setting the empty flute back down on the tray, wiping my lips with the back of my hand. Then I close my eyes to lean my head against the headrest.

Silas starts laughing again and I squeeze one eye open to glare at him.

"What?"

"It's nothing."

"What?" I insist louder.

"Need another?" he asks, pointing at the empty flute. "Sometimes, at certain moments in life, this one possibly being one of those moments, it's okay to drink a bit *excessively*." He emphasizes my own word back at me, not bothering to hide his amusement.

I fight back an eye roll.

"I already have my backup right here," I say, smirking, tipping my second glass toward him. "I hate flying. You know that." I close my eyes but go on. "I just want to shut my eyes and be there so I can get that next letter from Grant as soon as humanly possible. The more the merrier. Then head back home in one piece."

"Makes sense. There's a bed in the back of the plane you can go lie down on as soon as we're high enough. Andy will let you know when we're clear."

I crack my eyes open to look at him straight on.

"That sounds fine," I say, trying to soften my voice while failing miserably. I hope I fall asleep before the plane starts edging higher so I don't have to speak to him again. At least until we land.

I'm pressed into my seat as the plane races toward liftoff, making the second full glass of champagne Andy left on my tray slowly slide across the surface toward my lap. Silas and I both lurch to grab it and our hands clasp onto the glass and onto each other momentarily, quick as a wink, before I can pull mine away again.

Silas keeps his hand stretched across the aisle, steadily holding the glass in front of me.

I take a deep breath and force myself to exhale slowly, steadying my nerves.

I should probably spend the remainder of the flight taking advantage of that bed in the back of the plane to put more distance between us. Sure, I could use a nap, but also because I'm not sure what I hate the most: the fact that I'm about to take off in a tiny airplane owned by Silas Davenport, or the way my stomach jumped when our hands touched just now.

CHAPTER 11

Silas

I focus on the feeling of the jet's wheels lifting off from the ground in order to stop my thoughts from racing, but I can barely keep my eyes on the wall ahead as we hurtle down the runway.

It's jarring every one of my senses to be this close to her again.

I didn't treat her well after I lost my father. But it wasn't just her. I didn't treat *anyone* well during that time of my life, including Grant. In hindsight, I gave her so many reasons to dislike me.

From the outside looking in, it should have been an unthinkably bittersweet moment for me: the passing of my father, laced with the inheritance of his empire. I always knew I'd inherit the family business if I wanted it, and rightfully, I always figured I would. Knowing I was set for life financially made me feel safe enough to screw off at school, treating Harvard like my own backyard playground. I broke all the rules while doing exactly what I needed to do in order to carry a high enough GPA to graduate. I inherited the type of cushy societal background that gifted me one thing: the privilege of never having to take life too seriously. Always knowing I had the family business to fall back on if I screwed up enough, which I did, time and time again.

However, I hadn't expected my father to die so young. He was the backbone of the money-making machine that funded my entire lifestyle. I thought I had at least another twenty years or so to screw around before inheriting the business that kept him working eighty-plus hours a week just so I could race off to Ibiza on the family jet at the drop of a hat.

It was the stress of that money-making machine that killed him one night at a business dinner at Hyacinth's on Eighth. A heart attack, right there at the table, while some poor waitress attempted CPR — probably for the first time in her whole life. It didn't work, obviously, but I gave her enough to retire on ten times over for trying.

I've imagined the moment he died on the cold tile floor of that restaurant with a stranger trying to save him a thousand times. Probably more. Him clutching his chest, eyes growing wide, face turning red. The whole thing. The way his tablemates probably didn't understand what was happening at first, before calling out to see if any doctors or nurses were present. I've wondered countless times how long he lay there, writhing on the ground with an invisible tourniquet squeezing his chest before the waitress finally realized that no one else was going to even attempt it. And finally, the moment she knelt on the ground and pinched his nose to deliver that first breath. Probably too late already.

He was gone before the paramedics arrived, proving once and for all that it doesn't matter how much money you have. You can die right there at the table before the dessert is even delivered.

Grant was with me when I got the call. I'd taken him on yet another boys' trip away from home, and away from Jules, just days after they got engaged. This one was to Aruba. We were with three other friends, walking down the boardwalk to a strip of seedy bars outside the main touristy area when my phone rang.

"Your father's passed." His assistant had delivered the news of his death to me just like that. No pretense, no apologies. No *hello Silas* to start. My father was no saint, but I still remember how little care she'd taken in sharing the news with me that day.

"The company is yours now. We've sent a car to your GPS location to pick you and your friends up. The jet will be waiting for you all to return to Boston immediately. You'll need to start approving the funeral arrangements when you return."

I heard nothing after that. Instead, I handed the phone to Grant. Slack-jawed, my face white as a sheet, or so he told me later.

"He's dead," I told him. Plain and simple, just like she told me. "My dad. Dead."

The rest is hazy. From what little I remember, Grant stood a few feet away from me on the sidewalk, holding my phone to his ear, making the rest of the arrangements with my dad's assistant while I tried to hold down the acidic bite of bile rising up in my throat. We just stared at each other, neither one of us blinking, while he calmly gave one-word answers to God knows how many questions being asked of him on the other end of the line. He continued to be there for me that day and every day after, more than anyone else had ever been, or would be again.

My asshole attitude from that moment on certainly cemented that.

I was twenty-six years old, standing on a cracked sidewalk just outside a dirty-looking bar with a sign that proclaimed *Cold tequila and hot girls!* when my whole life picked up speed, swirling around me like a tornado. From that moment on, responsibility and adulthood came hurtling toward me from the sawed-off barrel of a shotgun.

A week later, I buried my father.

Afterward, when I peeled out of the cemetery in his blacked-out Pagani Huayra instead of the dowdy town car with a driver that his former assistant had arranged for me, I felt every moral code inside of me snap. Like puppet strings pulled too tight, for too long, ripping apart at the seams.

I shot out of his funeral like a bat out of hell, allowing his legacy empire to run off the expertise of everyone else he'd hired and worked beside for years. I wanted nothing to do with it and buried my head in the sand. I had no idea what I was doing, and the thought of it absolutely terrified me. Paralyzed me. Without Davenport Media, I was nothing, yet, I had no idea how to run it. Any of it. There was supposed to be more time for me to learn, more time for me to show up and give my father the attention to detail that he'd begged me so often to have while ignoring how to handle the ropes of the company. *His* company. *Our* company. I always thought I'd have more time.

He wasn't supposed to die when he had.

Yet, neither was Grant.

Important people rarely pass when they should — a lesson I've learned too many times now. Yet, it's always unsettling when it comes around again.

My mother's death was exactly that, especially since I was only eight years old at the time. That one sent me spiraling, rebelling fiercely, especially while at Fox Glenn.

I may have rebelled after losing my mother, but it was my father's death that destroyed me.

That was when so many of my relationships went up in flames in the aftermath.

I study Jules out of the corner of my eye as our jet climbs in altitude. Her hands are clasped across her lap and her eyes are squeezed shut, though I can tell she's still awake.

I try to imagine where she must have been when she got the news about Grant. Whether she was sitting right next to him when he inhaled for the last time, or who might have been there to see pain dilate her eyes when she got the phone call, like Grant was there for me when I got the call about my dad.

As much as I like to think that I know this beautiful woman sitting next to me, I don't anymore. We purposefully shut each other out of the most important moments of our lives. I have no idea who held her while she cried, or made sure she ate on days when she couldn't get out of bed. She was surrounded by a sea of well-intended supporters at Grant's funeral, but I didn't know who most of them were, only recognizing her best girlfriends from college in the seats closest to her, with her parents flanking her other side.

I don't even know if she's started dating in the past year, or moved on entirely in other ways.

She carefully plants her hands on the armrests on either side of her body once the plane begins to even out, increasingly more parallel to the ground. Her long, slender fingers are splayed out across the soft leather trim as she clutches the edges like that seat might actually protect her if we start spiraling back down toward the earth.

I don't know much about her now, but I do know that following my father's death, I was not someone Jules wanted to be around. Not someone she wanted Grant to be around either. I wish I could take it all back. At the time, I'd become the very definition of an ugly, grief-stricken cliché. A party-boy orphan flung into a multi-billion-dollar empire, the exact week they got engaged. The timing of it all was the perfect storm for reckless behavior, and one I tried so hard to drag Grant into with me.

I understand why Jules pushed away from me as hard as I pushed away from her.

Seeing her now with a clearer head than I've had in years, I want nothing more than to be someone she allows near her again, instead of keeping me at arm's length. I only hope she gives me the chance to show her how much I've changed. And if she walks away from this trip knowing nothing but that, it'll all have been worth it.

CHAPTER 12

As soon as the pilot mentions we've reached cruising altitude, Jules makes a hasty beeline for the back of the plane where the bed is already made.

"Let me know when I need to buckle up again," she calls back before disappearing behind the closed door.

I manage to get a bit of work done, and six hours later, after Andy has retrieved her from the plane's only bedroom, she's back beside me, buckling the seatbelt over her hips.

"How was your nap?" I ask. Her hair has been tied back at the nape of her neck and long tendrils spill out across her delicate collarbones. Some color has returned to her cheeks, and she looks more rested than she did all morning.

"Fine," she answers, yawning.

"Good afternoon," the pilot's voice crackles over the loudspeaker. "There's going to be some moderate turbulence as we make our descent into Bern. Please stay buckled until after we land. Attendants, that goes for you too, especially you, Andy."

I hear a loud chuckle from the service kitchen.

"Roger that!" Andy hollers toward the cockpit, and I smile, once again, glad to have a bit of humor on the plane with us.

I glance at Jules. Her eyes are closed again.

"Wonderful," she murmurs without stirring. "I love a good rollercoaster ride forty thousand feet up."

"A little turbulence never hurt anyone," I say, doing my best to sound reassuring. "Nothing's going to happen."

"No offense, Si, but I don't think you're going to be able to do a damn thing if this plane decides that it doesn't love whatever air pockets we're coming into at five hundred miles an hour." Apparently the long nap didn't sweeten her mood.

We hit a pocket of air that makes the plane feel like it's in freefall for a fraction of a second. She gasps and her hand instinctively shoots over the aisle between us. She digs her nails into my forearm. The plane dips again and she holds her breath, squeezing tighter, like her hold on me might actually save her if this thing goes down.

When the plane rights itself, she relaxes a bit.

"Sorry," she says, loosening her grip, still keeping her eyes shut, then wraps both arms in front of her chest.

I'm reminded of how odd it is for her to be here with me — to be reaching out to *me* right now instead of Grant.

Another air pocket jolts the plane down, then up.

"Oh my God," she murmurs under her breath, grabbing onto my arm again. This time tighter than before. "Tell Gloria to calm the fuck down."

"Ol' Gloria is keeping us in the air, and besides, Carl is a former military pilot I recruited. He's flown through worse while dodging combat fire. I also have a team of engineers prep the planes before every flight. You have literally nothing to worry about." I pat her hand just as she pulls it back.

"Don't do that," she snaps.

"Do what?" I ask.

"That." She points to the hand I've just used to pat hers. I thought it might make her feel better but clearly I got that wrong, too. "I get that Grant told you that you have to do this trip with me. I'm not totally sure why you agreed, since there's nothing in this for you. But you don't have to act like you care more about me now than you used to just because we're here. I'm not one of the girls from your tabloid photos who might be impressed with all this." She waves her hands around the jet. "So, you don't have to try and impress me by talking about engineers and fighter pilots you found." She settles back against her seat again. "I think you know me a little better than that. Or at least you did at one point."

"Sorry," I mutter, shifting in my seat. I'd like to argue back, tell her that she's wrong but I'll leave it at that for now. "I'm just trying to reassure you that it's going to be fine."

She relaxes her shoulders a fraction of an inch. "Well, I'm glad you're on top of safety — just don't feel like you have to flaunt it."

Flaunt it? I narrow my eyes. "I'll add it to the list, Jules," I murmur, possibly too quiet for her to hear, then add a bit louder, "And I do, by the way."

"You do what?"

"Care. About you. Now. Then. Always have," I tell her smoothly and calmly as if I'm reciting an indisputable fact from a history book.

Another pocket of air makes the plane dip, harder this time, before righting again. Jules' hand shoots back to my forearm, grabbing it even harder.

I look down pointedly at her nails digging into my skin, then up at her face. Her eyes are still closed but she cracks a discreet smile, as if she knows she's being ridiculous. She might want comfort right now, but she's not going to pretend like it's okay coming from me.

I smirk in her direction, even though she can't see it, before straightening my face to stare at the back of the seat a few yards in front of me. I'll play the game. I'll allow her hand to squeeze my arm harder with each passing moment without acknowledging that it's even there.

I peek one eye over at her.

She must feel my gaze and the obnoxious grin that accompanies it.

"Shut up and just let me hold your arm," she mumbles. Then she yelps when the plane takes another sizable dip.

I chuckle and shake my head toward the front of the plane when Andy pops his head out of the galley to check on us. I wave him off silently, wondering what Grant might think if he could see us right now. Probably happy that we're together, if not still on rocky territory.

"Sure, Jules," I say, under my breath, still smiling to myself. "Whatever you need."

* * *

Things don't get much better once we arrive at the hotel.

"What do you mean we're staying in the same suite? Monica said she would look into changing that."

Jules is staring at me like I've just thrown a glass of ice water over her head, both annoyed and wildly unimpressed.

"I believe she said it was too late for this hotel," I say, getting a nod from the attendant on the other side of the check-in counter.

We're standing in the lobby of Interlaken's most beautiful luxury hotel, right in front of the reservations desk. The opulent motif in here is like an old-world chalet sandwiched between two glowing turquoise mountain lakes, each fed by the towering snow-capped mountain peaks surrounding them. But Juliet's excitement and awe for the scenery subsided the moment the attendant behind the counter mentioned our one and only suite reservation was ready.

"You can't be serious, Silas. You have more money than God, which we don't even need to discuss. Just get another one so I can have this one."

She turns back to the attendant and slaps her credit card on the counter.

"You know what? I'll just pay for another room," she says, throwing a bit of cheer into her voice.

The attendant doesn't move, clearly waiting for our squabble to end.

"This is how Grant asked Monica to set up the reservations," I remind her, pushing her credit card back toward her. Apparently, Monica gave her false hope. "You won't even know I'm there once we're checked in. There are multiple rooms in the suite. This is how Grant set it all up so let's just go with it."

"Well, Grant's dead." We both cringe at the word *dead*, but she continues, turning back toward the worker behind the counter. "So, he doesn't get to make the arrangements anymore. I'd like my own, please."

She slides the card back across the reservation desk toward the woman checking us in.

"I'm sorry, it's the only suite of rooms we have open currently, but it's a two-bedroom setup so there's separate sleeping quarters, a living room, and a dining area," she tells my surly travel partner. "It's quite private for you both."

"You heard her. It's quite private," I repeat.

She glares at me, nose flaring with every inhale, like she'd rather bolt from this hotel than stay in any room that's connected to mine.

She turns back to the attendant.

"I'll take a non-suite then, please. And there's supposed to be a letter waiting for me here?"

"The only other room I have open is . . . *quite* nice."

Jules lets out a long breath and pushes the credit card to the edge of the counter, nearly tipping it onto the worker's keyboard.

"Wonderful. I'll take it."

"It'll be eleven hundred per night, plus taxes and fees. And I'll need your passports to check you in as well."

Jules' jaw drops.

"As in, dollars?"

"As in Swiss francs. That's roughly thirteen hundred dollars per night, plus the taxes and fees."

She clears her throat while I swallow down a laugh. Then she tilts her chin toward me, eyes wide. I'm busy restricting another chuckle while I watch her face morph into a defiant grin.

"I'll take it," she announces, keeping her eyes locked on mine.

I grab her card off the counter.

"No, she won't," I tell the attendant. I turn to Jules. "Juliet Hart, you're being ridiculous. Just follow his plan. I won't go near your room. Why would I, seeing as you've been so *fun* to travel with this far?" I add, sarcastically.

She sighs, then silently debates her options. Finally, she takes her card back and stuffs it in her wallet.

"You've got to be kidding me," she mumbles under her breath. "Fine. Whatever." Then she rummages through her handbag and slaps her passport down on the counter before turning toward me. "Do you have yours?"

"Does this mean we're checking in?" I ask, removing my passport from my briefcase. I hold it above the countertop until she confirms. "Just one suite?"

"Just give her the damn passport, Silas," she mutters, rolling her eyes. "Let's get the key to the suite so we can get our hands on the letter, and then we'll talk about accommodations. I'm too hungry to argue about this anymore."

The attendant's face brightens.

"Yes, I see a note about that here in your reservation. It looks like the letter has been left in our hotel safe for quite some time now. If I can get both of your passports, please . . ." She pauses to eyeball me. "It says you both need to sign for it." The attendant is calm, ignoring the spat we've just had, as if she's watched thousands of couples argue at check-in. Even though Jules and I are definitely not a couple. "And it looks like it will be released to you once you've checked into *the suite*."

I place my passport next to hers. Andy, Carl, and the rest of the flight crew are staying at another hotel in town — giving them much needed privacy from the two of us. Fortunately, it's just Jules and I here now in the lobby.

"It's not about having a fancy set of rooms," I tell her. "I won't go near your side. It's just how the reservations were made. For whatever reason, this is how Grant planned it."

"Don't you think it's a bit late for that? It's not like he can jump out and scold us for disobeying his almighty travel plan. It was probably just an oversight anyway. Grant was always very frugal."

"You're not going to be this big of a pain in the ass the entire trip, are you?" I ask before I can stop myself.

The attendant tucks her lips behind her teeth, but continues to check us in silently.

"Are you?" Jules shoots back. The corners of her mouth rise, her angry facade cracking ever so slightly as if she's slightly enjoying this.

I'm about to respond, but her lips widen. It's the first semblance of a smile since we landed here in Switzerland, and I decide to just let her have this round.

"Fair," I tell her. "I promise not to bother you once we're checked in."

"Fine. But don't expect me to come out of my side unless it's to eat. Or drink. *Excessively*," she adds.

I hold in a laugh.

"It's a deal."

"What are we doing here in Interlaken anyway?"

"Skydiving," I tell her matter-of-factly while grabbing both key cards off the counter. "We're jumping out of a plane in the morning."

She turns, eyes bulging, just as the attendant places a familiar-looking envelope down on the counter between us.

The stiff yellowed paper is marked with Juliet's name, scribbled across the front in Grant's telltale writing. Seeing this little piece of him again pulls something apart inside me. Right before she can snatch it away and head off toward the room.

CHAPTER 13

Juliet

After getting the keys and taking an elevator up what felt like eighty stories, even though it was under a dozen, I shut my bedroom door and crawl under the big, fluffy down comforter stretched out across the bed.

To think that just yesterday I was finishing up my last round of coaching sessions, naively walking away from Pete and back to my house, completely unaware that this whole thing was about to explode open in my face.

Now, I'm sitting a world away from Boston, unable to enjoy a place I've always dreamed of going because Silas is ruining every spare moment I've had here so far.

Not that he's ruining every spare moment, exactly. Just that he's confusing the hell out of me. So many things about him remind me of the man he used to be, back when we were all friends. But I feel like it's just a facade to get through this trip in peace together. To prove to me that he's not as bad as I know deep down he is. It's hard to know what's real about him anymore given everything that's happened.

It annoys me to no end. The fact that today was supposed to be the first day of my new year. The three hundred and sixty-sixth day to get through with no red X to mark at the end of it.

This is the day that I told myself the world would all start making sense again.

But, instead of waking up to a fresh calendar and a home cleared of reminders, I'm surrounded by nothing *but* reminders.

Reminders of Grant.

Reminders of Silas.

And perhaps most of all, reminders of the girl I was before everything in our lives went sideways. I'd forgotten how quick-witted and awake I could be when faced with an equal sparring partner like Silas *fucking* Davenport. Someone who isn't afraid to challenge me, or call me out. And every moment I'm around him, it feels like I'm saying *hello* again to the person I was before. Finally able to come back out of a long hibernation, tearing my way out of a thick layer of bubble wrap I've been trapped in all year.

I can recall the exact moment everyone in my life started treating me like I was suddenly fragile. Whispering quietly in the next room. Oohing and ahhing over me each time I smiled a real smile, or was "*brave enough*" to go out and do something — *anything* — I used to love to do.

Ever since Grant was declared terminal, I'd changed. Deeply. Of course, nearly every part of me had changed. But it wasn't just *me*. Something else I never could have predicted happened: Everyone else *around* me changed, too. Namely in the way that they treated and interacted with me. I lost everything familiar to me, even the relationships that were solely there to support me.

It's unreal how much I've missed being treated like a whole person who's strong and capable, instead of just a fraction of one — like I might dissolve into thin air at any moment, should someone utter the wrong thing around me.

But today with Silas, all he's done is say the wrong thing. A lot of wrong things. In fact, he hasn't treated me like I might break at all, and he definitely isn't afraid to tell me when I'm being a pain in the ass. Which I have been, in all honesty, since the moment he picked me up.

I know everyone around me changed in how they treated me because they felt like they had to. They did it out of love, and probably because I needed a soft place to land once we knew Grant was dying. But those days turned into weeks and those weeks into a year, and now, feeling what it's like to be treated as a whole person again, instead of just the girl who lost her fiancé? The girl who's fragile when I know deep down that I'm not? I don't want to give that feeling up.

I know I'm deliberately challenging Silas — sparring more than I might — simply because it feels good to have someone challenge me back.

It's absurd. I settle into the mattress, reveling in the softness of the sheets. The dusky view out my window. The feeling of something that Grant himself held, now safely tucked inside this room with me.

I can hear my suitemate thumping away at something in the other room. His shower turning on, a faucet turning off. A suitcase knocked to the floor. So much for Silas being completely undetectable while we share this place together.

I roll onto my back, drag the comforter up to my chin and settle deeper into the cushy mattress and pillows, slowly ripping the envelope open, one little tear at a time.

Then I take one more deep breath, before finally pulling out what's inside.

CHAPTER 14

Grant
One year ago

>   Dearest Jules,
>   If you're reading this, you've made it to Interlaken, which means you agreed to this whole harebrained idea of mine. Well done! Silas must be right on the other side of your wall, unless you banished him to his own suite, which I hope you didn't.
>   I know I swore that going on this trip would be my final request, but I have one more. Although this request is much simpler, and I hope easier for you to agree to . . .
>   Enjoy yourself.
>   Have fun.
>   That's it.
>   It's been a whole year since I've been gone, so if you haven't given yourself permission to do so yet, enjoy a good belly laugh or two. Do it often and without reserve. If I were there, I'd want you to laugh so often that your face feels permanently sore from stretching itself out with pure, unadulterated joy.
>   Be the girl you were before all this stupid stuff happened. I sent you on this trip with Silas because he's the best

person I know for letting loose, for changing the very makeup of a person when they need it the most.

When I met him at boarding school, I was a shadow of the man you met in college. I was painfully shy and I think that's the real reason my father sent me off to live elsewhere. To grow. Silas and his father were practically estranged from the time his mother died, so boarding school was the obvious choice to get him out of the house, but my own upbringing could not have been more different from his. You know my parents and I are close, so I think it nearly killed them to make the decision to send me off to Fox Glenn, but they did it to bring me out of my shell. Nothing they could give me at home could compare to the social immersion I would experience while away at school. There was no one to speak up for me, or to make necessary changes to my schedule when I needed it. I was on my own island there, which was exactly what I needed to find my voice. Except I figured out how to be alone while surrounded by other people.

And maybe that sounds familiar to you by now? Or maybe it doesn't.

At any rate, when Silas introduced himself as my new boarding school roommate, I was this nerdy kid with coke-bottle glasses and tube socks pulled high, almost up to my knobby kneecaps, when in walks the coolest kid I'd ever seen.

Most of the other kids at Fox Glenn were polished and clean, or a little nerdy just like me, but then comes this striking example of what Fox Glenn's admin would never want invading their brochures. He paraded into our room like he owned the place. Skinny arms hanging out the sleeves of his cut-off tank, big headphones covering both ears, and his too-long hair curled over the nape of his collar — well past what the dress code policy would allow. Which I would know because I'd studied the school handbook before arriving, like there was going to be a special exam over it.

Nothing about our friendship made sense. He was too cool for school while I was the type to memorize the handbook.

But we quickly became as inseparable as boyhood roommates often become.

When people saw Silas, there I was, and he to me. He brought me out of my shell. Gave me permission to break a rule here and there, as long as it wasn't too big of a deal. We balanced each other out. Me, keeping our borderline expellable adventures small enough to maintain enrollment, while he made sure our time there was memorable in all the best ways. Late nights out on the track field, eating stolen leftover chocolate cake from the cafeteria under a blanket of stars, or sneaking out past curfew to meet the girls from the school down the road. I think even my parents were secretly half-giddy every time I got a demerit sent home because it meant I was having a good time. That I was straying just enough from the absolute straight and narrow path I'd been on since birth to have a fantastic childhood. One I never would have gotten as an only child of two woefully busy parents. They knew that if I'd been paired with any of the other kids, whose noses had practically been flattened from being stuck inside textbooks from sunup to sundown each day, I never would have crawled out from my thick shell, or gained any confidence as a kid to carry me into the world with any sort of backbone.

The truth is, without Silas, I would never have become the man you fell in love with. A lot of the things you love about me were brought out by him.

Let go of your misgivings about the past where Silas is concerned, stored up in your most recent memories of him. He was better than that before his father died, and you had a front-row seat to the old him for so many years. Let him breathe some life into you as he did for me. You have only the future to look forward to now, and your future can be everything you dream of, as long as you're willing to let go of what you thought it would be with me.

Only onward and upward! Quite literally, Jules.

Tomorrow you'll board a plane that you won't be landing in. Remember me trying to convince you to do this back home? And you said, "Why do I need to see Massachusetts from a parachute when I can see it with my own two feet on the ground?" Here, in Interlaken, you're going to see it all from the sky. Mountain lakes, as light as the turquoise stone in your grandmother's ring. Glacier milk, they call it, surrounded by towering mountain ranges and glowing green hillsides draped in tiny yellow wildflowers. There's no way to get that view with your own two feet planted firmly down on the ground, so, wheels up at 10 a.m. No arguing. Silas has done this before. You're in good hands, my love. Always. Remember that.

Imagine me getting giddy from above as you earn your own demerits on this trip, doing everything you possibly can to surprise yourself — rebelling from the straight and narrow path you've always been on. There's fun to be had when you step outside the lines, so find your lines and blow past them, sweetheart.

Just live.

And when you feel the wind whip past your face tomorrow, know that it's me, rushing down to join you. And that I'm so proud of you.

Above all (no pun intended), thank you, always, for letting me love you,

Grant

CHAPTER 15

Silas

The moment we arrived at our suite, Jules disappeared into her side and locked the door. I heard the ripping of the envelope followed by a stone-cold silence. Silence that stretched on for an hour while I paced around and tried to keep myself busy, wondering what she was going through on the other side of that door, until I finally heard her shower turn on.

At some point, she must have ordered room service, because shortly after hearing the water turn off, there's a knock at our door.

A tall, lanky man wearing a smart maroon uniform rolls in a cart with two silver domes sitting beside a bottle of dark, red wine and a few empty glasses.

"Danke schoen," I say to him, slipping the worker a few extra bills for delivering the food before shutting the door behind him.

Then I hear Juliet's bedroom door crack open. She appears in a fluffy white robe with her wet hair combed back from her freshly scrubbed face.

"Did you order dinner?" I ask.

"Oh," she says, not moving to get the tray. "I ordered that thinking I'd be hungry by the time I got out. But that hasn't happened yet. I starving until I read that letter. Now, I can't tell if I'm still hungry."

"Jules," I say, sounding more stern than I mean to sound.

Her eyes flick up to mine, but she looks exhausted. All the fight — the bravado and toughness from earlier — is gone.

"You read it?" I ask, walking toward the cart to open the bottle of red wine to offer her a glass. I don't want to scare her back into her room, afraid her disdain toward me will keep her locked up in whatever bedroom she's checked into over the entire length of our trip if we keep going like we are.

"No, I thought I'd fly all the way here and then toss it out the window," she says, sighing but staring longingly at the glass I've filled. I side-eye her for a beat, not handing her the glass until she cuts the sarcasm. "Sorry," she relents. "Yes. I read it."

Without a word, I close the space between us and hand her the glass, then grab another empty one for me.

"And?" I ask.

"He said he wants me to have *fun*," she deadpans.

I snort before I can stop myself. Her head cocks to the side.

"Sorry," I say into my hand. Then I bring the glass up to my lips, distracting myself from unleashing into a second full-blown chuckle. The irony of that statement, mixed with the deflated look in her eyes, is too much. I quickly pull the glass back as a wide smile stretches over my face, and, before I can stop it, I let another snort roll out.

"What's so funny to you?" she asks, but when our eyes meet, I can see humor lifting her eyes too, fighting to stay hidden.

"Jules," I start, "I can't think of anything less fun than taking a trip with a guy you hate in place of your late fiancé. So, for him to suggest that to you is almost comical. No, not *almost*. It *is* comical."

I take a big swig of the wine, before clenching my teeth in an effort to stop laughing, but I can't. Another chuckle escapes me.

Her lips turn, tempting a smile, but she holds strong by biting her lip back before it can go full-blown rogue.

"Glad you get a kick out of that," she deadpans again.

"What else did he say?" I ask, hoping she'll let it all out instead of keeping everything about him bottled up. I know from experience how toxic that can be.

"That you were a real piece of work at school," she adds before making her way over to the couch in the sitting area. She plops onto it and takes a long gulp from her own stemware, turning the inner half of her lips a deeper shade of red.

"Is that right?" I ask, following her lead. I sit in the chair farthest away from her, fully aware that I'm treating her like a caged animal. One wrong move and she might retreat back into her habitat, only to be coaxed out again with red wine and sustenance.

"He said you brought him out of his shell." She looks down at her glass and swirls it around a bit. "And that every time you two got in trouble at boarding school, he believes his parents were slightly proud of him because it meant that he was having fun. With you, he enjoyed a memorable childhood, which is what they really wanted for him when they sent him." She finally smiles and her blue eyes pool in mine. "I'm glad he got to have that experience with you."

I think back at the memory of meeting Grant for the first time. That day I walked into our dorm room and saw this stiff kid sitting with his back to me. His maroon tie all cinched up around his neck, even though classes wouldn't be starting for two full days. Then the way he looked at me like I was an undiscovered specimen from one of his biology slides — something he'd never seen before.

I'd only ever felt invisible while home. What I'd never told Grant in those early days of our friendship was that he was the first person to look at me like I was anything worth seeing. I needed him as much as he needed me, and we fed off each other from the moment we said hello. Him needing someone to pull him out of his shyness, and me needing a true friend, which is exactly what he turned out to be.

"I might have pulled him out of his shell, but he gave me what I needed the most back then," I admit to her, taking another long sip of my wine. It's going down smooth and quick. We may need to dive into whatever's under those silver domes pretty soon so we don't immediately get drunk off this burgundy.

"And what was that?" she asks. "A wingman? Someone to follow you around on all your silly antics just like you needed after—" She cocks her head, stopping before she says *after your father died*. And although it's not exactly an invitation for a full-blown conversation, or really one I want to have, I'm happy she's willing to talk to me at all right now.

"I needed a friend," I answer, shrugging. "If I think back at my life before meeting Grant, the first word that comes to my mind is *lonely*. Then *invisible*. I was an only child, raised by a collection of nannies and a father who was married to his business. I always had a hunch that I reminded him of my mother, so Dad rarely looked in my direction. By the time I arrived at Fox Glenn, the only long-term companion I'd had was trouble. Grant was the first friend I ever had. He kind of took the place of family *and* friends in my head. And my heart. He was like a brother to me."

She lowers her glass onto her lap and scrunches her nose.

"I never knew that about your childhood," she admits. "I only ever heard stories from after you met."

"I'm sure Grant never really talked about my past all that much," I say, brushing it off, wondering why I felt the need to disclose something so personal right now. "When I came in and saw him in my dorm room that day . . . oh boy." I pause to laugh. "I honestly didn't know what to think. He was the textbook definition of a dork. But I loved that about him. You know how some people just fit together like a puzzle piece? Even though nothing about it makes sense?"

She nods, amused. "Of course."

"That was us. We were meant to fit together, even if none of the edges matched."

"Opposites attract," she agrees and her eyes shine. "Grant had a way of fitting together with lots of people who weren't like him."

"That's because *no one* was like him." I smile.

She looks wistful for a beat. Almost, *almost* with a tinge of admiration thrown in my direction, like I understand something she thought only she understood.

"He was good in practically every way, which is not a quality many people share," I tell her.

She laughs. "He was the better part of me, too. I don't know what's gotten into me since he died. I'm like a raging bitch that can't rein it in. And don't tell me I'm wrong." Her eyes fly to mine, looking slightly alarmed. "But also don't agree with that either, please."

I purse my lips, not allowing myself to agree. "No, I get it. Losing someone can change a person past the point of recognition." I wait until our eyes meet, hoping she gets what I'm trying to say. "But I don't think you're a raging bitch." She cocks a brow at me, making me laugh. "You really don't have to explain it to me, Jules. Of all people," I remind her.

We sit in silence for a moment, both feeling the weight that comes with missing the one person we both loved the most — his absence, hanging in the air between us. Lighter though, somehow, like just having someone else to hold the weight of it with you somehow eases the load.

"He also wrote that we're jumping out of a perfectly good plane tomorrow." She brings the wine glass back up to her lips, taking a bigger gulp this time. "So, you weren't lying about that part after all."

"You're going to love it," I tell her. "Promise."

"Wholeheartedly doubt that." She drains the glass.

"You're welcome to squeeze my arm anytime you need it tomorrow, though."

She shoots me a look, but the beginning hints of a smile take over before she can stop it.

Ha.

It dawns on me that I haven't actually seen her eat anything today, and the way she's downing the wine makes me think she may regret it once we're zooming across the runway in a tiny prop plane tomorrow morning. Plus, the Jules I used to know wasn't one to shy away from the inevitable downward pull of being hangry.

I get up to see what's hidden under the silver domes on the cart. There's a wedge salad under the first one, so without a word, I pull the plate down and hand it to her with a fork along with the little silver dish of dressing on the side. She sets it down on the coffee table between us, then pushes it away.

"Jules, eat," I scold, staring at the plate. "Trust me when I say you're going to want something in your stomach before you go to bed tonight. Little planes feel like a rollercoaster at takeoff, but that's nothing compared to free-falling from thirteen thousand feet up. At the very least, get some lettuce between you and that red wine before bed, please."

She cracks a smile, then pulls the plate back onto her lap, setting her empty wine glass on the table in favor of a fork.

I lift the other dome off the tray, surprised to see a thick steak sitting on the plate, with a mound of roasted veggies beside it. A cloud of peppery spices wafts up to my nose, making my stomach rumble. I wouldn't have guessed Jules would order a steak in addition to that salad. She must be hungrier than she's letting on.

I grab the plate and turn to put it on the coffee table in front of her, but she puts one hand up to stop me, her mouth still full.

"No," she mumbles between bites. "That's for you."

I look at the rib eye, then at Juliet, who's gone back to arranging her next bite.

"For me?" I figured she'd rather I starve to death so she could collect my death certificate and finish the trip without me.

"Don't make a whole thing of it," she huffs, still chewing. She waves her fork at me without looking up. "I figured you'd be hungry too."

Instead of saying another word, I sit down beside her on the couch, the plate of food balanced on my knees. Then I reach behind me to grab another set of silverware off the tray and cut into the steak, trying not to smile or read too much into the fact that she was thinking of me when she ordered this food. It might be the smallest gesture, but it's not nothing. I'd had a late dinner planned at the hotel's five-star restaurant downstairs, but I can tell that she doesn't want to get dressed to go do that right now.

I saw the steak in half and plop the thicker portion down on her plate, right next to her salad.

"I don't need that—" she starts to protest.

"Shhh," I whisper, not turning away from my plate. "Just eat it. You'll thank me in the morning."

We sit in silence, both working away at our steaks, while I start to think that maybe, just maybe, there's still hope for this trip after all.

CHAPTER 16

Juliet

The next morning, we've gone through a long safety briefing at the private hangar that basically covers all the ways we can die, including the very traditional *my chute didn't open* option, before signing all our legal rights off to the skydiving company.

The whole thing has me feeling like this is the stupidest thing I've ever gotten myself into.

I glance over at Jett, the tandem diver who will be strapped to my back, his name really quite fitting. Jett has an ever-present smile on his face, with shoulders that are around four times the width of mine. He looks to be in his early twenties. I wish he looked a little more seasoned or experienced, but I'm doing my best to ignore what we're about to do while I select a bright purple jumpsuit with a pink stripe up the side from a rack of flight suits they set out for me. My brain silently adds quippy comments while I try to make my selection.

Is that really the best choice to die in?

What will that purple look like when splattered out across the ground?

Could I possibly push Silas from the plane once the door slides open?

"First time?" Jett asks, pulling me out of my head.

He grins at me as he jumps up and down a few times to stretch himself out, looking more like an Olympic athlete or Roman statue cut from a solid hunk of marble than a skydiving partner. His navy-blue eyes match his own vinyl jumpsuit, and they're shining at me like a kid in a candy store. He's cute. Okay, he's well-beyond cute. And, unlike most of the men I've talked to in the last year, he's not a client. Or an annoying old friend.

"Yes, first and probably only time." I nod, reluctantly stepping into my purple jumpsuit before pulling it up past my hips. The vinyl hangs loosely over my spandex leggings — courtesy of Katie for this particular adventure.

"Nervous?" he asks. His grin grows wider. His accent is cute and I wish we could make less stilted conversation before I trust him with my actual life.

My fingers shake as I pull the sleeves over my arms and I try my best to zip the whole thing up. It takes a few tries, before he grabs the clasp from my hands and slowly pulls it clear up to my neck.

He's grinning at me when I look up, holding on to the zipper a beat longer than necessary, and I realize, with a start, that this guy might actually be attempting to flirt with me.

Oh. Oh, okay.

It's been a minute, and I feel a bit rusty, but this guy doesn't know a thing about me, or my past. Why not give it a momentary go?

"Do you remember your first time?" I ask, squinting at Jett, wishing so badly that I spoke better German. Or *any* German, really.

"First time? Me?" He puts his hand over his thick chest and I nod.

He gets a funny look on his face then throws his arms out to the side, pretending to fly toward the ground with a terrified look on his face. He stops and breaks into a smile, nodding sheepishly.

"I remember," he adds. "*So* scary."

I wish I hadn't asked. My stomach doubles the knot that's already there.

"But so fun!" He scrunches his face and gently grabs my arm, like he wishes he hadn't added any fuel to my ever-growing nerves. "You'll need to hang on tight." He pats his shoulders, which makes his biceps flex enormously.

"I can do that," I tell him, feeling a hint of blush creep across my cheeks.

God, I'm so awkward at this.

I glance across the room at Silas, who has already selected a cherry-red jumpsuit from another rack holding his size options. His hair is still mussed from last night since he worked from his laptop right up until our car arrived this morning and he didn't have time to shower.

He's not watching Jett and I, but instead he's talking with the tandem diver assigned to him — a guy named Ethan, who looks older and much more experienced than Jett. Silas' green eyes are giddy and glowing, without a hint of nervousness, right above his white grin. Ethan looks to be twice the age of Jett, and I'm more than a little envious that they've been assigned to jump together. Instead I've been assigned to jump with someone who could pass as my much younger, meathead brother.

I smile at Jett, who's still jumping around, full of as much nervous energy on the outside as I'm feeling on the inside.

"You want Ethan?" Jett asks, apparently noticing the wistfulness in my eyes while I stare at the other diver.

"No." I brush him off quickly, wishing I could stop a deeper blush from seeping into my cheeks. The last thing I need to do is piss off the guy in charge of securely strapping me to him.

He grins until I relent.

"Okay, I mean, he just looks much older. More experienced?" I say, nervously laughing, then add a shrug like it's a question. "Can't blame me for wanting someone who has loads of experience."

"I'm experienced," he tells me, nudging my arm. Then he hops back and forth like a track star heading into a big race. "Experienced in *everything* that matters."

He winks. Like, actually winks.

"Oh!" I don't know what else to say. *Jesus, take the wheel.*

He has the guts to wink at me, the look on his face saying more than his words, and I give Silas a withering glance. My heart starts to pound.

"Don't be nervous," Silas says, saddling up next to me.

"Your boyfriend?" Jett asks, pointing to him.

"Boyfriend?" I repeat before a high-pitched sputtery laugh comes out. "No!"

"Lucky man," Jett says to Silas, nodding appreciatively.

"No," I insist louder. "Definitely not boyfriend."

I step back from both the men. *What would give him that impression?*

Silas only laughs, completely unbothered.

"Please," I huff, rolling my eyes at them.

We all turn to watch a few more crew members who have appeared in the hangar. They're pulling a tiny prop plane out of a private bay using a dolly.

A *dolly*.

I'm about to make it very clear that Silas is not my boyfriend when I realize that the plane they're pulling out is meant for us.

"That?" I point at the plane as it's wheeled out of the enormous half-dome building. I don't know what I was expecting, but definitely not a plane that's small enough to be pulled out of a hangar by a guy with a little lever in his hand. "You have got to be kidding me. No way. Nope."

Immediately, I start walking back toward the rack to pull my jumpsuit off, but Silas keeps up, jogging beside me.

"Oh, no you don't!" he says, passing me.

I nearly bump into his chest when he darts in front of me, blocking my path to the rack full of jumpsuits. I put my hands on my hips and jut my chin out while I stare up at him, our chests nearly touching.

"I'm not getting in that tin can of a plane," I say, pointing at what appears to be a toy instead of an actual flying machine.

"The worst part is the flight up. But you'll already have a parachute on so—" He stops as my glare intensifies. He tries again. "Okay, you know, this location is probably why Grant chose this spot anyway. It's meant to be a distraction. People go on helicopter tours of this area for the incredible scenery. Once the wheels are up and you're floating in the clouds above those glaciers . . ." He points to the mountain range just beyond the runway. "Once you see those lakes again from above, you're going to forget about being scared at all. I promise."

"Oh, I highly doubt that," I tell him. I pull my jumpsuit zipper down past my crotch to step out, not giving him another chance to persuade me.

Before I realize what's happening, Silas has grabbed my zipper, and he's fumbling around, trying to zip the jumpsuit back up. But it's stuck.

His hands are working shockingly close to me, barely brushing against me each time he yanks, but the zipper won't give.

I step back, but he comes with me.

"Trust me," he huffs, finally jerking the zipper up past my belly button, but it sticks again at my chest.

"Silas, really?" I ask, widening my eyes, slapping his hand away.

He's already turned red.

"That was supposed to be much faster. It got stuck. I didn't mean to, um."

"The zipper sticks," I deadpan.

"Well, you could have told me that."

"When? In the split second you were lunging toward my crotch?"

"Well, yeah."

Jett steps up just behind Silas and points at the zipper, still stuck at my bra line.

"You need my help again?" he asks.

Jesus Christ.

"No," I exclaim, pulling it the rest of the way up myself.

"Ready?" Jett asks, blinking happily.

"No," I tell him, realizing that I just zipped my suit back up when what I really wanted to do was take the whole thing off and run out of the hangar.

I try to get the zipper to go down again but now it's stuck up at my neckline.

Silas grins, then bites his bottom lip.

"Come on, Jules. What did you think we were going to fly up in? A space ship? Just trust me on this."

"Why?"

"Because you used to," he says, as if it's the most simple answer in the whole world.

I swallow, not really expecting that.

"Key words being *used to*," I remind him. I try to jerk the zipper back down again while I go on, but it isn't budging. "Tell me why I should trust you *and* that toy plane, Si."

He laughs, hardly bothered, before grabbing my shoulders, giving me a gentle shake. Then he releases me and walks backward toward the plane with his arms outstretched, drawing out the distance between us.

"Because I would never take a chance with your life, babe."

I scoff. *Babe?* Before I get a chance to protest, he goes on.

"But just to put your mind at ease, I'll give you a little shake down of how I've got you covered. Even if you hate hearing about this shit, but only because you asked. Before we even got here, I flew my own personal mechanic out to go through the safety mechanisms of this plane, and to test out all the gear himself. He spent a week out here observing and checking everything about this top-notch operation. Then he was out again early this morning going over the entire safety checkpoint list with the crew, making sure it was in perfect condition. And I had these guys here," he goes on, pointing to Jett and Ethan, "train with an extra seventy dives this year alone, on top of their regular strict certifications, just to prep for this one and only dive with us today. Besides that, the parachute packs are mine. Jett and Ethan have the most up-to-date certifications which includes the special mechanisms used in these packs, which just so happen to be the best that money can buy."

My mouth is slightly ajar by the time Silas is done.

Is he joking?

I shift my eyes to Jett, who's smiling broadly, then Ethan, who's nodding. The rest of the crew is all watching me now, waiting for me to get into the tiny plane after all that.

Fucking hell.

"However, to be fair, it's not just me that you have to trust today," Silas calls out, smirking happily, knowing he just schooled me. He flicks his eyes over to the two tandem bros now standing by the door of the plane before looking back at me. His smile grows a bit more wild while they all watch me.

"I don't know if I can trust them either," I whisper loudly, wishing Jett and Ethan couldn't hear me right now.

"And the pilot is the most experienced pilot in the entire country of Switzerland. Jules, you're doing it. Period. I'm not doing this alone. You're going to be fine. Cross my heart and hope to—"

"Don't say it!" I shriek, clasping a hand over my mouth like it might stop the final words from coming out of his.

"—*not* die," he finishes, drawing a big X across his heart while an even bigger smile spreads across his face.

I fold my arms over my chest, breathing heavily, so not impressed.

Okay, I'm a *little* impressed. Silas somehow thought of every possible safety precaution before we arrived.

"Time to board," Ethan announces, pulling the sliding door open on the side of the plane.

I don't move. It's like my feet are cemented to the floor.

Without warning, Silas switches directions and marches right back in front of me until he's a mere six inches from my face. Then he takes another step, bending down until his nose is practically touching mine. The heat of his body courses out of his jumpsuit and pours into mine. His stance is intimidating, but his eyes are unrelenting, like he understands my hesitancy without being willing to let me off the hook.

"Get in the plane, Jules."

I refuse to step back.

It's a standoff, him against me, but his eyes are the first to betray him, glimmering at the edges just as his lips start to twitch, like he's actually enjoying this.

God, he's infuriating.

"I'm not taking no for an answer. You didn't come all this way to chicken out now."

"I didn't even know this was happening until we got here so it's not like I came all the way here to—"

"And?" he interrupts. "You're here now."

I lick my top lip before biting it.

If Grant were here, he probably wouldn't fight me on this. He'd probably say, "If you don't want to do this, you don't have to." Then something in me would unravel. Deflate. Regret would fill me, and I'd insist that I'd do it anyway against my better judgment, because I don't want to disappoint myself any more than him. I always craved for him to fight me on things a little bit more. To push me when I needed it. Especially things like this. Sometimes I need a push to get out of my own hard-headed way, but Grant never pushed me the way Silas is pushing me now.

His eyes dance in front of mine, egging me on, and I know he's not going to back down. I won't be getting out of this. My heart picks up speed and my stomach drops.

No one has had the guts to push me past my boundaries in, well, a very long time, and against any type of logic, I like it.

Even worse, something in me kind of loves it.

A big, substantial part of me *wants* to be pushed.

"Okay," I relent, shaking my head in disbelief that I'm actually going to give into this and to him.

Instead of stepping back, he grabs my shoulders and plants his face right in front of mine as one more shit-eating grin comes out to play.

Then he palms my cheek in his hand and for one hair-raising moment we stand there just like that. A silent agreement playing out between us.

This is happening.

He holds his index finger up in front of my face, now chuckling.

"Jules: Zero. Silas: One."

Then he turns and pumps his fist over his head all the way back to the door of the plane.

My jaw opens.

I scoff and roll my eyes at the back of his head.

"Real classy," I mutter.

Insufferable.

I can see how Silas managed to pull a very shy Grant out of his shell years ago. The man is relentless when he wants to be.

He points the finger at me while I shuffle toward the plane. "And you're jumping out of the plane first before me so I can make sure you don't chicken out at the last second."

"And if I don't?"

"Then you owe me dinner."

I scoff again.

"That hardly seems like a loss," I tell him. "I'll gladly buy you dinner instead of jumping out first."

"Alright then, I'll up the punishment. If you don't jump first, you'll owe me dinner *and* a dance at some point before we're back home."

"A dance?" I ask, narrowing my eyes, grateful for the light distraction as Jett draws closer. "Not happening."

"Not here, but in Spain, maybe," he says, rubbing his chin thoughtfully. "Or Italy. My choice."

"You want me to dance with you in Spain or Italy if I refuse to jump out first once we get up there?"

I watch the pilot climb into the cockpit. He starts pressing random buttons, then clips himself in.

Okay, deep breaths, Jules. This is happening.

"Absolutely," Silas says, throwing an arm around my shoulder while we wait our turn to climb in next. I wiggle out from under his arm, but he doesn't seem to care. He's too busy grinning at Ethan, who has a harness strapped to the front of him with an attachment for Silas' harness to get clipped in over his front. Jett has the same contraption strapped across his body, and suddenly, despite Silas' best attempts at distracting me, everything feels far too real right now.

We're about to get into this plane, but we won't be landing in this plane, just like Grant said in his letter. That is, if I can force myself to jump out of it before it comes back down.

"Okay," I say. My entire body begins shaking as the next chain of events draws me in. "If we make it out of this alive, I'll dance with you in Spain. Do you hear that, God? I'll dance with him in Spain!" I shout up to the sky dramatically.

Silas' face morphs while he watches me, now beaming.

Ethan attempts to clip Silas into his harness while Silas does a little makeshift salsa, swinging his hips back and forth with his eyes still glued to mine. Ethan eventually tries scolding him to stand still.

Which, of course, doesn't work.

I find myself watching Silas do a ridiculous hip-swinging dance while Ethan chases his shoulder clips. A billionaire being scolded by an older man in a jumpsuit while attempting to salsa dance on a tarmac. The whole thing is such an out-of-body experience that, before I know it, my crooked smile turns into a real laugh.

Silas maintains his grin, mouthing idiotic things about dancing with me until I feel a little tug at the back of my shoulder blades.

I turn.

I'm strapped into Jett's harness.

Silas distracted me through the whole thing.

It's happening.

He beams at me triumphantly while I start mouthing my own mindless threats back at him.

I better not die today, you asshole.
I don't know how you talked me into this.
Is dancing in Spain really worth all this?

But something flashes in his eyes that makes me think that, to him, it really is.

The stakes we've set feel like a nervous end-of-life type of promise, like I'm not going to have to dance with Si because I'm not actually going to survive this. My breath starts to pick up speed as I climb into the plane with Jett tethered on behind me.

"Atta girl," Silas calls out, grinning from ear to ear.

A moment later, the four of us awkwardly manage to sit on the floor of the plane. Then, before I can comprehend what's happening, the heavy metal door slides shut, latching us all inside.

CHAPTER 17

Everything starts happening too quickly for my comfort.

The plane door latches shut.

I'm sandwiched in between Jett's knees on the floor of the plane, both of us sitting near the door. Silas is sitting between Ethan's knees right next to me, and their long legs are sprawled out in front of them on either side of us with the side of Silas' body pressed into mine. It's cramped in here, and despite everything that's happened between us, I'm thankful to feel him beside me. Some familiarity in a moment filled with heart-pumping adrenaline and the real possibility of sudden death just minutes away.

The back of the pilot's head is directly in front of me. His hands fly over a dashboard of foreign instruments, flipping switches at random, and adjusting his headphones, then his mouthpiece. I've never seen the view out of a plane windshield while taking off, and, if I'm being honest, I'm not entirely sure that I want to. I prefer to be in the back with my eyes closed, praying as hard as I can.

Once the engine fires up, the plane jolts forward before falling into a steady hum, slowly coursing toward the runway.

Every fiber of my being is screaming at me to jump from the plane *now*, while it's still on solid ground.

Trek, another guy we met back at the hangar during our safety briefing, is sitting on the floor of the plane too, hunched near the door. I'm not sure what his role is besides operating the door and making sure we're all fastened properly to each other before careening our bodies outside.

I shudder, realizing that it would take just one of these thick straps or buckles to malfunction for me to dislodge from Jett and plummet to the ground alone, without a backup parachute on my own body to save me. I nestle in closer to my tandem partner, more thankful now for his solid frame behind me. I realize that it's been a minute since I was tucked in so closely to a man like this, and I'd prefer the circumstances to be so much different than they are right now.

The pilot pushes forward on the throttle, steadily picking up speed, making my stomach dip back into my spine. The propellers roar, and I can hardly hear anyone around me as the tiny engine starts racing us faster down the runway.

I'm having an out-of-body experience. I can't possibly be sitting in Switzerland, flying down a runway, completely out of my own control in this moment.

The nose of the plane starts to lift, much faster than any large commercial jet I've been on, and within seconds, we're airborne.

My ears pop as the wheels dislodge from the runway and begin to glide up toward the clouds, racing faster as we really pick up in altitude, suddenly tipping left to avoid the mountain range that has been growing steadily closer through the windshield.

It feels like I'm being pushed into the floor under a deep surge of water. My head spins from the sheer force of gravity, and I lean into Jett as the Gs take hold, dragging us down from below. I close my eyes. But that's a bad idea when a stronger wave of dizziness rolls through me. I force my eyes back open, but keep my gaze focused on the interior of the plane which seems to be spinning slightly with vertigo.

"Look out the window!" Jett calls into my ear, like he can tell from behind that I'm losing focus to brain fog right now from the force of gravity as we push up toward the sky.

I obey.

Looking out the little window next to me, I'm instantly hit with a postcard view sent from heaven — like a swift spiritual awakening has taken hold of anything left in me. The tiny plane's interior fades from sight and the world around us takes over. Jagged, snow-capped mountain peaks, as far as my eyes can see, flank two turquoise lakes below. Each body of water reflects the mountain range beside it, and the sun beyond that, like a perfect mirror image against the smooth blue surface. I hold my hand up to the window, comparing the color of my grandmother's turquoise ring to the blue-green hue of the water. Grant was right. It's a near-perfect match. I've never seen anything so awe-inspiring, and for a few precious minutes, I forget why we're on this plane at all, simply grateful to be here, losing sight of the fact that I won't be sitting on it when it comes in for a landing.

I turn to look out the other window and catch Silas watching me instead of the view. He breaks into a grin, knowing he's been caught, then quickly squeezes my forearm before letting go, just like he did on his plane yesterday, except this time it's oddly comforting instead of just plain annoying.

"I'm glad you decided to come!" he shouts over the ruckus of the engine. "You won't regret jumping!"

My insides twist at the word *jumping*, quickly bringing my body and mind back into the reality of why we're on this plane. *To jump*. Or, in my case, to fall out the side once Jett makes up his mind to go.

I force a tight-lipped smile, but continue to look out the window without answering.

"Twelve hundred meters," the pilot says into his mouthpiece that feeds the speakers in the back of the plane.

Jett jostles me between his knees.

"Feel good?" he shouts into my ear. I can't see him, but I can hear the smile in his voice.

I lean back and yell, "Maybe? I don't know!"

"Eighteen hundred meters," the pilot states calmly into loudspeakers a few minutes later.

Silas grins at me like a little boy.

"You've got this!" he shouts.

"What were we thinking?" I yell back, but the noise of the engine devours my voice.

"That we wanted to live!" he shouts. Then he winks at me, reminding me that this is what Grant had truly wanted for both of us.

"To *live*! Not *die*!" I mouth the last word, nervously.

"Don't say *die*!" he yells, clasping a hand over his mouth after the last word is out, but his eyes still sparkle over the top of his hand, like he knows the superstition is mine, and only mine.

I widen my eyes back at him. *Insufferable Silas*. Now is not the time to be making jokes about dying.

"Twenty-four hundred meters," the pilot announces.

My stomach takes another lurch toward the ground nearly eight thousand feet below. I thought it would take much longer to reach proper jumping altitude, but I'm quickly realizing that we're going to be hopping out sooner than I hoped.

"Oh my God!" I yell at Silas, then repeat it again and again, leaning back into Jett. Sixteen hundred meters to go until we're cruising at just over thirteen thousand feet when it'll be time to jump. "Oh dear God what are we doing?" My heart pumps wildly while I study the latch on the door just a foot away. The lakes outside are quickly turning into mere puddles while we climb up into the sky.

Jett begins tightening the straps across my shoulders, pulling me closer. I feel like a rag doll being dragged into his body, as close as he can get me, but it still doesn't feel close enough, knowing he's the only thing saving me from plummeting. Ethan adjusts their straps and I watch as Silas allows himself to be jostled around, getting them as close as possible, appearing completely unbothered. If he's nervous, his face doesn't give him away. Instead, he looks like he's about to take a joyride around the block on a moped, thoroughly enjoying himself, instead of about to fall toward earth from thirteen thousand feet up in the air.

The pilot's voice comes over the loudspeaker again. "Three thousand meters, and the weather is holding. Prepare the doors."

Prepare the doors?

"One thousand more!" Jett yells into my ear.

Trek pulls down a pair of plastic goggles over his eyes, then unhooks a huge latch from the door. He places one hand on a wide lever, grinning at me. My face twists into what feels like a polite smile while I try not to imagine what it's going to feel like when that thing slides open across its track with us sitting right next to it, though at this point, it's unavoidable. Even if I decide at the last minute not to jump, Silas will. That door is going to open up either way.

I might be sick.

"You first!" Trek shouts over the engine, pointing squarely at me.

I throw Silas a panicked look, but Jett is already scooting us toward the door. My legs turn to Jell-O and my heart pounds. My whole body is launching itself into fight or flight mode.

"Oh my God, oh my God," I repeat to myself, too quiet for anyone else to hear over the roar of the engine.

Every time Jett scoots, I'm brought closer and closer to the door that's about to open.

I start disconnecting my brain from my body as everything in me instinctively fights against what's about to happen.

"Jesus Christ, what the hell have I gotten myself into?" I mutter under my breath. I imagine Grant here instead of Silas. Knowing I'd probably still be back in the hangar if he was.

"It's going to be okay, Jules!" Silas yells behind me. "You wouldn't be here if it wasn't!"

"Holy shit. Holy shit," I repeat to myself, gulping in air, trying to stay calm.

I can't hear him, but I can tell from the way Jett's body bounces against me that he's laughing; then he goes rigid again when the pilot's voice comes over the speaker one more time.

"Thirty-seven hundred meters."

I look back at Si, feeling totally helpless.

"I hate you!" I yell at him, breaking into a nervous grin, forced out by a hurricane of terrified energy welling up inside me. I don't know whether to laugh or cry. I might do both.

"See you on the dance floor!" he yells back.

That wide grin is the last thing I see before I turn to the door and pull my goggles down over my eyes. Terror mixes with forced excitement. If I'm going to die, I may as well try to enjoy this.

The pit in my stomach starts spiraling over and over toward my toes while every part of me trembles with adrenaline.

"Four thousand meters," the pilot says steadily into the speakers and my stomach spins out of control.

Then Trek gives me a nod before pulling the door wide open.

CHAPTER 18

Juliet

Nothing could have prepared me for the blast of air that hurtles into the plane the exact moment that door slides open a few inches from me. Traveling one hundred miles per hour at the height of those towering glaciers, I'm thrown into mental chaos. There's suddenly nothing between me and thirteen thousand feet of thin air down to the placid lakes below. Not even a seatbelt to stop me from slipping out, should the plane tilt just so.

Jett scoots us another three inches toward the door until my feet are dangerously close to dangling outside it.

"Ready?" he shouts over the force of the wind exploding through the plane. It's like a tornado has been unleashed in here and we're going to be tossed out one way or another.

I squint out the open door while my heart thumps wildly out of my chest. Cold wind whips fiercely against my face, pulling my hair out of the braid I'd carefully made this morning — long strands flapping around my eyes, goggles pressing into my cheeks — while I close my eyes to exhale.

Grant.

For just a moment, in the thrill of it all, he's here. In the wind, whipping past my face, in that heavenly view outside with no glass cover between us.

I open my eyes again to see a string of mountain peaks sitting at eye level. The world, peaceful and calm outside this frigid airstream crashing all around me. I want to be out there with them. With *him*. Spiraling out among the clouds.

Just live, sweetheart. His words echo in my mind.

"Ready!" I shout back as the adrenaline coursing through me wins, taking over what's left of my better judgment.

I place my hands against the cold metal doorframe.

"Divers up!" Trek says into his mouthpiece.

"Prepare for departure," the pilot answers calmly through the speakers. "Divers are clear."

"Go!" Trek yells to us, pointing out the door.

Jett pushes my chin back so my head is nestled tightly under his jaw.

This is it.

I take it in, knowing I will never forget what it feels like to sit on the edge of this doorway, straddled between safety and survival, that beautiful world at my toes.

It's time to join it.

I force myself to let go of the plane; then, following one deep breath, we slowly fall forward.

Spiraling out into that breathtaking tundra below.

I force my eyes to stay open, to see every nanosecond of our sixty-second freefall, our bodies racing down together at one hundred and twenty miles per hour toward the ground.

I'm whooping and screaming with whatever breath I have left in my lungs, but the wind is carrying it away so fiercely that my voice doesn't have time to reach my ears.

Falling.

Floating.

Spinning above the most incredible view.

It feels better than all that — a wind tunnel that takes my breath away. We pick up speed as Mother Earth wraps her fingers around us so swiftly, so tightly, reclaiming our bodies into hers as we careen toward solid ground, while the clouds gently beckon us to stay.

And that view.

I don't know whether to study the way the jagged mountain peaks and valleys are racing past me, closer than any land traveler will ever see them, or to settle my eyes on the lakes. They grow bigger and less serene as we race straight toward them too. Waiting to swallow us up if our chute doesn't unfold like Jett promised me it would.

And just as I'm about to question when — and if — the parachute will explode to catch us, Jett tilts my chin back toward his neck again, and taps my shoulder — the signal to spread my arms and legs out to the sides, preparing me for the jolt we're hopefully about to have from the backpack unfurling.

I hold my breath until—

Whoosh.

I hear it before I can feel it. The chute explodes from the pack. A snap of thin vinyl uncurling from its careful placement, finding a pillow of air to land us safely back on earth.

Relief crashes through me when we're suddenly shot upright, no longer falling parallel to the ground, but perpendicular, with our bodies hanging down from the straps.

Safe.

"We did it!" I scream out into the beauty around us, flinging my arms out to the sides. I'm suddenly filled with a new rush of powerful adrenaline, the hit of dopamine awakening a part of me that's been left dead and dormant for too long. My face already feels sore from the way it stretched — screaming and smiling my way through the ride.

I did it.

All too soon, we're back on the ground, coming to a hard stop in a field of wildflowers and soft grass in a wide meadow beside the bigger of the two lakes. My heart is still pounding when I turn to search the sky while Jett begins to unhook us, my entire body still shaking, thanking him profusely.

It's then that I spot them.

A red dot under an orange and white canopy, floating down gently a few dozen meters behind us. Silas with Ethan strapped securely to his back, their parachute quickly dropping them down to rest in the meadow a few yards away. They've made it too.

I rush to greet them while Ethan quickly unstraps their tandem harness. Then, without thinking clearly, I race straight into Silas' arms and he snatches me up, spinning us both around, laughing in the emerald sea of green.

"I can't believe I just did that!" I yell, pumping one arm over my head. "That was fucking incredible!"

Adrenaline can be a powerful drug, causing people to do things they'd otherwise never do — like jumping out of a perfectly good plane, or throwing myself onto a guy I normally can't stand while he spins me around in circles. At this moment, I don't even care. I want to celebrate this with him — my partner in this incredible crime — who just defied all sense of logic and gravity right there with me. I wouldn't have done it without him.

"That was unreal," Silas says, bringing my feet back down to the earth for the second time today.

"Why have I never done that before?" I ask, still beaming at him.

He looks untethered in the best way, and I can't remember ever seeing such joy spread across his face. Out of pure adrenaline, he grabs my cheeks and turns my face down to plant a kiss on my forehead.

As quick as it happened, he turns and slaps Ethan across the back. "That was incredible, man. Thank you." Ethan beams back at us, and throws his hand out to Si for a hearty handshake.

"My pleasure," he says, his German accent thick through his warm smile.

I can tell Ethan's and Jett's veins are coursing with the same excitement that Silas and I feel, and I wonder if it ever gets old for them — doing this every day. From the look on their happy faces while they gather the parachutes back up, I can tell that if it does get old, today is not that day.

As we make our way to the SUV that will drive us back to the hangar, I make a mental note to never let the day come where I stop feeling adrenaline from new adventures either. And to never let this length of time pass before I give myself that gift again.

CHAPTER 19

Silas

If I've learned nothing else about Jules today, I've learned one thing: Adrenaline agrees with her.

All the way back to the hotel, she's been a flutter of excitement, reliving the freefall and every second of the incredible view during our ride back to earth. I can't take my eyes off her, and I don't know which is more thrilling — the adventure we've just had, or watching her relive it all over again right next to me. I've missed this. Doing things with someone I actually care about.

But by the time we arrive back at the hotel, the adrenaline has started to wear thin. She grows quiet as we walk toward the elevator that'll take us up to our penthouse suite. I do my best to keep her talking, but her answers become shorter, more clipped and strained with each passing second. When I unlock the suite for us, she's silent all over again.

Take what you can get, I remind myself as we walk in, especially if it means seeing little glimpses of the old Jules screaming back to life like she did today.

She sets her purse down on a table when I shut us both inside.

"I had Monica make us reservations at the lounge downstairs," I tell her, slowly, praying she won't just retreat back into her bedroom again for the rest of the night. "They have a patio that overlooks the view and a little birdie told me that the sunset there is absolutely surreal. I thought we'd start there and then—"

"I may just order room service again," she interrupts, kicking her shoes off one by one. Then she paces around the room until she finds the slippers she left beside the television console this morning. She quickly slips her feet into them, looking absolutely drained. I'm not even sure if it's the adrenaline crash or jet lag taking hold of her right now, maybe both. Of course, it may very well be something deeper, maybe something she read in the letter yesterday that she's just now remembering again as we return back to this space, but she raises a brow at me and crosses her arms, like she's waiting for a response.

"Room service?" I repeat, staring at her like I couldn't possibly have heard her right. I get that she's probably tired, but she can't be serious. We're in one of the most beautiful places in the entire world. It would be an absolute sin to sit in here wasting another evening with a wedge of lettuce sitting under another silver dome.

She purses her lips and lifts her face a fraction of an inch, not speaking yet, but the message is clear. My heart begins to pound a warning in my chest that I already know I'm going to ignore.

"Yes, I think I'll order in. Do you have an issue with that or something?" she asks.

Definitely a challenge.

Fuck.

I've known enough women over the years to know that this sudden change in her attitude, paired with a not-so-subtle hint to debate about something as insignificant as ordering room service, is not about her ordering room service at all. And it's not about me challenging her to come out with me instead. There's a proverbial wet towel on the bed, and she wants to talk about it.

I should just let her retreat to her room. Let her win this one because clearly arguing with her in this moment is going to lead to a much bigger conversation than what our dinner plans ought to be.

But I don't do a lot of things that I should do.

And I'm not really one to let wet towels rot on the bed.

"You're in Interlaken, Switzerland, for the first time in your life — possibly the *only* time in your life — and you're going to order room service for the second night in a row?" I ask, pushing a smile onto my face, hoping to soften the nudge. I'm opening a door that I might regret. But I also know that if we're going to stop this whole surly cat-and-mouse game we've been playing since I picked her up at her townhouse back in Boston, it might very well have to happen by walking through whatever deep shit I'm stepping into right now. "At the very least, go out to dinner at the restaurant alone. Without me if you don't want to be in my company. That's fine. But don't stay holed up in your room eating a hunk of rabbit food again. Have just a little more respect for Grant than that."

Her eyes narrow to burn little holes into mine.

"What the fuck?" she spits out. "What the fuck is that supposed to mean?"

I shouldn't have added that last bit about Grant, but instead of taking it back, I dig my heels in.

"He didn't send us around the world to sit in a bedroom eating dinner off a TV tray, Jules, and you know it."

"Be that as it may, I'm fine ordering in," she says gruffly, but she doesn't move from her spot on the carpet. Nor does she make any movement toward the room phone to order food. Instead, she blinks at me once. Then twice. Then practically taps her foot at me to say something back.

Here we go.

"You may be totally fine about it. But not everything is about being *fine*. It's about taking advantage of where your feet are planted. Today. Right now," I tell her calmly. Then I slip off my jacket and lay it across the back of a nearby chair. "And you just so happen to be planted in some of the most beautiful scenery in the world. Grant would have a heart attack if he knew you came all this way to go lock yourself in a padded room."

"What do you mean? It's not padded."

"Well it may as well be, considering the inhabitant's state of mind right now."

She laughs, though the normally melodic sound of it is laced with something more ugly. For the second time, I regret pushing us into this conversation.

"Well, Si, lucky for you and me, neither of us have to worry about giving Grant a heart attack over my dinner choices now, do we? Although you would know that more than anyone."

She places her hands on her hips and glares at me. I respond by kicking off my shoes.

"What does that even mean?" I ask.

She doesn't answer. Instead, she shifts her weight and re-crosses her arms without moving her eyes off me. I tilt my chin down and eye her, prodding her silently. Another stand-off I'm not going to let her win.

"What?" she asks, angrily.

I cross my arms, matching her stance.

"You tell me, Jules. I came back here feeling like I was living on cloud nine. You did, too, if you've forgotten. Now you seem to have lost all interest in having an easy night that matches the excitement of our dive today. You tell me *what*."

"Have you ever considered the part you played . . ." she starts, but then she drops her hands and shrugs. "Whatever. I don't know if I even want to go there right now. Or ever."

I sit down on the chair closest to her, hoping the subtly submissive gesture cools some of the lava bubbling up between us.

The silence is deafening. Instead of backing off like I should, I poke the bear.

"The part I played in *what*, Jules? You've been pissed off at me since you got Grant's first letter back home in Boston.

Monica told me you wanted to fly around the world with a fake death certificate of mine, just to get Grant's letters without having to be anywhere near me. I know you haven't really enjoyed my company since I lost my dad, but *this*? Frankly, I'm a little shocked by the level of hatred here. It seems pretty intense for a few stupid mistakes I made back in our mid-twenties. I get that this sucks. Hell, everything about this situation is about as bad as it gets, but can't we just put a cap on all that and *try* to enjoy ourselves?"

"You aren't having any trouble enjoying any of this," she says, waving her arms around the room. "Don't you think that's a little weird?"

"If sharing this suite was a bad idea I can just go tell the front desk to move my luggage to the other room on my way down to enjoy that dinner reservation by myself. We're leaving in the morning anyway, so I can—"

"No, this isn't about that," she interrupts, looking even more frustrated.

I puff out a sigh and lean back, feeling like she's got me tied in a knot I can't get out of.

"Then what? Get it out in the open. It's what we're here for, isn't it?" I eye her, wishing she realized that none of this is easy for me either.

She's seething now, rising up on her toes, opening her mouth to reply, as if she can hardly contain what she's about to say. Then she takes a deep breath and rocks back on her heels, leaning in toward me before speaking again. This time her voice is low and eerily controlled.

"Don't you find it just a little bit ironic, maybe even self-serving, that you're sitting here halfway across the world, sharing a hotel suite with your dead best friend's *fiancée* — making fancy dinner reservations to take me out for God's sake — when it was *your* building that fucking killed him?"

CHAPTER 20

Juliet

My words hit Silas like a nuclear missile, right on target.

He looks stunned.

"You think..." he repeats to himself then stops. His eyes widen, like each side is a laser ready to burn a hole into the floor between us. "You think that building had something to do with it?" He stands up to take a step toward me, a growl coming from somewhere deep in his throat. "Are you out of your damn mind?"

I instinctively step back, blinking. I've never seen Silas this mad, and I'm suddenly not sure if I want to, but it's too late for that now. I've said what I've wanted to say to him for months and I can't believe he has the gall to play dumb right now.

"Don't be daft, Silas. You can snap your fingers and have the Rockettes high-kick at your next fucking birthday party if you feel like it. Plus you're ivy league educated, not to mention one of the smartest men in the world according to every one of those stupid articles singing your praises across the entire fucking globe. Don't tell me that it hasn't crossed your mind, or God forbid, that you've already come to terms with it and you just don't care." My voice is now near a yell. "It took me a while to figure it out, but that's why you came to my house after his funeral to offer me money, isn't it? Because the guilt was already eating you alive?"

He looks like I've just physically assaulted him.

My heart is pounding out of my ears.

"What the hell are you talking about? Grant died of complications from a lung condition."

"From that fucking building, Silas. The one you gave him to work from." He shakes his head like I've lost my mind, so I go on. "How else would he have managed to die of a lung condition before the ripe ol' age of thirty? You gave it to him to use when he was starting up the Starlight Foundation. Remember? That was your big, fancy contribution to get his nonprofit off the ground."

I cross my arms over my chest and dig both feet into the floor. There's no way I'm letting him walk away from this. I've secretly harbored this hunch since the very last week of Grant's time on this earth but by then it was too late. I was too focused on giving him a few peaceful days without diving into this hunch, and then after he was gone, what was the point? It's still too late to change any of it, but I can't take one more second in this room without telling him what I believe happened. And how it very well might be his fault that Grant's gone.

Silas paces the room, wrapping a hand around the back of his neck like he's been shot from behind, before answering. This time more slowly and deliberately.

"I gave Grant that building to use because I believed in the work he was doing. Even when his parents wouldn't support him on it, and our business professor thought he was out of his mind for wasting his privileged leg up in the world by starting it. I wanted him to take his shot without having to worry about pooling the resources or taking a loan out for a building or lease. His parents wouldn't back him up on it so I . . ." He pauses, running a hand through his hair like he's confused, thinking back over every detail in his mind. "You already know all this, Jules. It was exactly what Grant wanted."

"That building was old and decrepit and full of all the toxic shit that I'm guessing killed him. You know it as well as I do. How else would he have gone from being young and healthy to—" I can barely get the words out when I think of Grant's final days. My voice cracks when I try to finish. "To a wasted *shell* of who he was. And as fast as he did, too. There's just no other explanation. What else could have caused it?"

Silas' mouth hinges open and his eyes dart back and forth, searching mine. All the air in his lungs looks to be sucked out by what I've just accused him of.

He shakes his head.

"Let me get this straight. You're convinced that the building I gave him is what caused him to die?"

That's not exactly right. It's just a theory and one I'm not even entirely convinced of myself given the gravity of it, but I nod my head and point my finger at him anyway. Needing to know if he's ever thought about it too.

"And you know it, which is why you showed up at my house just hours after his funeral. Flashing your money around, promising to *take care of me* in his absence." My veins burn like they're filled with acid as I spit every word out across the room at him. "The guilt was already eating you alive which is why you came over." I stop, catching my breath. I don't know whether he looks closer to crying or tearing the walls down in here. His shoulders are heaving like he can't contain the anger ripping through him.

"That's *not* why I came by that day," he interrupts, pointing back at me. "And you know it. It was more than that." He shifts his eyes at the floor, searching his memory. "I had that building tested before I gave it to him. I would have known if there were any issues."

"You gave him a shithole you *think* you tested? What was wrong with his old office? Why did you have to give him that stupid building in the first place?"

"Grant's business was going through a rough patch around the time my dad died. Growing pains, a slump. That building helped relieve some of the foundation's overhead. I had offered to renovate it before he moved in, but he wouldn't let me. I had to talk him into taking it in the first place."

"Ah, you had to talk him into it so you could get the tax write-off that a building donation like that got you?"

"Jesus Christ, Jules. Not everything is about money. A deduction like that would have been a drop in the bucket to—"

My glare stops him mid-sentence.

"And you handled the testing? Personally?" I demand, wondering why I'd never heard about any environmental testing being done before Grant took everything over and moved in. I didn't hear the deep ongoing details of his everyday business, sure, but I feel like I might have heard something about testing a whole damn building *if* this testing had actually taken place. "What did the report say then? I want to see it."

"I-I don't actually know," he stammers. "My assistant Ryan handled it. All of it. The one who—"

"That fucking nineteen-year-old you had deliver suitcases to my house a few nights ago? He was the one who handled something so important?"

"He's not nineteen," Silas starts to say, before I give him a look that makes him stop talking. His hands stretch toward me like he's drowning under my accusation and I'm supposed to pull him out. "Ryan did hire the company that tested Grant's building for anything that might be harmful before I let him move in. I knew it hadn't been occupied since, God, I don't know when my father last had someone in that building . . ."

"And you saw the results? Personally?"

I wait, watching the color drain from his face so quickly that he doesn't need to answer.

"You never checked the report." My voice cracks, confirming my worst fear. I cover my eyes and collapse down to the couch, unsure whether my legs can hold up under the weight of the news. "You stuck him in a decrepit building and then watched him die."

"That whole time of my life is foggy," he admits, looking bewildered, still shaking his head. "It was the year my father died . . ." He trails off, looking absolutely tortured like he's morbidly reliving the months he spent plastered across every tabloid as the little rich boy driven off the rails with his dead daddy's money. There wasn't a soul in the world during that time who wasn't aware of his mental state. It was a tumultuous time for Grant — helping Silas get through that phase of his life as he found himself to be the most famous orphan in the world. It's also when I started to hate him. And that was long before I knew what he was capable of letting happen right under his nose out of sheer laziness.

"How many people have you told about this?" he asks, weakly.

"How many other people?" I repeat, nearly shouting back at him. "Is that your greatest concern about what I've just said? How your public image might be dragged through the mud again? Whether or not your floozy groupies are going to catch wind of this and hate you for it? Not whether or not you're responsible for how he died?"

"No," he shoots back, looking like I've just slapped him across the face for a second time. "I want to know why you never asked to have the building tested yourself after he died."

"After Grant passed, I sold the nonprofit to Velon Development who took the whole operation across town to their own building. I then sold the Smithfield for next to nothing and told the new developer that I felt like it was unsafe. I was in a fog at that point. A complete haze. I put it in writing, then just wanted it gone. All of it. There were so many loose ends to tie up, and given the location of the building, it was easy to hand over to someone else with the caveat that it may need further testing. Grant's parents had no interest in knowing whether or not their son might have lived if that building was the issue. They told me to just let it go after the sale, and I did at first. It wasn't until a few weeks later that I drove by and it was already demolished. The new developer destroyed it soon after taking possession to build something else on the parcel."

"I remember," he whispers. "I drove by and saw that it looked as if the building had never existed. Why didn't you tell me that's how you felt?"

"Everything happened so fast. It wasn't until after he was gone and his parents stopped coming around that I finally had the energy to look into it more. I was trying to find answers about how it happened so quickly. I read that it may have been prevented *if* the cause was truly environmental, which there was no medical test to determine whether it was or not. Just a hunch when you look at the history. Which means he would be here with me right now instead of *you* if you hadn't been so irresponsible with that stupid building. He trusted you, and your lazy ass kill—"

My words hitch in my throat and I drop my eyes toward the floor. I've said nearly everything I've wanted to say for months, except that. But instead of feeling better like I hoped I might, I couldn't feel any worse.

CHAPTER 21

Silas sits back down in his chair opening his mouth and closing it again, like a fish gasping for air as he absorbs my accusation. Fighting to find the right words.

I wait as my heart pounds out of my chest.

It sounds so loud in this deafeningly quiet room.

Finally, he speaks. "Why didn't you tell me sooner?" His voice comes out controlled, like he's measured each word before letting it out.

"By the time I had any energy to try and connect the dots, the building was gone. Right after he died, I listened to his parents. I wanted to forget about everything and never think about those last few months again. I figured why make things harder for everyone — me, his family, our friends — by proving my hunch was right? Would it change anything if we knew that it could have been prevented? No. And adding that extra layer of pain didn't seem worth it."

"Until now?" he asks. "Why now?"

I shake my head and my voice bends as the truth finally comes out. "Because I don't know how to be here with you in all *this*—" I fling my arms out, waving at the room we're sitting in — "without knowing for sure. How can I enjoy it — your fancy jet and your ridiculous hotel rooms — if the money that bought all this might have also killed him? I tried to follow his letters, to be a good sport. To come along and not destroy what he clearly wanted us to do. But now that I'm here, and I felt so happy today after that skydive, I'm wondering how I can be so awful to actually enjoy this?"

"The money?" Silas asks, weakly.

"And the fact that you might have been the one to know about the building's condition, but didn't care to change it," I nearly whisper. "I don't know how to be in the same space as you without knowing if it's your fault or not. I've tried. I swear to God, I've tried. But I don't know how to be here with you and your money without an answer."

"You want to know whether or not you should blame me?" he asks.

I nod.

"For retribution?" he adds, calmly.

I don't answer, but instead stare back, watching his face grow cold.

I don't want to cry, but I don't know how to get through this conversation without it. Silas has never looked at me like he is now. Like I'm the monster instead of him.

"Ah." He sits back silently. A grave understanding washes over his body and he sniffs toward the floor. "So, you're looking for a settlement? You want to prove I'm guilty?"

"Christ, not everything is about money, Silas," I nearly scream. "Can't you see that? Money has nothing to do with what I'm looking for right now."

He either doesn't react, or he's too locked up in his own thoughts to hear what I've just said.

"Of course, you're entitled to quite a bit if the report shows anything was connected. I just find it odd that you've been harping on my lifestyle for years while secretly wanting to take me to court the first chance you get just to get a piece of it. I totally understand why. Just say it out loud though. You don't have to act like you find me appalling then come out with something like this. Just say what you want and it's yours."

When his eyes find mine, he looks as if he's seeing me clearly for the first time. But it's all wrong. He's wrong about all of it.

"No, lawsuits don't do anything when it comes to things like death. There's no changing what happened to Grant in a courtroom. Just a pile of money exchanging hands at the end of it. And I wouldn't be able to spend a dime if I knew that's where it came from."

"So you've already thought about the pros and cons of suing me."

"Of course I have but—"

"But, it's not about the money, it's about telling me that I may have been careless enough to cause my best friend to die. So I can live with that for the rest of my life? That's the point of this conversation instead of just asking me to see the report?"

His green eyes morph to steel and I hate myself for bringing this up. Haven't we both been through enough?

"It's not about that either." My eyes fill with tears. "I just don't want to hold on to this question alone anymore."

"Tell you what, we can just skip over all that. You can have whatever you want, Jules. Regardless of what the report says, fucking take it." He extends his arms out to the sides as if offering himself up to me. "Take everything. I already told you that you could have anything you wanted last year. All you had to do was ask instead of acting like I was a horrible friend for even offering."

"If I was after your money, I would have come for you a long time ago. But there's nothing you can give that'll make up for what I lost," I shoot back at him.

"For what *we* lost," he corrects, quietly.

My tears finally spill over. Deep down, I know Silas would have never done anything to hurt Grant. If I'm right about this, and I hope I'm not, it would have been a horrible, unthinkable *mistake*. I just needed someone to blame, and now that I'm sitting here blaming him, it feels awful.

Tiny beads of sweat line Silas' forehead. The last time I cried in front of him, he'd offered to order takeout and stay with me as long as I needed to calm down. This time, he just pulls his phone out and hits a few buttons on the screen.

"I'm calling Ryan," he says.

He switches the phone over to speaker mode when it starts to ring, and we stare at each other, both scarcely breathing. I have no idea what time it is back home on the East Coast, but it feels like an eternity before something clicks over and Ryan's voice comes through.

"Hello?"

"I need you to send me the environmental report from the Smithfield building," Silas says, not bothering to greet him.

"The Smithfield building?" Ryan repeats, sounding confused. "The original report from . . . from over five years ago?"

A twang of anticipation lurches in my stomach. I feel queasy. This is it. Silas wasn't lying about doing a report. I knew when I brought this up to him that he may want to do an inspection on whatever rubble might be left beneath the former building. I'd expected that it might take weeks, possibly months, from the time I brought it up until I had a clear answer.

I always stopped short of pushing for clarity on this. Unsure whether blindly blaming Silas for his death was better than knowing the real truth behind his illness. But now, knowing that the answer has been sitting in someone's computer all this time?

Fuck.

Nauseating guilt washes through me. I could have had closure. I should have asked about this a year ago. If for no other reason than to confirm my suspicions and put a stop to the endless agonizing and research over all the horrific *what ifs* that have plagued me for the last year.

"Send it over." Silas' voice is uncharacteristically sharp. "Now."

"Of course. I just need to locate it," Ryan answers quickly. "Give me five or ten minutes?"

"Thank you," he answers, looking nervous but determined.

He hangs up.

I'm a bit taken aback that he's so eager to confirm how guilty he might be but grateful that he's willing to uncover the truth right in front of me.

I watch as he drops his face to his hands. A revelation like this could destroy him, I realize. Possibly for good this time.

It's not what I want to happen, but the ball is already rolling.

Without a word, I stand and walk into my bedroom but leave the door open and begin packing the few things I got out of my suitcase since arriving. I want to be ready to fly out of here the second Silas is able to confirm what I think is in that report.

CHAPTER 22

Silas

By the time my phone pings with a message from Ryan, Jules has thrown everything into her suitcase and is back to sitting on the couch across from me, waiting. The air between us is thick as we wait to find out whether or not my building had anything to do with Grant's death.

My phone pings with a text.

The report is in your inbox.

I text Ryan back:

We may need separate planes out of here. Make the arrangements then stand by.

"What'd he say?" she asks, sounding breathless. She looks like she's practically crawling out of her skin right now, having to sit across from me while we wait for the truth of that report.

"He sent it," I confirm, trying to stop my hands from shaking when I hit the email icon on my phone screen.

I see it immediately at the top:

Subject: Smithfield building report

I tap it and nervously clear my throat. Terrified of what I'm about to read. Afraid of what it will mean for Jules if I confirm her worst fears: that everything about Grant's illness could have been prevented, and that I was the man who didn't do a thing to stop it.

I tap the PDF attachment and scan the summary page of the report. A rush of air escapes my lungs all at once when I get to the end. I hold the phone out to Jules for her to read it herself.

She's white as a ghost when she takes the phone from me, her hands trembling just as much as mine. I can't imagine how hard this last year has been for her, agonizing over what she believed was a preventable death. I wish she would have told me sooner.

I move to the spot on the couch right beside her, careful not to touch any part of her right now. She's too engrossed in what she's reading to notice. No one should have to read something that they've agonized over for a year sitting all alone on a couch. Even if she hates the person beside her.

She scans the document for what feels like an eternity, her breath rapid and unsteady, before scrolling through it a second time. Finally, she places the phone back down on the coffee table between us and the screen goes black.

I sit quietly, letting her digest everything she's just read, giving it a chance to sink in for a minute or two. Maybe more.

"I don't understand," she finally says.

"I'm sorry you've been torturing yourself. I wish you'd have told me what you suspected sooner so I could have—"

"Proven your innocence?" she finishes, closing her eyes tightly. "Oh my God, Silas, I'm so sorry."

I turn to her just in time to see a flood of tears stream down her face. As much as I want to wrap her up in a hug, like the one I held her in last year, to do anything I can to stop the relief that probably feels more like pain, I don't.

I don't move.

"I knew Ryan would have told me if something had come back as abnormal in the report," I continue, more slowly, and as gently as I can. "I know how consequential it could have been if he hadn't been diligent, if I had just assumed . . ." I pause, unsure of how to word what I'm trying to say without wounding her more. "But he *was* diligent. There's nothing in that report to suggest the Smithfield building had anything to do with Grant's illness."

She turns to me, her eyes already swollen, but she looks less angry than she did a moment ago. All this time, she's been able to direct her anger about Grant's passing at me, and I know from my own experience as an angry kid after my mother died, and again as a lost twenty-six-year-old after my father passed, that sometimes grief needs a physical outlet for the pain. Something, or in this case, *someone* to blame for the tragedies that turn your insides out and threaten to eat you alive.

If Jules had needed an outlet for her grief, someone to blame for Grant's death, I get it. I don't blame her for wanting that. But all this time, I wish I'd known that it was *me* she was blaming so I could have put her mind at ease a lot sooner.

I study her face, unsure of what to say. Not at all certain that I should be the one to say anything to her right now as the truth of his passing finally comes to light.

No one was responsible.

"Sometimes unexplainably awful things just happen to the best kind of people."

"How can that be possible?" she whispers, releasing a fresh waterfall of tears down each cheek. She wipes them away slowly. "How could he just be fine one day, and then gone a few months later if it wasn't that?"

"I remember the doctor saying Grant was more susceptible to it, right? Asthma as a kid, then into adulthood, plus they suspected a genetic deficiency on top of that, which they were about to do a genetic test for right before he . . ."

"Right before he got worse," she finishes for me, reluctantly. "Before they decided he wasn't going to make it through the treatment." She finally brings her eyes back up to search mine, as if looking for a place to anchor her thoughts, likely spinning out of control right now.

I nod, wishing with everything in me that this conversation never had to take place. That it really was Grant sitting here, making her smile right now instead of all this making her cry. Both of them deserve to be here instead of me.

"I'm sorry," I whisper. I don't know what else to say.

"It's not *you* that should be apologizing," she says, weakly, pale. "I should have never . . . I'm so sorry I blamed you, I—"

I hold up a hand to stop her, not wanting her to have to go through what feels like an unnecessary apology. If I had truly been negligent enough to give a toxic building to Grant, I would have deserved every bit of the wrath she was ready to rain down upon me tonight. Hell, I probably would have been a hundred times harder on myself than she ever could have been if that report hadn't been negative just now.

I wish I could shut out the truth about that time in my life. If my assistant had missed something in that report, I probably would have handed the building off to Grant anyway because I wouldn't have been responsible enough to check it myself. It could have been that easy for me to neglect something deadly during that time of my life. She has every right to question the decisions I made.

I shake my head at her.

"It's alright, Jules. You don't have to explain it to me. I don't blame you for thinking I could have done something so careless, considering how reckless I was back then."

"I think I needed someone to blame. Like, if I could blame something for why it happened the way it did," she starts, then stops, like she's trying to shake off a mountain of frustration.

"You don't have to justify it to me," I tell her, but she goes on.

"Even when I was unleashing on you a minute ago, insisting that it was your fault, it only made me feel worse. And now, seeing that I was wrong? All that time and energy I spent *hating* you? Oh my God, how I've *hated* you, Si." Her voice cracks.

I give her half a smile. "I know. You aren't exactly shy about it."

She laughs as another tear escapes.

"How are you still sitting here?" Her face twists, like a leaf withering on its branch. "What the hell is wrong with me?"

I'm about to tell her nothing is wrong with her, but she starts laughing, quietly at first, then louder like she doesn't know where to take all this pent-up emotion that's suddenly spilling out of her.

"I wanted to push you out of that plane today without a chute," she says, barely able to get the words out. She holds her stomach, laughing like all the aggression has drained out and it's the only thing left to do.

I smile, remembering my recurring dream. "I wouldn't have blamed you if you had," I tell her, breaking into my own tortured grin, "at least if you'd been right about this."

"But I wasn't," she adds, sobering up. "I was wrong about all of it, thank God. I have hated you so, so intensely. Wrongfully. When truthfully — and don't give me shit for saying this Silas, or I swear I'll never say anything nice to you ever again — but . . ." She pauses, looking slightly alarmed that she's about to say something nice.

I sit a bit taller. "But what?"

"Silas, I am so, so sorry."

"Forget it," I tell her, meaning it. "I never want to revisit this conversation again."

"Just like that?" she asks, looking bewildered.

"Just like that," I confirm, nodding. "I don't blame you for questioning it. I just wish you'd told me sooner."

She studies my face and for the smallest moment it feels like I'm looking into the eyes of the old Jules. The one who doesn't hate me after all.

"You know what?" she says, suddenly shifting gears. "Let's get out of here."

My shoulders fall. "*Here* as in Switzerland?"

She stands up. "No, out of this room. We need some time out of this suite. Cleanse the energy. God, especially after that."

Her laughter has tapered off, and even though she's still swiping a few stray tears from the corners of her eyes, which are now as translucent and light as the turquoise lakes outside, she appears ready to roll out of this room. And I'd be lying if I said I wasn't too.

"Now?"

"Yes, now. I need to get out of this stuffy cave, like an hour ago. We're in Interlaken, for God's sake, Si." She smiles ruefully. "We need to go get a stiff drink and something other than a wedge salad."

She kicks off her slippers and locates her shoes.

"No lettuce in bed?" I confirm, standing to grab my jacket.

"Absolutely not." She rolls her suitcase back through the doorway of her bedroom. "I'm going to find a hat. What time is that reservation?"

I glance at my watch.

"You have forty-seven minutes. Enough time to change."

She turns around and gives me a wide grin, patting the top of her messy bun. Her nose is still red and her eyes are swollen from crying, but somehow she still looks beautiful.

"I hear wind-blown chic is in," she retorts, "and thank God for that because you're right there with me, I'm afraid." She points to my hair, still sticking straight up from the free-fall earlier, I'm sure. "You might want to find a hat as well."

"Unfortunately, this place has a dress code. You up for that?"

"Nope," she says. "Would you mind if we just found a pub or something? Somewhere that'll accept me in jeans?"

She shuts the door to her room and, without her eyes on me, I breathe a real sigh of relief.

There you are, Jules.

"Yeah," I call through the door. "I'll have Ryan cancel and find us a place nearby."

She peeks her head back out.

"Can we not?" she asks.

"Not cancel or—?"

"No, can we not bother Ryan again?"

I blink like the thought is foreign to me. "It's literally his job for me to bother him."

"Exactly. I'd rather just walk around and see what we run into."

I pull my phone out to see what's around the hotel on my Google Maps app.

"Okay, how much time do you need?"

"Do you not remember how fast I can whip myself into shape?" she asks. The door closes again but her voice calls out, muffled now through the wood. "Pretty sure I'm lower maintenance than you! Give me ten minutes!"

When I hear her bathroom tap turn on, I sit back down on the couch and run my face through my hands, feeling ill.

Thank God for Ryan's diligence.

I didn't believe Jules could have been right about us completely missing something that important in the report, but I could have never lived with myself if she was. That would have been the end of me.

I breathe in deeply, waiting for the raging panic-driven nausea to subside, wondering if Jules is doing the same thing on the other side of that door right now, knowing without a doubt that there's nothing either one of us could have done to save him.

CHAPTER 23

Juliet

An hour later, I'm sitting opposite from Silas at a solid wood plank table in a little fondue restaurant. A flight of white wines is out in front of us. I let him order since his German is nearly impeccable, thanks to an array of foreign au pairs and nannies growing up.

The waiter has just left us with a collection of bowls filled with crusty breads, pickles, and tiny boiled potatoes that are soft enough to spear with our long forks before dipping them into the simmering cheese pot in the center.

"Dig in," he says, handing me a fork. He looks somewhat aged after that discussion we just had, and I don't blame him.

"I've never done this," I tell him, choosing a cube of bread before sliding it onto the mini spear. I watch as he swirls a potato the size of my thumb around the white melted cheese.

"Never done fondue in Switzerland? What in the world have you spent your adult life doing?" he asks sarcastically. "You like your white dry as a bone, right?" He picks up one of the little carafes and pours a splash into my glass. "Try this one first."

"I've spent my entire adult life working," I answer. "Normal people work most of their adult life, Si. Not spend it eating fondue in Switzerland."

I smile. It's meant to be a joke but he sets the carafe down, stealing a breath before settling his eyes on me.

"Jules," he says.

"Yes?"

"I know I was an ass to you at one point, and I know you get most of your information about me now through tabloids, which, by the way, feature almost nothing but fabricated shit to sell clicks and subscriptions . . . But if we're going to spend the next few weeks together, I'd like to clear one more thing up."

I set my fork down.

"Fair enough. I'm all ears," I say, then take the sip of the white wine he's poured for me. "Damn," I whisper. "That's good."

"I know good wine." He smirks.

"Clearly."

"Okay, first, do I have a privileged lifestyle? Absolutely. But do I work my tail off for it now? Yes. Did I always? No. But did I ask for any of this?" He waits for me to answer this time.

I blink back at him. I've never considered that.

"No."

"You work hard at your job, and I work hard at mine. Let's just leave it at that." He picks his fork back up, ready to move on.

I frown, nodding. "That's fair," I concede. He has a point.

He takes a sip of wine, then drains the glass.

"Next," he says, pouring a splash from a different carafe into his glass. "Speaking of work, tell me what the hell a dating coach does."

I laugh, realizing that there's a lot for us to catch up on.

"Well, probably exactly what you'd think I do. Sit down with people, just like this, and tell them what they're doing wrong when it comes to attracting a partner."

He laughs then leans back in his chair.

"I can see how you would be good at that. People pay you to tell them what they're doing wrong?"

I grin. "Among other things, yes."

"Brilliant." He laughs again, but there's admiration in his eyes. "How did you decide you wanted to do that?"

"The idea started back in college although I didn't swap out my corporate HR job for it until a few years ago when I saw how much fun Grant had getting his nonprofit off the ground. I wanted to be my own boss, too. I'm not the first person to become a dating coach, so I can't claim the idea as my own, but I used to watch people flounder in the dating pool back in college. I always felt like I could have helped them out if they'd asked."

He eyes me, the hint of a joke running across his face. "Let me guess, I inspired you?"

I laugh. "Yes, you did. Not because you were hopeless in dating, but because the friends I matched you up with were always dumbfounded that you didn't stick around very long. I felt like they were all a bit desperate for you and nobody likes desperate."

A deeper shade of amusement slides across his face while his mouth curls up.

"Go on," he says, taking a long swig. He tips his chair back, looking pleased.

"I don't necessarily mean that as a compliment though. I never saw you get in a serious relationship with anyone and I always wondered why."

His eyes dim, but the smile doesn't leave his face. "Great question," he remarks, adding another splash of wine to my glass. This one is from the third carafe out of the six we have lining the table. We're having a self-selected wine tasting, I suppose.

"Have you been with anyone long-term? Ever?" I ask, trying another sip. It's more delicious than the last.

"Here and there," he answers. "Nothing like you and Grant had, but I've committed to a few women over the years."

I nod, suddenly struck by two things: one, I never knew that, and two, I wouldn't have guessed from what I've seen of him in the news. I feel a slight pang of regret at the distance we've allowed to grow between us.

"Were any of them special?"

New emotion flashes in his eyes.

"Not really," he answers. "The last woman broke up with me because I wouldn't stop talking about you in my sleep."

At first, I think he's kidding. I widen my eyes then burst into laughter when I realize he's not. "Why would you be doing that?"

"I had a lot of anxiety about our upcoming trip, I guess," he says, now laughing too.

"Do I want to know what was happening in your dream?" I'm a little afraid to know how his subconscious mind might paint me.

"Let's just say this reoccurring dream always ended with you shoving me out of a plane door, or off a cliff or something, so I'd wake up yelling out your name."

I gape at him, unable to wipe a ghastly wide-mouth grin from my face.

"That's awful! I'm so sorry!"

He laughs and tips his glass toward me. "It's not like you had anything to do with it, right?"

"But still, I've been giving you nightmares for a year, so much so that your girlfriend broke up with you? Did she know that the dream was actually about me being awful?"

"Raven never believed my explanation. She had her own ideas about what it meant." He shrugs and smiles.

I look away, embarrassed that I've caused so much havoc in his life without even knowing about it.

"Well, I'm sorry just the same." I scrunch my nose. "I can't believe she broke up with you over that. Or that you've known about this trip for the past year while I only found out about it a few days ago. No wonder you had anxiety about it. The last time I saw you . . ." I trail off, remembering the way he'd shown up on my doorstep looking like he had so much to say, but filled the awkward silence instead with comments about flowers and being exhausted and offering money. I cringe at the memory. I don't think he knew what to do with himself that night, either. "I can understand why your dream entailed me pushing you off high places."

He nods, remembering too. "I should apologize for what I said that night. I was trying to make good on the promises I made, but nothing was coming out right. My timing couldn't have been worse. I was trying to run back to the car when you opened the door because I already knew what a horrible idea it was."

I blow a stream of air out the side of my mouth.

"I was pretty awful to you," I admit.

"And what I said was . . ." He pauses, thinking through his words. "Well, I had told Grant I'd be there for you, but obviously how it came out was all wrong."

We smile sadly at each other. We both have things we regret.

"God, grief can really fuck with a person, right?" I ask, and although it's not an excuse for either of us, it's the truth.

"You have no idea," he says.

"Actually, I think I'm starting to," I admit.

He nods, and this time, when our eyes meet, I see nothing but the friend he once was staring back at me. Full of compassion, understanding, and most of all, a second chance at making everything right between us.

CHAPTER 24

We've been racing through the Spanish countryside toward the bay in a blacked-out Bentley limousine for over an hour to get from Seville, where we landed ol' Gloria, to the coastal town of Cádiz. The views out my window have been incredible the whole way, but now, as the deep blue of the bay comes into view, I find myself gasping out the window, speechless in the most wonderful way.

If someone had asked me a few days ago, I'd have sworn that nothing could beat Switzerland's majestic skyline of snow-capped mountain peaks and crystal-clear alpine lakes. However, the medieval architecture of this once tiny village set against the glowing turquoise Bay of Cádiz might tie it.

I open my window to inhale the fresh sea air. It hits my face along with the familiar heat of the sun and I smile to myself that we've finally made it. Another bucket list item nearly crossed off.

"You've sailed before, haven't you?" I ask, turning to Silas, who's sitting beside me, still working on his laptop. He's been working the entire trip over to Cádiz, so I've been enjoying the scenery in near silence. There's a polished walnut console between us where I lean to look out his window next.

"I was on the sailing team at school," he reminds me, moving his gaze from the laptop screen to the open window.

Years ago, after viewing a race on TV, I'd mentioned to Grant that I'd always wanted to try sailing. It looked like one of the greatest adventures I could ever imagine — coasting along the water's surface in a sleek vessel, totally at the mercy of the wind while the team onboard tries to harness it. However, I never imagined I'd actually get the chance to try it in one of the most picturesque locations in the world.

I figure whoever's sailing the boat will just set me up with a nice seat on the side, out of the way and hopefully not messing anything up. But I'm curious whether or not Silas will be sitting with me or participating in pulling ropes and tying off jigs with the rest of whoever's been hired to take us out on the water.

"Are those boats similar to what we'll be sailing in tomorrow?" I ask, pointing at a collection of them out on the water.

"Similar enough," he tells me. "Have you never been on a sailboat?"

I shake my head. He immediately grins.

I grin back at him.

It's impossible not to when he's giving me that particular look. It's similar to the one he gave me last night after telling me about his absurd reoccurring dream. Utterly ridiculous.

"Well, now you're in for it," he says, his voice deep.

He pats my knee but I don't move it away this time. Something about clearing the air between us last night has drawn Silas back into my comfort zone. He might not be exactly who he was before his father's death, but who could be after a loss like that? I'm starting to understand that now.

"Why's that?" I ask.

"Just be prepared to fall in love." His eyes wander. "With sailing," he adds. "I remember my first time like it was yesterday. It gets in your blood real quick. I'm glad I get to be there for your first time."

My stomach does a little flip and I go back to staring out the window, soaking up our view. I can't wait.

When we arrive at the hotel, we finish checking in after being ushered to a separate VIP room just for us. Unlike our accommodations in Switzerland, the flight crew is also staying at this hotel but in a separate wing of the building.

"Here are your separate room keys," the receptionist says to us, smiling warmly.

"Separate suites?" I ask, throwing eye contact at Silas instead of her.

"I thought that's what you wanted after your reaction in Interlaken..." He trails off, clearly not wanting to repeat the scene I'd thrown at the first hotel. "I asked Monica to split our reservation up here. I mean, unless you wanted to bunk up with me again, in which case—" He winks at me with a smirk instead of finishing the sentence.

I hold up my hands, catching the laughter in the attendant's eyes.

"No, that's perfect," I tell them both, quickly. I'm shocked that something in me wishes he was going to be right outside my door again instead of possibly down the hall or on another floor entirely. But this is a much better arrangement. "Thank you for listening, and for making the swap."

"You sure?" he asks, studying me closely when he slides my key across the counter, before pocketing the other one meant for him.

"I'm sure," I tell him. "And the letter?" I ask, turning back to the woman behind the counter.

She hands me a stiff envelope bearing Grant's handwriting across the front.

The reason we're here at all.

Just the sight of it makes my heart thump harder. This one has fared better than the other two, looking nearly as crisp and white as the day it was written. I hold it up to my chest, exhaling deeply before turning back to face Silas again.

"You doing room service tonight, then?" I ask, sarcastically.

"Wouldn't fucking dream of it, Jules." His voice is tight, like something in him just shifted from a moment ago.

I clench the letter tighter.

"Join me back down here in one hour, or I'm coming to find you," he adds, smiling gently. He eyes the letter tucked to my chest and rubs a quick circle around my back with his knuckle, adding a bit of unspoken empathy to his words.

I'm here for you, if you need me.

The whole thing makes me laugh quickly — crisply — then for some odd reason, tear up. His hand pressed to my back like that.

I've missed this version of him, the friend he'd been to me, so much. The one who used to give me a load of sarcasm and crap, but was so intensely there for me, always, and without hesitation. It's no wonder that the loss of him during a time I needed him the most felt nearly unbearable.

"In that case," I tell him, "stand by."

He leans in and plants a firm kiss on the top of my head, the letter crunching between us.

"Just call if you need me to come up."

I nod.

He pulls back and starts off toward his room.

"One hour, Jules!" he calls out over his shoulder before turning the corner down the hall toward his side of the hotel.

Then I take off toward my own room, the unopened letter still clutched in my hand.

CHAPTER 25

Grant
One year ago

> *Jules,*
>
> *Your parachute must have opened if you're reading this, thank God. Either that or you've somehow survived a harrowing skydiving experience and carried on to collect this letter at your next destination. In which case, good girl.*
>
> *Either way, bienvenido a España!*
>
> *Let's hope you took the advice of my last letter to heart and are thoroughly, unabashedly, enjoying yourself by this point.*
>
> *I hope that the staggering views of Interlaken followed by the stunning seascape of Cádiz has left you utterly spellbound by the world again, and you're permanently wondering why you don't live in this intoxicating part of the world year-round. In other words, I hope this trip is doing exactly what I wanted it to do for you — getting you out of your comfort zone. Stoking a loud, inescapable yearning to experience life outside the mountain of grief you've carried all year, caused by yours truly.*

I also pray to God that you are no longer questioning why I sent you on this trip with Silas.

Do you remember when we went on that camping trip through the Adirondacks a few years after graduation? You, Silas, and me, plus Ryeson and Dax?

The five of us had ventured out for just a night or two, mostly because I don't think any of us could bear to be away from working plumbing any longer than that. You were the only girl to join, and it was on that trip I told Silas I was planning to propose to you.

We'd been backpacking all day to set up camp out by Dorian Lake. You'd had the worst time, twisting your ankle on that overturned log halfway through, and then you were eaten by the army of mosquitos that bombarded our camp. We'd all joked that you must have had the sweetest blood among us because you were getting absolutely eaten alive. You were like a Maglite, drawing every last mosquito to you instead of to the rest of us. But it was too late to hike back to the cars to give you any relief. It was getting dark by the time we arrived at the lake. We'd had no choice but to stay the night and leave first thing in the morning.

You were miserable. I could tell that you were just trying to be a good sport about it because you didn't want to be the weakest link, or ruin the good time we were all trying to have, even though I knew that any one of us would have been pissing and moaning about it much more than you had. You'd put on a brave face and coated your entire body and sleeping bag in mosquito repellant before lying down and pulling the sleeping bag up over your face until the smoke from the fire got thick enough to keep the bugs at bay while you slept.

After you finally drifted off to sleep, Ryeson and Dax passed out too.

When Silas and I were alone beside the campfire, crickets and mosquitos being our only company, I told him that I was going to propose when we got back home. I already had the ring from my grandmother and everything. I just needed to psych myself up enough to do it, vowing to find the perfect moment to ask you for your hand.

At first, he'd grown quiet. Then he stayed quiet for a long time, which, as we both know, goes completely against Silas' nature. We both sat there, just him and me and the crackling fire with you snoring quietly beside us — your head sticking out of the top of your bag.

Now, as if you could forget, Silas was the biggest ladies' man on campus. He could have had any girl he wanted, and he did. But when he found out I was going to propose, he just watched you sleeping, only your face visible from the top of your sleeping bag, already covered in red bites from earlier in the day. Then he finally looked at me and said something I've never forgotten.

He said, "I'm glad you chucked that coin in the Charles River. You were right not to back off from that stupid coin toss. You were right to call dibs and fall in love with her. Jules is perfect. Every bit of her is worth fighting for. You were just the one who was smart enough to do it."

Which brings me to the coin toss.

I've never told you about The Coin Toss.

It's uncharacteristically Neanderthal-ish of us, I know, but basically, after you'd asked us for a pen in World Civ, Silas and I left class that day and flipped a coin to see who got to ask you out.

Silas won the coin toss, between the two of us, fair and square. It was my job to back off and let him ask you out. But I'd angrily chucked the coin in the river and called dibs anyway.

I know, it's awful, and I'm sorry. Young boys are stupid and archaic, and nothing makes our caveman tendencies surface quite like a beautiful woman sitting in our midst.

But the point is, for the first time in my life, I'd thrown all integrity into the wind and told Silas that you were mine anyway. Coin toss be damned.

So, when he told me that he was glad I'd chucked the coin in the river instead of getting his chance to ask you out, I was offended. How could he be telling me he was glad he didn't get his shot with you? How could that be his response to what I'd just told him? That I planned to ask you to be my wife and he didn't think that you were good enough for him? I thought he was being arrogant and off-putting, but it wasn't until later that I actually understood what he meant.

"I'm glad it was you," he'd told me over the sound of the crackling wood. Everything dark around us. "She deserves to be with someone like you."

I figured he didn't like that I was cementing his place as our permanent third wheel, so I left it at that.

Soon after, I'd passed out in my sleeping bag, still rolling his words around in my head, not totally sure what he meant by any of it. But a few hours after I fell asleep, I woke up to see Silas — still awake — still sitting up all alone to stoke the fire. It was almost daylight by then, and he hadn't even unrolled his sleeping bag to try to get any sleep at all.

I was totally confused. Was he mad? Why hadn't he slept?

He didn't know I'd woken up, and I lay perfectly still in my bag, watching him, wondering what would compel him to not even try sleeping.

But after a few moments of watching, I knew.

Silas added another log to the fire, then looked over at you to make sure the pillars of smoke were still keeping the mosquitos at bay. Fanning them away from you every now and then while making sure the flames never went out. Ensuring you had as much protection as possible.

He'd sat up that whole night making sure enough smoke came off those logs to keep the bugs from attacking you while the rest of us slept soundly, blissfully unaware.

I don't think he saw me wake up to see him staring down at you early that morning, but I'll never forget it.

He may have thought that he'd never give you what you deserved, but that was just Silas being Silas. Never truly believing he was ever enough for anyone, let alone someone like you. But as I watched him take care of you, seemingly all night long

— without recognition, without an audience to see it — just out of the goodness of his own heart when even I couldn't stay awake long enough to do it — I knew that he would have found a way to deserve you if he'd taken the chance.

I get it. You're probably wondering why I'm wasting all this time painting this picture for you that doesn't exactly show me in the best light: me sleeping away while my best mate was caring for you instead.

It's because I want you to know that no matter how brash he can be — no matter how bizarre, or outrageous, or arrogant Silas comes across, you have always had someone looking out for you who wasn't me. And you need to know that even when you feel very much alone in the coming days and I'm not there to be with you, he will always be stoking some type of fire to keep you safe. That's just who he is. Who he's always been. That night showed me how truly important you are to him — that he'll always be right there taking care of you, usually when you're blissfully unaware that he's doing it at all.

I wish I could have stayed up all night to keep the fire burning for you, but knowing that I didn't have to and that you were warm and safe from anything that could have hurt you brings me more comfort than most other things can these days. Because I know that even if I won't be there to see it, you're going to be okay. You're going to have someone who loves you, who's always going to be looking out for you, even when I can't.

So, please don't hate me for seeing what you might not have ever seen, and for knowing who would be there to take care of you when I never could again.

That's the reason he's with you on this journey.

And why I couldn't have imagined it being anyone other than him.

Now, go live, sweetheart. It's the only thing left for you to do.

As always, from the bottom of my heart, thank you for letting me love you,
Grant

CHAPTER 26

Juliet

I read his letter twice more, not yet ready for my time with him or his words to truly be over for this leg of our trip. Then I breathe in the scent of the paper, praying that this one still has any small trace of him left clinging to the papyrus since it was so much more well-preserved than the last two.

But there's nothing left of him anymore.

Just the words that I haven't had time yet to process.

I roll to my side on the bed, dragging my knees into my chest.

Needing to delve into the picture Grant's just painted of the three of us — but especially of Silas — while I try to close the freshly opened wound in my chest.

I feel inexplicably guilty for leaving Silas to struggle all alone after his father died. Knowing, now, how unmooring the experience of losing someone can be.

I always knew how important he was to me, but could never have guessed just how much the feeling was the same for him too.

I remember that night. I remember waking up all stiff and smoky in the morning, telling Grant how shocked I was that I didn't get attacked even worse while I slept.

"Some kind of miracle," I'd told him.

Then I'd asked Silas how he'd slept that night as we all made instant coffee over the fire and rolled up our makeshift beds.

"Pretty decent," he'd said, not really looking at me.

He hadn't mentioned what he'd done, or bragged to the other guys that he'd been the only gentleman among them to stay up all night stoking the fire.

This is the first I've ever heard of it.

I have so many questions I want to ask them both.

Why did Silas stay so far away from me this entire past year?

And why did Grant choose this exact timeframe to tell me everything he thought I should know?

CHAPTER 27

Silas

An hour later, I'm pacing the lobby, still waiting for Jules to come down. Each time the elevator dings, I watch the doors, hoping it's her standing on the other side when they open.

But another ten minutes goes by without her showing up, and I'm starting to worry that whatever Grant wrote in that last letter was too much for her.

When the elevator chimes once more, I hop into it and ride up to her room, locating the room number that the receptionist said aloud when handing us our keys. I walk down the hallway and pound on her door.

My phone buzzes in my pocket with a text from Jules:

That better be you pounding like a maniac on my door. Because if it isn't, you might need to come up here.

I smile before typing back:

Would you be mad if it was?

Within seconds, the deadbolt slides over and the door opens. She's standing behind it, still wearing the same sweatsuit she wore on the plane ride this morning.

It's a stark contrast to my crisp dinner suit, the one I know I won't be eating in anytime soon, and my stomach growls in response.

She shrugs, taking a step back. "I was about to text you to come up."

"Hangover still going strong?" I ask, knowing damn well her appearance has nothing to do with her hangover from the wine last night.

"Not hungover anymore."

She walks back into her room and collapses down on the bed.

I sit on the edge right next to her, me sitting and her lying, while we study each other's eyes. I wish I could read her mind.

I wish this trip didn't have to unfold like this — a letter at every stop. Dragging her through the mud again each time she's finally starting to enjoy herself. It's a byproduct of the trip's design that I'm sure Grant didn't account for. If she didn't know about the letters already, I'd be tempted to steal the next two before she can retrieve them, just to relieve her of the weight she still has yet to bear.

"What'd it say?" I ask, gently.

"A lot of things." She pauses. "One being that you stayed awake to stoke the fire so I wouldn't get attacked by mosquitos all night. That night we all camped by the lake?"

She watches me intently, already knowing the answer.

How would Grant know about that? And why would he write it into one of these letters?

I chuckle nervously then reach in front of me to tuck a loose strand of hair behind her ear.

"Of all the things he could have chosen to write to you about, why waste time on that weird detail?" I'm hoping to make light of it, although it has my own mind racing.

What else was in that letter?

I lie down too, facing her with some space between us, on my side. If she's going to be curled up while we have this chat, then I will be too.

"Why did you do that?" she asks. "There were three other guys there that night and none of them felt the need to stay up to do that, including my own future fiancé. Hell, I could have stayed up all night to take care of myself. You didn't need to, but you did. Why?"

She chews her lip, studying me as if this will be the moment that my face finally gives it all away and shows her exactly how I feel about her.

"Well, you'd already been having the worst day. First your ankle, then we found out that you apparently had the most tasty blood among us. Not surprising, given the company you had around you that trip."

I pause to grin at her, coaxing out the sweetest smile. It spreads across her face like sunlight. My heart pounds, knowing that that look in her eye right now is meant for no one else in the world but me.

"Keep going," she whispers, hugging her knees to her chest.

"Those bugs were ruthless. If that fire had gone out, you never would have made it through the night. I just felt bad for you."

"Is that all?" she asks, gently.

"Why would Grant want to tell you about that, of all the things to spend his time writing to you about?"

She shrugs, but looks like she might have some idea.

"Was it because that was the night Grant told me he was proposing to you? Is that why he felt the need to include that detail? I didn't even know he was aware I'd done that."

"He said something else about that night," she adds.

I think back, racking my memory for anything else that might have transpired while everyone else slept by the lake. I shake my head, coming up blank.

"You told him that you were glad he'd won the coin toss."

She watches me even more intently after saying it, like she doesn't want to miss a single micro-reaction.

I smile faintly, controlling my face as best as I can, and sigh.

"Grant's really letting all the cats out of the bag with these letters, isn't he?"

She doesn't return the smile, but continues watching me, like she's finally seeing me clearly.

"You don't have to be embarrassed," she adds, running her tongue over her lower lip before biting it, releasing it slowly so that the tender flesh bounces back, more pink than it was before. "I think it's sweet you did that."

My body sinks deeper into the mattress. I don't have a good answer for her. Instead, I reach over to tuck another strand of stray hair back behind her ear. She tilts her face up a fraction of an inch toward mine and I let myself steal a look at her lips, parted just barely, a sliver of white teeth visible beneath the pink. Finally, our eyes meet somewhere in the middle.

"What else did Grant's letter uncover for you?" I ask her, not wanting to dive into the details of that camping trip if we don't have to. There's a second reason I stayed up that night and it had nothing to do with mosquitos. But right now, I don't want to tell her that I couldn't even fathom sleeping, knowing that she was going to be getting married. We had always been a ragtag team of three, but my third-wheel position felt a bit more serious, knowing they were going to be husband and wife with me on the side. Something about the pending engagement cemented a bond between them that I could never mount up to or truly be a part of. They were my chosen family up until that moment. As dumb as it is, the only emotion I could process that night — surrounded by my best friends and a cloud of thick smoke — was loneliness.

"He's pretty adamant that he sent me off on this trip to *live* again." Her voice pulls me out of the memory of that night.

"And that annoys you?" I ask, catching a hint of frustration in her voice.

"No. I mean, yes? I guess? I don't know. This is the third letter I've gotten to read from him, counting the first one back home, and each time I read one of them, it's like he knows exactly what I've spent the last year of my life doing. Like he was there to see it for himself." She laughs ironically. "He knew me so well, he even knows me postmortem."

"He's been right about everything?"

"Annoyingly so," she confesses, smiling faintly. Then her lips twitch into a broader smile. "I wish I could have surprised myself by bouncing back. Not sitting home most nights watching old *Schitt's Creek* episodes when I couldn't sleep because it was the last series we watched together. Sometimes I still start laughing and look across the couch, expecting to see him laughing too. And I know it's not good. Living in the past like that."

Her eyes settle into the space between us as a collection of memories stirs within.

I want to open up her mind and let every thought spill out across the room, like a thousand tortured microcosms that need to have their moment in order for her to be at peace again — instead of having been locked up there in her head all year long with nowhere to go.

"He's pretty convinced that I've spent the last year hiding out alone and that I need you to remind me that this big ol' world out here still exists."

I smile, knowing that this is exactly what the last year has been like for her. That she's been holding back from taking part in the world fully, partially out of grief, but partially because no amount of living feels right when you're wrapped up inside a storm.

"I tend to agree with Grant," I tell her. She narrows her eyes at me, but then I go on. "I was only eight when she passed, but it felt like I was insulting my mom any time I laughed or forgot for even one second. I spent years being angry because it didn't seem right to be anything but angry. Offensive, even. Then, well, you saw me after my dad died.

I basically jumped off the deep end. That time, there was no moral compass left. I was an utter disaster."

"And after losing Grant?"

"I hate to say it but I sort of felt like a seasoned pro by the time we lost him." I tilt her chin up with the pad of my finger. She blinks a few times, confused.

"How can you say that? I can't imagine it ever gets easier."

"Easier, no. *Never*. I struggle with his loss every minute of every day, Jules. Losing Grant gutted me in a way that was different from losing my parents, and in a lot of ways, it was somehow more painful. I loved my parents, but I *chose* Grant to be my family. He was irreplaceable to me, just as much as they were."

Her eyes well up with tears. "I think I've needed to hear you say that."

"And I'm sorry if I haven't shown you that part of this journey for me. But what I mean is that I gave myself some time to go off the rails for a shorter window, then slowly swam through the parts of grief that I knew I could do without — like all the idiotic coping strategies I used in the past. And then went straight to the better part of the whole train wreck."

"The better part? Excuse me if I think you sound crazy right now."

She rolls her eyes, and I swallow down a laugh.

"You're on your way to figuring that part out for yourself," I tell her. "Even if you think you're not, because against all odds, it'll come next if you're open to it."

"Enlighten me."

"I forced myself to skip past the scalding anger that comes with losing someone. The part where you wish the whole world would swallow you up with it so you don't have to keep going. This time, because I knew I'd get there eventually, I made myself live better *for* him. More meaningfully. Because at some point, you'll see the awful, gut-wrenching, life-altering, mindfuck of a gift that it can be. You see what can happen when you stop taking each day for granted like you did before losing them. Knowing they never got a February 28th, or a June 2nd of that year, but you did."

"What's so special about June 2nd?"

"Everything."

She furrows her brows.

"The simple fact that you get to wake up each day with air in your lungs when someone else that should have didn't makes that day extraordinary," I tell her. "You're not living and breathing just for yourself anymore. You're doing it every day for them too. Twice as hard. For the people you loved that don't get to."

She wipes a lone tear from her temple as it slides off toward the bed.

I've never talked like this to anyone.

"Silas Davenport," she says quietly. The saddest smile creeps across her face. "I never pegged you as such a deep feeling, little softy."

"Even assholes have feelings," I say, tapping gently under her chin.

She finally laughs at that, sniffing back future tears.

"I think that's what Grant has been alluding to in all his letters," she admits. "Like he somehow knew that I'd need you. But not just that, it's almost like I need . . ." She pauses, trying to find the right word.

"Permission?" I finish for her.

"Exactly. Permission to enjoy my life again. Which is why these letters have been so cathartic, I think."

"Permission from who though? If Grant's already giving it in these letters?"

"Maybe from other people. People who knew him. It's like I can be myself around total strangers or anyone who has no idea what happened because they just see me as another normal person functioning out there in the world. People who don't know me don't see me as a victim of my circumstance. But everyone else who knows what I've gone through looks at me like I should be eternally broken. Like they're so damn happy to see me crack a smile because they believe deep down that I shouldn't be smiling at all. Like it's against the moral code of grief or something. It feels suffocating being around that all the time."

I know exactly how she feels.

"How do I get past that without having to move away from everyone I've ever known, just to get away from that awful look in people's eyes when I try to be me again?"

"It'll get easier with time," I tell her. "And in the meantime, you go on living exactly the way you want."

She watches me for any sign of disgust or judgment about what she's just admitted, but I know she won't find any. Not with me.

"Jules, if you need a formal invitation to rejoin the world again without a hint of judgment, then please, by all means. You have it."

She sits up on the bed.

I sit up too so our knees are touching while we face each other.

The beginning of a smile curls the edges of her lips, but she straightens her mouth into a thin line when I start to speak, saying the exact words I wish someone had said to me after I experienced my first loss so long ago. As ridiculous as it is.

"Juliet Hart," I begin and she sits up straighter. "Would you please, by all fucking means, not just honor his memory, but honor the amazing woman that you are by laughing until you snort, smiling until your face hurts, and making those godawful jokes that you love without reserve, or fear of judgment from people who think you should spend the rest of your life crying over something you had absolutely no control over?"

The smile on her face finally breaks through the mask of uncertainty she's been hiding behind, like the sun itself starts pouring out of her. Soon, she's beaming. Nodding.

"As stupid as it sounds, I think I've needed that," she admits. "God knows I will *always* miss him, but sometimes missing him feels like all four walls are closing in. Part of me hated that you were joining this trip because I was so ready to turn over a new leaf and feel like myself again, without judgment from anyone that knew him. Having you come along meant that I felt like I had to sit and continue suffering in silence, to continue actively mourning him every moment of every day, just because I knew that's what you'd be expecting me to do."

"You don't need to explain it," I tell her, and she nods. "This whole trip can be a safe place for you to come back to yourself. You don't need my permission in order to do that, but I'm here for it anyway. I pushed everyone away after my dad passed in order to get that space to heal and grow past it, which was the wrong way to do things. I know that now."

"But I don't have to push you away in order to be me again," she says.

She leans toward me, wrapping both arms around my neck, hugging me closer to her while digging her face into the crook of my shoulder. Then she exhales the weight of everything she's just revealed.

I close my eyes and we sit like that for a minute before she slowly lets me go, happy that we've finally managed to break down whatever walls we'd both built around ourselves and each other.

She brings the back of my hand up to her lips and plants a kiss there before pressing my palm into her cheek.

"I've missed this," she says, smiling. "This version of you. Promise me you're not going to morph back into that other, out-of-control Silas the second we get back home."

"Other out-of-control Silas is gone," I tell her. "This might come as a surprise to you but I kind of hated that version of myself, too."

She laughs and starts to pull my hand away, but I hold it there.

"And Jules?" I pause, waiting to have her undivided attention. When I do, I lean in another inch so I know that she's listening. "I've missed you too. Welcome back."

CHAPTER 28

Juliet

We decide to explore the boardwalk for a late dinner. I've never been to Spain and from what I could see coming into Cádiz, it's going to be even more gorgeous now that the sun has gone down. The whole city is springing to life in a new way.

After walking down the boardwalk near the marina, we dive into the nearest eatery without even looking at the name on the door and are surprised to see the rest of the flight crew is already there.

"They live!" Andy says when we all spot each other.

I laugh and give him a hug, happy to welcome his comedic relief, after finishing such an honest conversation with Si earlier. I can't explain it, but I feel much lighter. More like myself than I've felt in a while.

We all end up sitting together. After ordering four heaping dishes of the freshest bluefish tuna I've ever tasted and a collection of tapas to share, the pilot and Silas decide to play a round of pool, leaving just Andy and me alone at the table.

We watch them play for a bit and Silas looks just like the kid he was back in college. Carefree and handsome, his laugh ringing out across the mostly empty bar each time Carl says something that makes him double-over. Even from here, I can see that his pilot has more skills than him. It's probably from plenty of nights out at pool halls while trying to fill his time during the rigorous flight schedule Silas has him on, but Si is still managing to keep up with him. If I didn't know them, I'd never guess that Silas is Carl's boss. Playful banter ping-pongs back and forth between them and they quickly clear the balls from the table.

"What's it like to work with him?" I ask Andy, nodding toward Silas. The crack of Silas' pool stick breaks another set apart. Balls fly toward every pocket.

"You want my honest opinion?" Andy asks, tipping his chin down before taking a swig of his tangerine-colored whiskey sour.

I nod and he watches them for a moment. I think he might be making sure they're out of earshot.

"That man can be a tough nut to crack. Wants everything a certain way, his plane stocked with certain things, his bedroom on every flight done up just right. And he'll definitely let us know when it's not."

I nod, feeling a bit deflated, wondering if I should have asked. Especially as I was just starting to see him as the guy he was before.

"But when business travelers are on the road as much as Silas is, it's understandable that they'd want each detail of their home away from home to be as predictable as possible. Those planes are his home when he's on the road, and the crew is almost like his family. We're what he comes back to time and time again. More than anywhere or anyone else in the world."

I hadn't thought of it that way.

"I can understand that," I admit. "It sounds kind of lonely."

"Lonely, yes. But not in the way you might imagine. At first, he operated exactly like his father had — bringing women back to the plane with him from all over the world, flying them home the next day while he slept off some rancid hangover in another exotic hotel or vacation villa off a tropical coast."

I cringe, definitely wishing I hadn't asked. Just hearing that stirs up something I hate. Like I'm peeking through a window into Silas' sordid past — the one I never want to look at again.

"But I haven't seen that side of him in a very long time," Andy says slowly, seriously, making sure to catch my eye when he does. And he must notice the look on my face because he quickly adds, "Silas was dealt a terrible hand when his father died, having to step up and take on well over a hundred thousand employees overnight when he was still a kid himself. We all had to parent him a bit to get him through it. Myself included. I think that's why he's so meticulous now. He doesn't like to make mistakes. Doesn't like to let any of us down. He's experienced enough mistakes and disappointment to last him a lifetime."

"That's the Silas I remember. The one who didn't want to let anyone down and was there for the people he loved," I tell him, watching the pool balls fly across the table when Carl begins another round. "The change in him after his father died is what tore us apart. I don't know if what I'm seeing now is a permanent change, or just an act he's putting on while he has my undivided attention here. This whole trip was a promise he made to Grant. I know he wouldn't want to let him down."

Andy pats my hand with a smile.

"Trust the change. Mr. Davenport may be a lot of things — the best types of people often are. But he's now one of the best men I've ever known. Sure, he's wildly particular, a workaholic, and can have a tongue on him that most people would be nervous to go up against. And rightly so. He's as quick-witted as the day is long. But he's also incredibly kind, impossibly generous, and honest to a fault. That man is incapable of lying. Not to mention a real hoot to hang out with. Truthfully, I never want to work for anyone else. He might not be exactly who he was when he was younger, but, honey, who is?"

He's not wrong. I'm certainly different than I was back then, too.

Silas slaps Carl on the back after Carl hits a few balls in. He dips into a mock bow.

"You really think he's changed?"

"A diamond doesn't become a diamond without a little pressure, hon. He's gotten a few more years of maturing under his belt since you've seen him. Men need a few more years to mature than women sometimes." He winks. "At some point, Silas knew he couldn't keep going the way he was while maintaining the business his father had built. And deep down, that boy doesn't want to disappoint anyone. Especially you."

"Me?" I ask, confused.

"Yes, you. His old girlfriend was sweet and all, but I knew it wouldn't last." He shakes his head with a sour look.

"You mean Raven?" I ask. "Silas told me she broke up with him because he kept saying my name in his sleep."

Andy smiles like he knows exactly what I'm talking about and I wonder if he ever heard Silas talking while asleep on the plane.

"Raven just wasn't right for him," he says, not confirming or denying it. "She just didn't have that *thing* Silas needs."

I frown, imagining what Raven must have been like for Silas to have a real relationship with her.

"And what's that thing Silas needs?" I ask, shifting in my seat. What does a man like Silas Davenport really need to be happy?

"You." He says it so fast, I think for a moment that I might have imagined it.

"What?" I ask, laughing. "A friend?"

Andy stirs his drink with a straw.

"You've always been what Silas needed. Lord, if you only knew. You're the itch that just couldn't be scratched. Believe me, because he's tried to scratch it without you over the years."

I blink at Andy, wondering how Silas' flight attendant could have such a strong view of us, of *me*, already.

"You just met me though."

"Doesn't matter." Andy twists an imaginary key in front of his pursed lips, then tosses it over his shoulder.

"Come on," I push. "You can't leave me with a cliffhanger like that."

"I've already said enough," he tells me, setting down his empty glass. "Oh good Lord, honey, here we go again." He juts his chin out toward Si and Carl, inviting me to take a look.

Two women have saddled up right next to Carl and Silas. One of them is so close to Si that her chest is practically touching his. Both of the women are giggling and making eyes up at him like he's on their dinner menu for tonight.

I eye Andy.

"What do you mean *again*?" I ask, carefully watching the four of them.

Andy sighs like this is an everyday occurrence.

"When you're traveling with a globally known billionaire, he's bound to get recognized here and there. Happens all the time. At first, it was like watching an all-you-can-eat buffet, but his appetite has tempered. Like I was saying."

A sharp spike of jealousy sends my pulse racing while I watch these two women try to flirt with him. One even reaches up to touch his arm, practically drooling onto his shoes. He smiles politely then glances over in my direction, nodding toward the table where Andy and I are sitting. Both of the girls instantly turn their heads. Their expressions change when they see me. I give them a halfhearted smile, adding a little wave.

Between gritted teeth, I ask Andy what's happening.

"If I had to guess, I'd say he's telling them that he's with us," Andy replies, giving me a triumphant grin. "With *you*, more specifically."

"Oh, he doesn't have to do that," I say, frowning. "He's single. We're in our own suites this time. He doesn't have to . . ." But I trail off, realizing that he might not *have* to use me as an excuse as to why he can't connect with these two women, but that I *want* him to use me as an excuse to walk away. And I'm not totally sure why.

"Oh, yes he does," Andy chortles, then gives me an exaggerated side-eye that makes me laugh.

"And why's that?" I ask.

The two women walk away like all the wind has just been knocked out of their sails.

"Because I have a funny feeling that he's been waiting his whole life for this," he tells me. "Whatever all *this* turns out to be."

CHAPTER 29

After the crew turns in for the night, Silas and I barhop our way down the boardwalk. We have an early sail in the morning but tonight Silas is everything I always loved about him: charming, charismatic, hilarious. Always two steps ahead, anticipating my thoughts before I even voice them, and by the time my jet lag is threatening to have me pass out cold, sitting at the last table, he's already calling the waitress over for the final check.

When we walk out of the bar, into the balmy night air, I'm acutely aware of his arm brushing against mine as we make our way down the street.

Grant's words fill the empty hollows of my mind, while Silas' words join in next, like a chorus of reminders, compelling me to lean into him even more instead of pulling away.

Live because they can't.

I link my arm through his like I've done a thousand times years ago, and he bends his arm at the elbow, locking me in. We walk like that, listening to the sound of the waves striking the rocky shoreline below while tourists and locals mingle on the sidewalk, weaving around groups still standing outside bars and eateries. The architecture here is pure magic and there's something more beautiful to see on each block we pass, dating back hundreds of years, with hidden alleyways and wooden doors leading to delicious-smelling food and drink carts or street musicians making the most of the crowds heading home in the dark.

The faint echo of a Spanish guitar rings out when we turn the corner onto an old, narrow walkway that'll lead us back to the hotel. There's a small group of people gathered here, listening to a musician pluck the strings with an empty guitar case sitting open at his feet. It's scattered with loose change and crumbled bills. A few couples dance on the cobblestone, gently swaying in each other's arms, illuminated by an old streetlamp flickering periodically overhead.

Silas pauses beside me.

"I think you owe me a dance," he says. It's not a question, but a command.

Before I can tell him no, he turns me toward him, pulling me in by the waist with one hand while grabbing tightly onto my free hand with the other.

"Si, you can't be serious—" I begin to protest, but he holds me firmly against him, making me forget the rest of my words. I swallow the rest away and let him lead me, chuckling.

"A deal's a deal," he says, reminding me of our negotiation back at the hangar in Switzerland.

I groan, remembering, looking around at who may be watching us awkwardly sway on the cobblestone but no one seems to care.

"Forget about everything else and dance, Jules."

"Forget?" I repeat.

"Focus on the music." His face curls into a grin. "It's gorgeous."

He's not wrong. The musician's fingers fly up the neck of his guitar as his other hand expertly plucks the strings. The Spanish melody is sexy and slow.

Silas' grip on my spine grows more firm. His body tenses against mine, and my heart begins to beat even louder.

I glance at the other dancers, positive that we'll stick out like a sore thumb. These people all look as if they might have grown up in a flamenco studio. My body feels stiff, but my feet slowly begin to follow his steps.

"Out here? In the open like this?" I bite my lip as we begin to move.

He leans down and rests his cheek against mine, his lips gently brushing across my ear when he speaks.

"Right here."

I swallow. The heat of his breath near my skin sends a shiver down my entire body starting where his lips brushed the space beneath my earlobe. It's gentle, like a feather. Barely whispering past my skin, so much so that I'm not sure whether it was meant to be or just a miscalculation of the space left between his lips and me.

I close my eyes and tilt my chin up toward the black sky filled with stars, giving him more access to my jaw, faintly wishing his lips would find that spot again. Not thinking about whether it's right or wrong. Just wanting so desperately to feel that simple jolt of electricity again. The one that reminds me I'm here. Living and breathing on a sidewalk, now in Spain.

He bends to speak again, and this time I know it wasn't a mistake. "Forget everything else, Jules. Just move your body with me."

There's no point in fighting a man like Silas when he wants something, so I do exactly as he says.

I forget everything that brought us here to this exact moment.

I let the people, and the sidewalk, and the waves crashing below all fade into a hazy background of noise, and instead of focusing on how we look, or who might be watching me dance with the one man I started this trip out loathing, it all turns to gray.

And we dance.

CHAPTER 30

At first, we dance like all the other couples around us. He plants his left hand just above my hip, and we glide in unison, swaying back and forth a few times while I grin into his shoulder, barely shuffling left to right on the balls of our feet. Then, he pushes me out gently by the hip and I spin around once under his arm while a few more unabashed couples walk onto the makeshift dance floor, giving us less room to move so freely, caught up in the small but growing collection of hopeless romantics dancing under this old street light in Spain.

He gently pulls me back into him following the spin, and I wrap both of my arms up around his neck. The closeness between us shields my face again from his.

Then he says what we both must be thinking.

"This is one of those moments that was never supposed to happen." His lips brush that sensitive spot just below my ear.

"But is it wrong to enjoy?" I ask, before I can think twice, flushing right after the words come out.

"No," he whispers back. "Of course not."

I lean into him when the music dips into a slower melody. The dancers around us sway back and forth against each other, just like us.

"We don't stick out like a sore thumb," I tell him quietly, smiling.

"Is that what you thought would happen?" He laughs quietly into my ear, and a layer of goosebumps spring out down both of my arms. "You know, I'm not completely awful at dancing."

"No, I remember you having moves back in college, actually."

"How else was I supposed to get any ladies with a mug like this?" he asks, sarcastically, pulling back.

He knows he's impossibly handsome.

I scoff, and push back gently, but he draws me in closer.

We sway for a few moments while my heart pounds in my ears.

The guitar, the dancing couples, the waves sloshing below — it's all too much. It's the kind of moment that makes me ecstatic just to be alive. My whole face hurts from smiling most of tonight. Laughing more than I have in well over a year.

"I want to have this memory. Dancing on a Spanish sidewalk with you. Right under the moon," he tells me. "I know, I know, you're probably hating this but—"

I lean back to find his eyes, then shake my head at him.

"There's nothing to hate about this, Si." And I mean it. "Maybe this moment was never supposed to happen, but I'm glad it is."

Before he tucks me back into him, we grin at each other as the song transitions into a slow Spanish rendition of "Moon River." The song is beautifully haunting and one of my favorites, but a few of the couples reluctantly meander their way off the sidewalk, moving on with their night while the melody drifts after them down the sidewalk.

Silas and I continue to sway together under the soft glow of the flickering streetlamp. Neither one of us quite ready to break the unexpected spell of the evening, or bid this exact moment farewell, because as long as we're still living it, we don't have to acknowledge that it's happened.

CHAPTER 31

Juliet

The next morning, Silas is back in my room and I'm doing my best to ignore the tightness in my chest from just having him in here.

Something unexpected switched in my head last night. And while he didn't end our dance on the sidewalk with a kiss, there was a moment when I certainly thought he might.

And with it came a moment in which I certainly wanted him to try.

I have no idea how.

I'm sure the drinks we'd had earlier with the crew made our decision-making capabilities a bit hazy, but I can't say I regret any of it.

"What do you mean we'll still sail in weather like this?" I ask. He can't be serious. After waking up to rain pounding at the window, I thought for sure the sail we had planned this morning would be postponed until tomorrow when it's dry and sunny again.

"I'm sure it'll clear up by the time we get down to the water."

Silas is standing in the sitting room of my suite with his hands on his hips. He's in full athletic attire, including a white backward baseball hat that looks far too attractive on him in this exact moment.

His eyes are shining at me like a kid on Christmas morning.

After our moment on the sidewalk last night, Si had dropped some bills into the guitar case, then we'd raced back to the hotel, arm in arm, when the sky began pouring out of nowhere. When I opened the door to my suite, our hair dripping down our necks, I hadn't known what to say anymore. It had suddenly felt too quiet, the space too intimate, and we'd sheepishly parted ways, tucking ourselves back into our separate rooms, muttering things about hot showers and needing to get sleep before the big morning sail.

I'd spent most of the night tossing and turning, trying to think of all the reasons other than *he was Grant's friend* in order to stay away from him.

The list was short.

He'd kissed me on the cheek before leaving, and I'm pretty sure that if I'd had the courage to ask, he'd have probably done more.

I couldn't actually be sure.

Did he always end the night by kissing girls on the cheek? Especially if they were just friends? Or was that the drinks at play?

Does he feel some loyalty to Grant? One that would never allow him to cross the invisible line between us? In the light of day, I don't even know if I want him to.

I was already a ball of nerves this morning after hardly sleeping, and that was before I saw the pounding rain outside.

"Get your gear on, Jules," he says, pulling me out of my head.

"My gear?"

"You might not be partaking in the actual work of sailing, but you'll still need a hat, a polo, tennis shoes with good tread . . . It was all in the clothing options on that list from Katie."

"I was thinking a sundress and thongs?"

He bursts into laughter, seemingly unbothered and unchanged by what unfolded last night. He seems as carefree as he always does.

I watch him squeeze sunblock onto his hands, even though the sky is gray, and he rubs it up and down both forearms, pulling up his sleeves to slather it onto his shoulders, tendons rippling each time he moves his fist up and down.

I look away, biting my bottom lip.

What the hell has gotten into me?

"You can do bare feet on the deck. I'd prefer that you didn't trip over flip-flops when the boat tips," he says, not bothering to look up.

"Tips?"

He stops what he's doing to stare at me. His nose and forehead are still painted white.

"You missed a spot." I point, scrunching my face at him while I wave my hand around. "Okay, you missed a lot of spots."

He doesn't move. It's like he hasn't heard me.

"What?" I ask.

"How much sailing have you seen?"

"I've watched sailing," I say, defiantly. "Like, from the shore. And once on TV."

"But you didn't know the boat tips?" he asks, looking concerned.

Now he has *me* worried. But, in true Silas form, he manages to crack a smile and continues rubbing in the sunscreen, now looking like a cat that ate the canary. Like I'm in for some type of secret reveal later on.

"I really just plan to sit there and enjoy the view," I assure him. "Do you think there will be dolphins?"

I toss aside the sandals I'd been planning to wear and start searching for a pair of sneakers with good tread.

"Dolphins?" he repeats.

"Kidding?" I answer, weakly.

"No, you're not."

"No, I wasn't. But I think I am now?"

"We're going to need to give you a crash course in what to expect while you're on the deck so you're not hit off the side by the boom. Or worse."

"What's worse than getting hit off the side by a boom? And what's a *boom*?"

"What's a boom?" he repeats, looking absolutely gutted that I didn't take one single minute of time to prepare for our little sailing adventure.

In all fairness, I really just pictured myself sprawled out across the front of the bow in a cute swimsuit, hanging on to a rope or something.

"Do you mean I'll hit the water with a *boom*." I clap loudly, like something's just hit me off the front of a boat. "Or . . . ?"

"It's the long log thing that swings back and forth and knocks people off. Anchors the sails." He smacks one hand into the other, like one is knocking the other over. "Boom!"

"Oh, God." I swallow. "Named appropriately then."

He glances at his watch.

"We should go. I'll explain on the way."

Silas steers me toward the marina from behind while I walk and watch a few quick sailing lesson videos on my phone the whole way there. Thankfully, the rain has cleared up and the sun is peeking out of a strip of white puffy clouds. Turns out, there's a lot more to know about sailing than how to look pretty on the front while admiring the view, and by the time we arrive at the marina, I'm feeling a bit more prepared.

"You'll be fine," Silas assures me. "I've got you."

"What type of boat did Monica rent for us?" I ask, looking around the huge array of sailboats and yachts lined up. There's every type of vessel you can imagine.

"Monica didn't rent us a boat," he says, walking with a purpose, like he knows exactly where to go.

"Should we go find a counter to rent one then?" I ask, looking around for someone who might work here.

Silas walks right toward two men wearing matching white-and-blue striped polos with white hats, stepping off the most beautiful boat in the harbor. It reminds me of his plane, all polished wood with sleek, masculine lines.

"Good morning, sir," one says.

"She's ready for you," the other adds, stepping onto the dock.

She?

"Thanks, guys," Silas says, swapping places with them.

"Safe travels, Miss Hart, Mr. Davenport," they say in unison as they walk past us toward the parking lot.

"Thank you?" I mumble like it's a question.

"This is it!" Silas says, turning to hold a hand out to me. I let him help me step on.

"This?" I ask, looking down the long exterior of the ship. "Are they coming back to help? Where are they going?" The two men continue to walk down the dock away from us. This boat has to be at least thirty feet long. Maybe forty.

"I always sail her alone," Si tells me while starting to inspect whatever roping system those two men just finished tying up.

"Right," I say, sinking down into a cushy captain's chair, right next to a giant pronged steering wheel, feeling intimidated. "What were they doing out here on the boat then?"

"Getting her ready. It's been a few months since I was here, so I had them freshen things up a bit. Make sure she was in top shape to sail today."

"You've already been here?"

He nods.

"Alone?" I press, trying to imagine Silas coming all the way to Spain by himself to sail a boat out of this very harbor.

He nods again, this time with a grin, before going back to testing various ropes around the boat's perimeter.

"So, you flew those two guys out just to prep the boat?" I guess. "Just like the mechanic you flew out to Switzerland for the plane check?" Instead of annoyed, I feel touched by his attention to safety and detail regarding everything we've done so far. Admittedly, it's a different feeling than I first felt when he'd let me in on his safety scope.

He pulls a coil of rope off the deck and starts untying us from the dock.

"I don't take any unnecessary chances. Not anymore," he says, looking focused as he kneels down to untie another long rope. The cuff of his white sleeves tighten around his biceps as he expertly works the thick coils between his hands.

I blink, unsure of what to expect with just Silas and me out on open water. But we're already drifting backward, out into the sea, as he mans the small outboard motor at the back of the ship to get us out of dock. And just like that, for better or for worse, we're sailing.

CHAPTER 32

As we slowly make our way out to open water, Silas tosses a thin lifejacket to me. I tuck it behind my feet, down under my seat, but he glares at me long enough that I finally pull it over my shoulders and clip the front.

"I'm not going to need this, am I?" I ask.

"I don't know how good of a swimmer you are," he says, winking.

I scold my stomach for twisting at that. Of course he's kidding.

He has to be kidding.

"No really, Si, I'm not going to need this, right?"

"Safety first, babe," he says, absentmindedly before leaving the motor to hop up on the stern to pull a few more ropes, lengthening a long tether attached to what must be the boom.

Watching him, I can't help but wonder what other women he's brought out on this boat. And if he has, did they know how to sail like this?

Silas heaves a rope attached to a pulley system, bringing the enormous sail to life overhead. The glistening white fabric puffs out and snaps open in the wind. I immediately feel the weight of the boat lifted up beneath it. The wooden hull begins slicing through the water as if it were a hot knife cutting through butter. The water rushes along beside us, deep and dark and blue. I look back at the harbor, realizing that not only is it starting to get farther away, but it's leaving us with the most gorgeous view of Cádiz from out on the open sea.

"We're sailing!" I exclaim, watching Silas as he mans the entire ship himself. *We* might be a strong word here, I realize.

He hops from one platform to the next, securing a rope while uncoiling another. His brow is furrowed in concentration, studying the sail billowing in the wind. Then he takes the impressive metal wheel in both hands and pushes it left, then straightens us out to the right.

It's like he's dancing with the ship in silent concentration. Just the two of them taking up all his thoughts right now, while I'm the outsider watching everything between them unfold. This side of him is serious and stern — something I rarely see in him.

Something, I realize, I want to see more of.

When the ship is finally on a course he seems to be pleased with, he relaxes a bit. His shoulders visibly uncurl beneath his jaw and he rocks his head from side to side, stretching out whatever tension the launch from the dock just caused. Finally, his eyes find mine watching him.

He smiles.

"Need help?" I ask, trying not to look embarrassed about the fact that I've just been caught staring at him.

"No," he says, but his grin stretches wider across his face. His eyes squint into the sun behind his steel aviators. He takes them off for just a moment, lifting his face to feel the full heat of it. When he opens his eyes again, I can see the amber flecks of gold simmering in the sea of green, even from here.

I bite my lip and look out at the sea. The wind hits my face and I inhale into the sunlight, feeling a light spray of saltwater rise up in the air. What is it about this place? It's like all my stress is melting away in the mist, floating off, as if carried by the breeze.

He was right.

This sailing thing would be too easy to fall in love with. Too easy to never want to return from.

"How do you ever leave this?" I sigh, watching him. "And how often do you get to come back?"

"Not enough," he says simply, falling serious again. "Come on up here," he adds, motioning for me to join him. He grasps the wheel with one hand while holding his other arm out to me.

As soon as I stand, he steps forward to cradle me between his elbow and palm, making sure I don't misstep as the ship tilts to one side. I carefully make the few steps over to the wheel.

"Put your hands at ten and two," he instructs, placing my hands on it, boxing me in from behind. "Feel that?"

It jerks hard beneath my hands and I grip it tighter, fighting the water churning around the rudder below.

"It's pushing to the left," I say, glad his hands are still hanging on to help right next to mine.

"So, pull it to the right," he tells me, shifting his hands so mine disappear beneath his, guiding them gently but firmly. Together, we pull the ship to the right. It's only a few inches, but the resistance of the water pulls harder than it did a moment ago.

I lean in and push. He lifts his hands so they're hovering now just above mine, letting me do all the work myself while balancing on the deck behind me. We're rushing across the surface of the sea, not touching in any way now, but just having him behind me makes me feel safe. And honestly, happy.

"You're sailing," he whispers in that same spot behind my ear, and I'm immediately transported to last night — his lips just below my jaw — right before we began to dance.

"And you'd better not go anywhere," I say, turning over my shoulder, making sure I can feel his body behind me without having to tear my eyes off the view ahead. "Where are the brakes on this thing in case something jumps out?"

He laughs. "It's just us out here," he assures me. "And it'd take a lot to bring ol' *Vivi* down, believe me, I've had enough time testing her out here to know."

"Vivi?" I ask, wondering what music icon — or worse, what girlfriend from his past — must have influenced the name choice.

"*Vivian*, actually," he says.

I search my memory for any girls we knew back in college or famous musicians named Vivian.

"Do you name everything you ride on after some random woman?" I ask, nearly shouting above the wind.

He chuckles louder, then sobers enough to answer.

"Vivian was my mother."

Shit.

"Oh my God. I'm so sorry. Ignore what I just said." Of course I'd ruin the nice moment we were having.

How did I not know his mother was named Vivian?

"This boat was my father's. He'd named it after her. I didn't know it existed until I learned about it in the will."

The wheel jerks to the right and I shift it to the left, trying to imagine twenty-six-year-old Silas finding out every detail of his parents' lives through a long will left to him by his father. Finding out there was a boat he never knew existed with a name he never had the heart to change.

"So, you came out here to see her for yourself?" I ask, twisting my cheek over my shoulder.

"More like I tried to drown myself out here, really."

I gasp and release the wheel, turning around to face him.

He plants his hands on the wheel, now behind me, while I struggle for balance and try not to fall into his chest.

"You didn't," I say, holding his shoulders, finding my sea legs.

"Of course I didn't." He cracks a smile. "I'm here, aren't I? I might have been a mess back then, but no. No part of me was actually trying to drown myself, Jules."

"Jesus Christ, Si." I smack him on the chest.

I whip back around and place my hands beside his on the wheel again, but feel him slip away from behind me.

"You're not going anywhere, are you?" I call over my shoulder. I'm definitely not secure enough to hold this monster of a wheel all by myself yet.

"You've got this," he answers, shifting to one side, still keeping one hand firm on the wheel, but planting his feet beside me where I can see him, and he can see me.

"I lived on this boat for a month after I found out about it."

"You what?" The wind whips around my eyes while I study his hardened features, suddenly aware of how little I see his face without a hint of humor in it. "How did I not know that?"

"You didn't know a lot about me back then," he says, smiling. "You only saw what I wanted you to see at the time. Which, turns out, was the absolute worst side of me."

"I had no idea you went and lived on a boat in Spain for a month. Grant never told me."

"I tried to get him to join me out here, actually."

I fall silent. *That's* the Silas I knew. The one who was reckless. The one who would have pulled Grant away from me for a month without thinking twice about what that might do to me, our jobs, or to our relationship.

"He never mentioned that."

"Probably for the best," he says, straightening up. "It left me to wrestle with all the demons I had to wrestle with, but completely alone and without him here to do it for me. That month was the beginning of the end."

"The beginning of the end?" I repeat. *What does that mean?*

"Hang on, let me shift a few things," he says, hopping up on the front of the boat before I can stop him.

"No, wait! I'm not ready to hold this without you," I yell after him, hoping he can hear me against the wind.

"Yes, you are!" he shouts back, ignoring my plea for him to come back. "Just hold her steady. Exactly like you're doing!"

I grip the wheel tighter, not allowing it to move even an inch while I watch each step he makes like a hawk. Tying a rope off here, clipping another over there, shifting the boom to the exact spot he wants it by tying off a pulley after drawing it taut. Each step is deliberate and smooth, and I can tell he's done this exact dance with *Vivi* a hundred times before.

When he's done, he carefully makes his way back to me, stooping and stepping over and under random ropes and pulley systems until he's beside me again.

"We'll anchor her here for a bit. It's calm enough right now," he tells me.

"What do I do with this?" I ask, still gripping the wheel like our lives depend on it.

"Lock it in place, so we can go up front."

A moment later, Silas has my hand, carefully leading me up to the front of the boat. I hadn't noticed before, but there's a dip in the bow, a little cut-out meant to lie or sit back on, it seems. He grips my hand tightly for balance as I make it over to the cushy spot, ready to sink lower when I make it there safely.

We sit down beside each other, and once I'm feeling steady enough, I allow myself to look around.

"Wow," I gasp, taking in the view around us. The sea is the deepest blue out here where we're anchored, but it grows lighter as it heads into the shallows leading up to shore. The city of Cádiz looks even smaller from out here, with its rocky coastline and whitewashed domes, like a medieval dollhouse showing off across its light, sandy shore.

"You should see it at night," he says, admiring the view beside me. "The lights reflecting off the water are unreal."

"I can't believe you stayed out here for a month," I tell him, pushing on his arm gently, hoping he'll tell me more about that time of his life.

"Off and on. I'd go into town when I needed more supplies. But mostly, I stayed on the water. Drove everyone at Davenport Media crazy." He laughs. "This was the one place they couldn't get to me with endless meeting requests and Zoom calls. The board was threatening to vote me out if I didn't, in their words, *grow up* and come back to run the family business. I almost didn't."

I stare at him, bewildered.

"You almost let it all go?"

All I saw of Silas back then was this cocky, arrogant, filthy rich playboy. Cruising in and out of our lives with a thousand-yard stare, dishing out shit as if his life depended on it. I didn't realize he'd been so painfully close to losing everything.

"I was numb. Numb and dumb..." He pauses, lost in the memory, but I continue staring at him, wondering how in the world he got it together enough to be as successful as he is now.

I stay silent, hoping he'll go on, but when I can't wait any longer, I ask, "What happened to make you come back?"

"There came a point when I realized that I either had to let it all go once and for all, or I had to do exactly what they told me to do: grow the fuck up and take what my dad had spent his entire life building."

"How did you decide?"

"Grant."

My heart twists at the mention of his name.

"And you," he adds.

"What?" I snap, wondering how in the world I had anything to do with the decision that saved him and his company when I didn't even know he was out here.

"I knew I was losing you. Both of you. I knew I'd fucked up past the point of forgiveness roughly eight thousand times already, and if I had any chance of earning back trust — yours or Grant's — then I had to dock *Vivi* and get back to my life. I had to go back to Boston. I had to try. I couldn't lose you guys. You were the only family I had left." He pauses, then side-eyes me as if he's about to confess something else. "That and he tracked me down."

I blink back at him.

"He — who?"

"Who do you think?"

"Grant was *here*?" I ask, dumbfounded. "When?"

"It was some long weekend that you were doing wedding prep with your girlfriends."

I stare at him. "The weekend Emma and Molly took me to New York?"

"For some dress shopping or something, yeah."

"And Grant flew *here*?" I press my finger into the wooden deck of the boat.

"Ryan had called him as a last resort. Knowing if anyone was going to get me back home, it was going to be him. He flew Grant out here to talk some sense into me."

I narrow my eyes at the depths of water around us, then lie back, my face growing hot beneath the sun.

"I wasn't sure if he ever told you that."

"No, he most certainly did not."

"That's the only thing he ever kept from you," he assures me, watching how my face has morphed with this unexpected news.

"How would you know that? He also planned this whole bloody trip right under my nose without me knowing."

"Because Grant always told me everything. Regardless, it worked. I flew back with him and got to work. For some things, it was already too late. By the time I returned, you wanted absolutely nothing to do with me. Grant and my friendship was hanging by a thread. I don't think he wanted me around you any more at that point. I was *unpredictable*, in his words. And now I'm aware that he always knew how I—" He stops talking to push a hand through his hair.

"Knew what?" I ask.

Silas lifts his eyes toward mine. He somehow looks apologetic and unapologetic at the same time.

Startled, I watch him until it becomes clear. He doesn't have to say the words out loud for me to know what he's thinking.

Neither one of us feels the need to confirm it.

He runs his tongue along his teeth then turns out toward the sea. I don't press him more, but my heart thumps louder.

"I get why you weren't okay with me by that point," he adds.

"I wanted nothing to do with you by then," I say quietly, feeling gut-punched. "I remember now. It was after that dress shopping weekend I had in New York."

He glances down at the deck, nodding.

"I deserved everything I had coming," he says, finally smiling ruefully.

"I'm so sorry," I tell him, shaking my head. "I didn't know what loss felt like back then. I had no idea how much it could change you. Like the actual DNA of who you are before and after can morph into something you don't even recognize in yourself."

"The whole time I was out here, the only thing I wanted to get back to was you—"

"And Grant," I finish for him, not allowing that sentiment to stand alone. Even for one second.

He laughs gently. "And Grant," he agrees, nodding.

"So, you came back."

"And the first thing I did was give Grant that building, hoping it would show you guys how much I'd changed. That, and I was trying to help."

"The Smithfield." I exhale the word.

"When you told me that you thought it could have had something to do with his illness—"

"But it didn't," I interrupt. "I'm glad I know the truth, but I do regret bringing it up like I did."

"It could have been the biggest fuck up of my entire life, Jules."

"It wasn't though. I wish we hadn't lost so much time to stupid mistakes and assumptions. We were so close," I say, sadly, wishing I could take back all those years we drifted apart over something, in hindsight, he had such little control over. Something I shouldn't have blamed him for at all. "I was too hard-headed to give you another chance," I admit. But then I add, "Until now."

He grins, looking like years of stress is finally draining out of him.

"Right," he agrees, leaning back so the sun washes over him. "Until now."

CHAPTER 33

Silas

I hadn't meant for it all to come out like that. Something about the sun, the water, the reflection of it all bouncing around in her unbelievably light turquoise eyes had me spilling everything I swore I'd never spill.

"When do we do this again? Can we just stay here forever?" Jules is practically bouncing off the deck as I swing the tail of the boat back into its slot at the marina. "How can we do this every day?"

I grin at her, trying to reconcile the fact that deep down inside I'm desperate to give her anything. She could ask me to buy that tiny island we passed on the water twenty minutes ago and I'd do it in a heartbeat.

Last night feels surreal. Like a dream I could never bring myself to have. I had to shove away all the doubts and second thoughts I had about dancing with Jules. It was supposed to be simple. The musician was already there. It was an easy way to fulfill our deal from back in Switzerland. Just one more way to remind her that there's so much more to look forward to if you're willing to live in the present moment. But it had all flipped as soon as we started moving across the cobblestones together.

I'd barely been able to breathe. That whole moment we had last night with the guitar playing under the lamplight — I promised myself that it wouldn't matter what happened between us next — that one moment alone could quench my thirst for Juliet Hart until the day I died. However, by the time I woke up this morning, I knew I was only fooling myself if I thought I could live forever off that memory alone.

I woke up in desperate need of seeing her again.

I pull the sail down hand over fist, using the ship's pulley system. The enormous swatch of fabric floats down onto the deck, sinking into a heap next to my feet.

"We can stay in Spain as long as you'd like. Teach you to sail. Live by the water. Hell, I'll even buy you whatever boat you want. A little dingy to practice with? Or you can just learn on this one," I tell her. Seeing her eyes glow like this, like she's falling in love with the same sport I've always had a soft spot for makes me happier than I've felt in a long time. She's the only woman I've ever taken on that boat. And the only one I ever want to see out there again. "I never took you to be such an adrenaline junkie, Jules, but now that I know, what am I going to do with you next?"

She throws her head back into the sunbeams and lets out a laugh. She looks more free from worry than I've seen her look in years. If she was beautiful in Switzerland, she is magnificent here in Spain.

"I guess since you started forcing me to jump out of planes and race in the ocean," she shoots back, laughing, "you've created a monster, Si." She hops to her feet. "What's next? Shark diving in Bermuda?"

I set the ropes aside and begin securing a second buoy off the starboard side.

"The next stop might surprise you, actually," I tell her. "We're learning to make pasta in this little stone house off the Amalfi Coast. Zero adrenaline required, if you're up for it."

Her laughter rings out across the front of the ship, and I chuckle while I watch her, wondering when it's going to dawn on her that I'm serious.

"No, really," she says, stooping down to tie her sneaker. I hop off the hull to give her a hand and she steps onto the floating dock.

"Really though. There's the sweetest little grandma in Amalfi who's agreed to teach us. She goes by Nonna Lisi. It's a small break from adrenaline and extreme sports, but it should be memorable nonetheless."

She pauses to regain her balance after having used her sea legs out on the water, but she quickly steadies herself and releases my hand.

"Nonna Lisi?" she repeats, then smiles, looking for the joke in my eyes. I wait, knowing she won't find one there. "Wait, you're serious?"

"I guess not all your bucket list items included a death-defying experience?"

She skips a few feet in front of me, swinging around to catch my eye again as she twirls ahead.

"I have absolutely no idea how you guys found this adorable woman to teach us pasta making in Amalfi," she starts, "but I can't think of a better place to go next!"

"Good, because we're heading straight to the airport from here. The crew already grabbed our luggage from the hotel."

She runs back and hugs my forearm into her body before linking her elbow in mine, like she did last night. We walk toward the car waiting off the dock, back on dry land, and I wish she'd snatched my hand again, like she did for just a second before the sky opened up above us last night. But, I'll take her arm linked in mine.

"Thank you," she says, looking up at me.

"For the sail today? You don't have to thank me for that. I love getting out there."

"Not that. *This.*"

She releases my arm and skips ahead again, swirling her arms up toward the sky.

"For not giving up on me before all this could even get started. For not leaving me in my house when I couldn't walk out that first morning." She walks backward, still facing me so she can hold my eye while talking. "For not hating me for what I accused you of." She plants her feet. "You have never given up on me, even when you've had so many chances to. And maybe should have at certain points."

I'm taken aback.

"I would never give up on you, Jules. You should know that by now."

I continue walking toward her until our knees nearly knock together. Then I take off my sunglasses so she can study my eyes. I'm not sure what's going through her head, but I stay quiet enough to find out. Hoping she'll tell me.

"I'm starting to realize that," she says, quietly. "You've always looked out for me, and you deserved better than what I gave you after you lost your dad. I shouldn't have given up on you."

"It's not the same thing," I argue.

"But it is," she says. "It can really be that simple." I begin to shake my head but she stops me. "Just let me have this round," she whispers. Then she wraps her arms around my waist in a hug, pressing her cheek to my chest. I've hugged Jules plenty of times as friends, but somehow, this feels different. I exhale into her hair and she giggles. "Your heart is like a drum circle in there."

I clear my throat. "Sailing always gets me going," I tell her, shifting my eyes up toward the sky. Will it ever not feel wrong to be utterly obsessed with her? "It's been a minute since I got out there, you know."

I pull back and start leading her toward the car and the driver that's waiting for us on the road.

"Let's get you off to Italy before I change my mind and carry you back out for round two since you seem so keen on sailing now. Keep you out there for a month? Maybe two?"

I lunge at her like I might make good on that promise.

She shrieks and runs down the dock, her golden hair trailing behind her as she skirts away from me. I suck in a breath and fight the urge to run after her, knowing it might not be the best thing for either one of us if I manage to chase her down.

CHAPTER 34

Juliet

Silas and I were rerouted back to the hotel after a flight delay kept us grounded in Cádiz. Now we're back in my suite after a delicious night out.

Five minutes ago, the hotel's room service staff dropped off an unexpected dessert just as Silas came in to grab the gear he'd left in my room before the sail this morning. We both came out of the rooms at the same time when we heard the knock on the door, him emerging from the bathroom in only the charcoal pants he wore to dinner earlier.

No shirt, and no socks. Just bare feet and the pants I saw him zipping back up as he exited the room to answer the door.

They dropped off just one saucer of molten lava cake with two scoops of vanilla ice cream, topped with two heaping mounds of whipped cream on top of that. Two spoons were nestled in beside the platter on the cart, though there was only one plate between the two of us.

Neither of us ordered it, so I'm not sure how they knew it was my favorite. But it smells delicious, even from where I'm sitting across the long table now from Si.

We're at either end of the long dining table in my suite, the one that could fit sixteen people, if we had fourteen other people traveling with us.

But it's just him and me, grinning at each other about the unexpected delivery now sitting on the table in front of him.

Silas picks up his spoon and digs in, not even asking if I want a bite.

Just like him to take what he wants, when he wants it, without asking first, I think, watching.

I'm not sure what I'm waiting for though. I should just go grab my own spoon and dig in too, but my feet are planted where I'm at, as if stuck in cement. All I want, I realize as he eats a second bite, is to watch him enjoy it.

As if he can read my mind, he looks up.

"You know you want it," he says, raising the spoon before scooping up another bite. He makes sure to get all three layers onto it before tucking it deeply into his mouth. Chewing slowly, and licking his bottom lip after swallowing.

"How do you know I want it?" I ask.

Instead of answering, he lets out a wicked sort of laugh, one I've never heard come out of him before.

"Is it that obvious?" I say, feeling silly for not just getting out of my seat to grab a spoon for myself.

"You *could* be more obvious about it," he tells me. "It's the only way to make sure your needs are met."

Then he wipes a bit of liquid chocolate off the corner of his lips with his thumb before pushing it back into his mouth to suck off the top.

That should not have been as hot as it just was. *This is Silas*, I remind myself. *What the hell has gotten into me?*

"How could I be more obvious?" I ask, my mind racing.

"Lie down," he demands, pointing not to the couch or to the bed tucked out of sight, but to the table stretched between us, the glossy surface as dark and molten as the cake itself.

I rise to my feet without thinking, heart pounding between my legs, and climb onto the table. I'm wearing pajamas I'd never wear back home — a cherry-red Agent Provocateur bodysuit that I don't remember packing — with a robe over the top. The bodysuit is a lacy, curve-hugging number that's high-cut over both of my thighs then built like a corset on top, pushing my breasts up until they're nearly spilling out the top, even more so now that I'm crawling my way across the table on all fours.

"Right there," he tells me when I get to the middle. "Don't go any further."

I stop and lean back onto my knees.

He slides the saucer across the surface, and I catch it before sitting on the tabletop with my legs stretched long between us, robe parting down the middle.

"Is that what you want?" Silas asks, his voice growly and deep.

His eyes trace down my body and I widen my knees just enough for him to see how I'm barely covered by a thin strip of delicate red lace, no wider than two of my fingers, or his.

I lick my lip and bite it.

"Maybe?"

He stands, and I can see that he's hard beneath those charcoal pants, the material already stretched tight across his lap.

"You know this is exactly what I want," I tell him, dropping my knees even wider, holding the saucer up.

"Then eat it," he demands. His eyes narrow darkly.

I don't know why, but I'm compelled to obey him. To not think for myself. To just let him take charge.

I dip my finger into the center of the cake before swirling it up toward the layer of ice cream, topping it off with so much whipped cream that a quarter-sized dollop falls onto my chest as I carry it up toward my lips.

Then I push my chocolate cream-covered finger deep into my mouth, swirling my tongue over my own skin and nail, tasting my skin along with the cake. Groaning before sucking it clean, then pulling my finger back out of my mouth again. It was as good as I had hoped. But I can do better.

I lick my lips before digging into the whipped cream again. Then hold my finger out to him.

"Want some?" I ask. I bend my knees wider, not really talking about the cake anymore.

My heart pounds in my chest as his eyes travel down to the tiny spot of whipped cream resting on my chest before heading south to a view I know he's going to like even more: a second dessert.

"Don't tempt me," he growls. "You know I can't touch you."

"What do you mean?" I ask, my mind blank as to why. "You can't touch me? Or touch me here?"

I drop my finger, still wet from my mouth, down to the lacy crotch of the bodysuit I'm wearing, pointing to the softness of my body beneath the sheerness of the lace.

"Don't," he says, weakly. But I don't believe him. He's watching my finger intently as I start to draw circles across the fabric, dipping my legs apart while the sensation starts to build, quickening my breath while I watch him, wanting more.

"I've been alone for so long," I moan, drawing tighter circles, pulling the fabric aside. Then I slip my own finger inside my walls, feeling the coil in me draw open as he watches it slowly disappear.

"Jules," he pants my name.

"I don't want to be alone anymore, Silas," I tell him.

I find the two little snaps of the bodysuit, holding the tiny strip of fabric in place, hoping that once there's nothing left between us, he'll climb across the table to finish what I've already started.

"Don't," he warns, louder.

"You don't want dessert?" I ask, arching my back. Teasing an invitation.

"It's going to be worth the wait," he tells me, not moving.

"Up, Silas," I demand, nearly lost to my own climax. "Up, up, up. Get up now."

He finally climbs onto the table like a hungry wolf, one knee drawn up to join me while his eyes stare intensely into mine. But he stops.

"Get up! Up!" I repeat, frustrated by his hesitation.

I can't wait one more second for him to reach me. I'm nearly there. Everything in me starts clenching and pulling apart. He's going to miss it if he doesn't hurry.

"Up! Up! Up!" I begin to shout. *Oh my God, this is it.* "Silas, you're going to miss it," I moan, desperate for him to make it to me before I unravel.

"Up!"

"Silas?" I groan.

Andy's voice enters the room.

"Up, Jules!"

Wait. What is Andy doing in here?

"Wake up, honey. I hate to break it to you, but you don't need one more second of beauty sleep. You're already putting the rest of us to shame as it is. Up, up, up!" Andy claps his hands each time he says *up*.

I groan and roll over on the enormous table.

But it's not a table. There's a pillow.

I can feel *two* pillows.

I squint one eye open.

It's a bed. I'm on a bed.

That wasn't a dream was it?

Oh God.

I roll over. I'm on the bed in the back of the plane.

Where I've just had the most incredible sex dream of my life. I practically came in my sleep.

But about Silas?

No.

No. No. No.

CHAPTER 35

Silas

I sent Andy to the back of the plane to get Jules up, since Carl warned us, ten minutes ago, of unexpected turbulence coming up, but neither have returned. We were grounded in Spain for the night due to a storm after driving two hours to the airport, so we left Spain late this morning, a day later than planned.

The plane's bedroom door cracks open behind me and Jules finally emerges from the back, practically being chased down the aisle by Andy.

"Get buckled back in your seat now, hon," Andy is saying in a measured tone, shuffling her up to where I'm already seated.

She slides into her seat and pulls the lap belt across her hips to buckle herself in. Andy is chuckling as he continues down the aisle and Jules glares at the back of his head, trying not to laugh, from the look of it.

"Good morning, sleepyhead," I say, smiling across the aisle at her.

She looks weirdly flushed and the tiniest bit guilty. Intrigued, I shift to face her full-on.

"Good morning," she says, stiffly, avoiding my eyes.

"What's that look for?" I ask. "You doing alright?"

"Fine," she says, exhaling loudly. She crosses her legs one direction, then the other. Then side-eyes me for a split second, before snapping her attention forward again.

I eyeball her back. "You sure?"

"Silas, I said I'm fine," she says, widening her eyes, once again crossing her legs the other way.

"Did something happen with Andy to make you upset back there?"

"No, what would happen with Andy?" she answers quickly. Her voice has risen an octave. Then she adds, "Why, what did you hear? Can you hear anything from here?"

"What was there to hear?" I ask, studying her harder, swallowing a laugh. She looks panicked in a very guilty kind of way.

"Flight attendants, please buckle up." Carl's voice suddenly courses through the speaker, causing Jules to jump.

"Little jumpy there?" I ask, now fully amused. "What are you afraid I'd hear in the back while you were sleeping?"

"Nothing."

"It had nothing to do with you dreaming about me, did it?" I guess, smiling in her direction. I watch her face to see if it'll give her away, clueless whether or not I'm right.

She twists herself toward me then glances toward the kitchen galley where Andy is probably buckled up behind the wall. "Who said I was dreaming about you?" she asks, a bit too breathlessly. "Could you hear me or something?" She blinks, way too innocently, then shifts again in her chair.

Christ.

"No one said you were dreaming about me. But your face just did," I say, laughing.

"Shut up," she says, staring forward again. "I wasn't."

"Happens to the best of us," I assure her. "Were you pushing me from the plane again or is that just in *my* dream?"

"Definitely not," she answers, forcing a frown to cover up her smile. Her face says it all. Whatever this dream was, it's not one she wants to talk about. "And if I was, it's not like I could help it."

"Okay." I settle back into the seat, wishing I knew what it was about.

"Sorry I took up the only bed the whole flight. You probably could have used some shut-eye, too," she says, changing the subject.

"Was it a good dream at least?" I press again, not willing to let it go.

"No," she says, too quickly to stop herself.

I chuckle and nod. "Yeah, mine never were that great about you, either."

She swallows but the look on her face is priceless. "You're welcome to take the bedroom now," she tells me, probably hoping I'll go and leave her alone.

"Can't," I tell her, feigning disappointment.

"Why not?"

"Seatbelt sign is on." I tap the illuminated sign above us. "I do plan to take a shower though as soon as it turns off."

She crosses her legs the other direction again.

"Unless you need one first?" I smirk. "A real cold one, maybe?"

"No," she answers, again too quickly.

I laugh and bite my lip. "Suit yourself."

CHAPTER 36

Juliet

I mentally run through the past week after the seatbelt sign is turned off and Silas gets up to use the shower in the back of the plane. I'm finally alone again when I realize that none of this could simply be a figment of my imagination.

Si and I were close before, but not *this* close.

The dance in Spain, the conversation while we were sailing yesterday morning, and now the dream I just had?

Am I so deprived of intimacy over the last year that I'm making things up in my head?

"You look like you could use something cold after whatever I just woke you up from," Andy says, coming down the aisle. He's holding a tall glass of sparkling water with a slice of lemon balanced on the side. "And since your travel mate is taking up the only shower onboard, this'll have to do." He grins.

"I don't know what's gotten into me," I tell him, shaking my head. Andy could hear me moaning Silas' name in my sleep when he came to wake me up.

"You want to talk about it?"

He hands me the cold glass and I immediately drain half of it, thanking him after.

"How am I ever going to go back to basic economy?" I ask, hoping to side-swipe the question.

"Oh, how quickly luxury becomes a necessity, right?" he says, winking at me. "You know, you might not need to go back to economy after this."

I nudge him gently on the arm, looking behind us toward the bedroom and bathroom suite where Silas might emerge from at any moment.

"Oh please," I say, sighing. "After this, I'm sure Silas and I will go back to living very separate lives, where I teach people how to date and Silas rules his empire from in the sky."

"I'm not so sure," he sings over his shoulder as he walks back up the aisle to tuck himself into the kitchen again.

"Andy, where did that blue shirt go that I had hanging in the bedroom?" Silas' deep voice suddenly rings out from a few feet behind me. I turn around to say hello, but I'm met with more bare skin than I was anticipating.

Silas is standing shirtless in the aisle with a fluffy white towel tied loosely around his waist. His smooth, taut skin is still damp from the steamy shower room he's just emerged from. I try to avert my eyes, but I can't seem to peel myself away from the thick eight-pack abs that are almost eye level behind me. Unfortunately, I steal a glance lower at the V of muscles between his hips.

Christ, Jules. Keep your eyes forward. You're just deprived of a man's anatomy. That's all.

I slowly turn toward the front of the plane, not making any sudden movements.

"Um, Andy's in the kitchen," I tell him, not turning around again to speak. My words come out a bit high.

When he doesn't answer, I turn to see what else he needs just as he releases the towel draped around his waist.

"No!" I gasp, then practically choke on a sigh of relief when I see a pair of black boxer shorts is underneath.

He laughs and lifts the towel up to catch a few drips off his neck.

I lean back and exhale, feeling myself redden.

"Andy?" Silas repeats, louder this time.

"Sir?" Andy pops his head out from behind the kitchen wall. His eyes appear to be dancing, even from here.

"My shirt?"

"Oh, I grabbed it to give it a quick steam. It's ironed and hanging up. I must have stuck it in the wrong closet! Let me grab that for you."

I'm pretty sure I'm not imagining the cheeky smirk Andy just threw in my direction.

I do a double-take, trying not to laugh.

"And the pants?" Silas asks, raising a brow at him, half amused.

I bite my upper lip, locking in a laugh.

"Oh, those are up here with me too," Andy adds, somehow maintaining a somber expression. But he quickly turns his back to fetch the pants.

I roll my eyes at Andy with my back still turned to Silas, doing my best to stifle a full-blown giggle from escaping my lips.

"I'll get those both right to you, sir," Andy adds, waving one hand through the air.

"Oh my God," I mutter under my breath. "You are too much."

"Thank you," Silas says offhandedly, as if he's still clueless to the little charade that Andy is playing out quite skillfully here, but I doubt it.

When Silas turns to head back to the bedroom, Andy winks subtly in my direction before pursing his lips into a tiny grin.

"Just like your dream," he mouths, then chuckles to himself.

"You are wild," I mouth back, shaking my head.

"I don't know what you're talking about, dear," he drawls, waving his hand into the air between us again. Then he starts whistling innocently as he grabs Silas' perfectly pressed pants off a wooden hanger near the galley. "But, as I was just saying before that man came out here all practically naked and standing a mere six inches from you, I dunno if you'll have to kiss this level of luxury goodbye, m' dear. Some things just stick. Even if they don't seem that way at first."

"Real amusing," I say, smiling, but still shaking my head.

"Now, do you want to bring these to him? Or should I?" He taps me on the shoulder with the hanger as he walks past, laughing quietly before disappearing into the suite of rooms where Silas is still waiting to get dressed.

CHAPTER 37

"That's right, *bambola*," Nonna Lisi whispers behind me. I smile to myself, dropping the raw eggs into the mound of flour piled high on the thick wooden butcher block counter in front of me.

Then I turn my knuckles over, mixing the raw, eggy concoction with my bare hands, kneading the freshly ground flour and creamy yellow yolks ever so slowly, just like Nonna Lisi showed us how to do a few minutes ago. The mixture grows slimy and smooth between my fingers so I tuck in more flour before turning the dough in on itself, again and again.

"You're a natural, *bambola*," she says, patting my forearm appreciatively, leaving a handprint of fine white powder clinging to my skin. Then she turns to Silas to inspect the pile of floury egg in front of him.

"Yours still needs some work, *uomo bello*," she says to him, her eyes sparkling. Then she grabs a hold of his forearms and shoves his hands deeper into his slimy ball of dough on the same countertop, grinning over at me as she does.

Nonna Lisi's weathered face is beautiful, as faces that have the good fortune to age during a long life built on a foundation of happiness tend to be. Like each smile has left its mark. Her eyes crinkle in long lines all the way back to her hairline when she smiles, and her mouth looks as if it's been stuck in a permanent grin ever since she was just a little girl. I loved her the moment I saw her, and haven't stopped smiling since we arrived at her house to make our pasta.

I watch Silas work the dough, his fingers lithe and capable, pushing into the soft mound before pulling it back from the wooden countertop, kneading it into submission with precise rhythm and skill.

Is there anything he's not good at?

I think Nonna was just giving him a hard time to make me laugh. Watching him work the dough like that is making me feel hot under the collar, so instead, I tear my eyes away to look out the stone-framed windows. Settling on the breathtaking view of the shoreline and similar stone houses neighboring this one.

I am *in love*. And not just with Nonna Lisi, who is everything I hoped she would be, but with her home — the stout little house that we're standing in overlooking a view of Italy's infamous Amalfi coastline.

Since we were delayed last night, we came here after landing at the private airport in Pontecagnano, taking off from the tarmac in an old Rolls-Royce convertible that took us here to Amalfi for a late lunch, and then Nonna Lisi's home. It's perched atop a rocky cliffside overlooking the sea, surrounded by a vibrant grove of green-and-yellow lemon trees. The cobblestone walkway leading up to her house was cracked in a thousand different places with each piece of stone settled deeply into the ground, colorful and worn, like painted concrete. It's as if the earth itself had simply grown in around them. Then, when Nonna Lisi had answered the door, I'd practically melted into the pavement myself too, seeing her for the first time.

Her face shows decades of sunshine and laughter. She'd greeted us at the entrance of her property under a smooth, stone archway. Crystal, nearly translucent, blue eyes, like two teal pools cut deep into an old leather cloth, shined up at us, ushering Silas and I into her humble abode which, like her, is weathered and worn and comfortable in every way.

I imagine we're two of a thousand guests or more who've made their way into this very house, into this very kitchen over the couple hundred years it's been here.

And then when we got to the worn wooden countertop, it was Nonna Lisi who had instantly made us feel the most at home, even more than our surroundings. It's as if she's an ancient fixture of the room itself, surrounded by a dozen or so clay pots and bowls without a single measuring spoon or plastic cup in sight.

"Who needs a measuring spoon when it's all in here," she'd said grinning at me, while tapping her heart. "I've been making pasta in this kitchen since I was a little girl with my own nonna. And now, I show you."

The three of us had quickly tucked ourselves into Nonna Lisi's kitchen lined with big square windows cut into the stone, surrounded by chestnut shutters, thrown open to let the hot rays of the evening sun inside.

The ocean glitters below, as if a big diamond has been ground into dust then thrown across the surface of the water, casting shadows and colorful prisms that dance and parade their way across her cream stucco walls.

When we first started our lesson, she'd spoken to us as if we were a couple, here at the start of a marriage or romantic journey together. When I realized her mistake, I'd quickly waved my hands in front of us all to correct her.

"No, no, I'm sorry, Silas and I are just friends," I told her.

"Friends?" she repeated, glancing back and forth between us. "Says who?" She nudged me, grinning.

"Says both of us," I assured her, glancing up at Silas, who nodded in agreement.

"You came all the way to Italy to my kitchen to make pasta with your *friend*?" she repeated, looking like we were out of our minds.

I shrugged and laughed. "I guess so?" It did sound absurd when spelled out like that.

"You won't be just friends after tonight," she said before pulling bowls and eggs out onto the weathered surface behind her.

"Oh, yes we will," I replied under my breath, glancing at Silas like she probably says this to everyone who comes to her kitchen.

"And I don't say that to everyone," she said, her back still to me, as if reading my mind.

My eyes had darted back to hers when she turned and smiled, taking both my hands in hers after setting everything down.

"Just make the pasta." She smiled gleefully. "You worry too much, *bambola*. I can see it in your eyes." Then she touched my cheek, beaming.

"I don't," I said at the same time Silas nodded, saying, "She does."

My jaw dropped at him, but Nonna Lisi had laughed and released my hands, shuffling around her kitchen to pull a bowl of freshly ground flour over next.

As our lesson started, I watched her hands, like expensive Italian leather — both soft and impossibly strong — pull one creaky wooden cupboard open after the next to extract buttery smooth carved utensils and wooden bowls, each one silky to the touch from decades of use as she held them out to us to take. I'd turned each one over, feeling the history in my hands.

She smiled and hummed as she worked, eventually pulling out three heavy goblets and a ceramic jug of red wine.

"*Cin cin*!" she'd exclaimed, pouring the glasses nearly full to the top, before handing two to us and keeping one for herself. Then she'd tipped hers back, letting at least a third of the wine pour down her throat before turning to us and asking suddenly — innocently — if we were in love yet.

I'd laughed and held my cup between my fingers, rolling it back and forth, suddenly at a loss for words. Silas happily stared at me, waiting for an answer.

"No," I'd finally said, when enough time had passed and Silas hadn't answered at all. "We're friends. Like I said. Not lovers. We're not here to — no."

"Okay," she said simply, then grinned with her back to the countertop, for a few beats. "We'll check again soon."

I'd laughed, choking a bit on my wine, wondering if this woman had some secret power that wasn't advertised with her pasta classes.

She tapped her temple. "I know these things," she'd said.

Silas had chuckled under his breath and I'd whacked him in the gut — gently, but enough to make him laugh even harder.

Then she'd grabbed our hands and shook them together, giggling like the whole thing was hilarious.

"Okay. We make pasta first! We learn to fall in love with that!"

I'd bit the inside of my cheek and squeezed her hand back while she beamed between us, as if she knew she was making a love match instead of Italian cuisine tonight, regardless of what we denied.

Now, Silas and I each have a pile of sticky white flour and egg in front of us, willingly participating in an unspoken contest for the most delicious pasta at the end of all this. I can tell she's quite taken with him, if her giggles over Si are any indication, clicking her tongue over anything he says like a proud mother hen, while finding any reason to leave white flour residue all over his arms, both dusted in white by now.

"You love it?" she asks, noticing me staring outside at the view again as we work the dough.

"This? Yes," I confirm, smiling. "What's not to love?"

"You love where you live?" she asks.

"Oh, do we love Boston?" I repeat slowly, stealing a glance at Silas, unsure of how to answer. She's been telling us tales all evening about how much she has never wanted to live anywhere else in the world, even since she was a little girl living here with her own nonna.

"I do love it," Silas begins, slowly. "But, I can see why you love your home here though, and have never wanted to leave. You have the type of place that begs to be adored. I can see myself missing this place for the rest of my life after only spending an evening here," he tells her, and I'm touched. Because even if I couldn't put my own thoughts and feelings about tonight into words as eloquent as that, Silas just nailed it. That's exactly how I'd describe our evening here too.

"Then stay here," she says, pushing a pocket of dough with his hands.

He doesn't look up. "I wish it were that easy," he says.

"You have to get your hands dirty, like this," she tells him. She sprinkles a bit of warm water over the top, making the mass grow stickier between his fingers. "You need to get messy. Sticky things aren't bad, you know. People are scared of all the messes nowadays. Want every little thing to make sense. Things I have loved the most? They don't make any sense." She smiles, as if remembering. "Perfection? No, no one can love perfection. You find the best things in the most messy parts of your life."

She pulls the mound of dough off the wooden counter, then slaps it back down again with a *thwak*.

"This is love." She waves her flour-covered hands around the kitchen, the worn, ancient walls and weathered clay pots. "True love is worn and messy." She draws out the word messy, like she's driving home a point, and part of me wonders how she knows our lives — our relationship — is as messy as it gets. "Why are you here if you're not in love? Is there someone else?"

Silas laughs, the sound of it echoing off the walls while she pulls his hands from the dough. She takes a quick turn with it, working her magic with the mixture until it looks just like it's supposed to look.

"Keep going," she tells him, pushing his hands back down again. "We make sure you fall in love—" We both narrow our eyes at each other over her shorter head, wondering how this funny little woman can be so outspoken — "with pasta!" she finishes, bursting into laughter at her own joke. Then she rises on her toes to tap a spot of flour onto the tip of Silas' nose, even though his own face towers high above her.

"You're too handsome, *uomo bello*," she grumbles. "But she's too *bellissima* for you."

Silas nods, breaking into a grin.

"Trust me, I know," he says, and we all laugh.

The remainder of the night unfolds like that. Nonna Lisi, charming as can be, teaching us every traditional way to roll pasta, gnocchi, and drink wine, while we all take small breaks to stare out at the shimmering sea below the home she's lived in her entire life. Until at last, the length of the horizon finally swallows up the remainder of the sunlight, and it's sadly time for us to go.

She ushers us toward the door. I've been given two giant yellow lemons picked from her tree out front for the long walk back to our hotel together. We've opted to walk since it's such a nice night and the little town against the coastline is stunning.

"Live in a city that doesn't beg to be adored, and travel with a woman who hasn't been loved by you? You're making mistakes, *uomo bello*. Life won't wait," she tells him, patting his flour-covered cheek. Then she winks at me happily, and reaches up on her toes to give me a tight hug goodbye.

Tears spring to my eyes when I remember that she isn't a long-standing part of my life, and I might never see her again.

"I've loved everything about this," I tell her, squeezing her back one last time. "I will never forget you, and I will do my very best to be messy." I smile warmly at her, holding up the giant lemons between us.

"And then I will come to the wedding," she says, patting our backs as we go.

I shake my head and laugh, but don't say another word, because something deep inside me twists her words around a memory I'll take with me forever. Forcing every last detail into my memory bank for safekeeping. And then we walk out into the night.

CHAPTER 38

Silas

As soon as the thick wooden door swings shut behind us, the light from Nonna Lisi's house fades too. Jules and I are left with a symphony of crickets and crashing waves under a full moon as we begin the slow walk to our hotel together under the dusky twilight sky.

I've already texted our driver to let him know that we prefer to walk instead of getting a ride. It's balmy, and the hotel is only a mile or so away. Plus, it means more time alone with Jules.

She walks beside me for a few paces, her giant lemons cradled against her chest, before speaking. "I liked the skydiving, and I absolutely loved the sailing, but I want to live in that house with her forever," Jules says dreamily as our steps fall into a slower pace beside one another.

"I agree," I tell her, wrapping one arm around her shoulders, praying she doesn't resist. Instead, she leans into me and we continue down the cobblestone path lit by street lamps.

"She's right, you know," she adds, not looking up at me.

My insides clench at her words.

The little elderly woman made so many comments about Jules and I belonging together that she was even calling me Romeo by the end of the evening.

"She was right about which part?" I ask.

"Why don't we live in a place like this?" She looks up at a lemon hanging heavily from a branch near the path. "Don't get me wrong, I love Boston, you know that, but this place? Spain? Switzerland? Why aren't we living in places like this? Especially you. You have all the money in the world, Si. What keeps you in Boston? Especially with that boat in Spain?"

"My work. My life." *You*, I want to add but don't.

"Same. My entire coaching business, all my clients, everything I've built for myself is back there."

"You could do that remotely, or build your clients back up in the location you want. The world is ours, Jules. Where would you want to go?"

"The world is *ours*?" she repeats, turning to look at me, but I just continue walking as if suggesting we leave everything behind to move somewhere else is the most natural thing in the world. Because I wish that it was.

"Well, neither of us would want to be lonely in a new place so I figured we'd go together." I break my facade and give her a slight smile.

"Good point. Alright. In this hypothetical world, we'd go to Amalfi first. Then maybe try a year in Spain next, to see if we like it any better."

"And don't forget Interlaken," I tell her.

"Or Geneva," she adds, wistfully.

"I could add a few homes to my investment portfolio here," I admit, quietly, allowing a more serious tone to fill my voice, hoping she doesn't find the offer of me buying homes in her dream vacation spots upsetting. Every time money comes up, she looks like she might throw something at me.

I eye those two abnormally large lemons she's still cradling, just in case.

"God, I can't imagine having that kind of money to throw around all willy-nilly. See a town you like? Oh, just buy a home there! It seems surreal to live like that. I don't know how you get used to something like that."

"It's easier when the money doesn't matter as much as what I'd trade it for," I tell her.

"Trade it for?" she sounds confused. "What *can't* you buy?"

"I used to bargain with God sometimes. Give me my parents back, and I'd give it all away. Especially if it meant I'd get to grow up with a mother and father who loved the shit out of me. Sometimes I walk by parks where all the moms are playing with their kids — you know, pushing them on the swing, or giving them a hug when they fall — just to live in that dream world for a minute. People may be envious of me, but I'm envious of anyone who grew up like that."

She's quiet before grabbing onto my hand and squeezing it. For a moment, I think she's going to hang on, but then she drops it, dropping my heart out onto the sidewalk along with it.

"I had to force myself to put one foot in front of the other for months after losing Grant, but you were hit with the responsibility of a billion-dollar company and thousands of employees the same day you received the news about your dad."

"One hundred and sixty-seven thousand employees, to be exact," I tell her, feeling the weight of every single one of those families who depend on a paycheck from Davenport Media to house and feed their families, not to mention themselves.

Her face falls serious, and she grabs onto my hand again, but this time, she doesn't let go.

"That kind of thing can break a person. I hate how experience can wise you up, but sometimes it's so hard to put yourself in someone else's shoes without it."

We walk, both of us deep in thought.

"And I think as long as you're there, I'll stick around Boston," I tell her. "I'd like to be near you, too. I always thought of you as one of my best friends. I hope we can still be friends when we get back. If not, and if my company allows it, then maybe I'll end up leaving the area one day."

She stops on the sidewalk and turns to look up at me, concern in her eyes.

"Silas, I don't think that I could lose you twice."

"You wouldn't lose me, I'd—"

But before I know what's happening, she drops the lemons on the cobblestone, grabs my face between her palms. And then, against everything I saw coming on this trip, she kisses me.

CHAPTER 39

It's the kind of kiss I've always dreamed about. The type you watch in movies and hope to experience one day for yourself, but after a while start believing that it's all made up for Hollywood magic.

But, this kiss is not made up for Hollywood magic.

And neither are her lips, her hands, and her body pressing firmly into mine.

Her lips feel desperate at first as her nails run through my hair, down the back of my neck, like she can't get as close to me as she wants or needs.

I stand there, too stunned to respond at first, and then, I give in.

When I do, her lips slow down against mine, pulling back enough to take her time, tasting my tongue slowly, running her fingers along my jaw, pressing her body into mine. I cup her waist, squeezing her closer. Then when I know she's not going to run, I drag both hands up her back and find her neck, the crook of her jaw, hooking my thumbs in that soft spot just in front of her ears to cradle her face in my palms.

Then our lips pause, less than an inch away, both of us panting like we've just completed a half-marathon over the course of the last ten years, and I force myself not to move. To let her bring herself back into me for more, or to step away, questioning everything.

This has to be her choice.

It has to be her wanting me as much as I have always wanted her in order for us to keep going.

For one solid moment and too many extra heartbeats, I think she might actually pull away.

Our breath mixes in the dark, crickets and waves suddenly coming back to life loudly in my ears — before all I can hear are my own thoughts screaming and cheering and wondering whether any of this is going to be okay.

Another ten seconds pass, but it feels like an hour. And then I feel her easing back from me, bringing both eyes up to meet mine.

She touches a few fingertips to her bottom lip, rubbing them absentmindedly, like she's already remembering what it felt like to have my lips there just seconds ago.

"Silas, I—"

"Don't," I tell her, smiling gently, hopefully. "Don't think about it. Don't try to figure it out yet. Not right now. It's just another moment that—"

"Shouldn't be happening—" she whispers.

"But is," I finish for her.

"I shouldn't have done that," she says to herself more than me. But when our eyes meet again, she inhales sharply. "Fuck it," she whispers on the exhale, then presses her lips back to mine, and I wrap my hands up in her hair.

One hint of doubt can ruin everything.

Turn our mess into something more. Something neither one of us will recognize.

I won't let her question it.

Not now, not ever.

She responds by grabbing my belt with both hands, pulling me into her, hooking her arms behind my back, then dragging them up toward my shoulder blades. My entire body turns to fire, wanting her, like the electric current that's been simmering beneath the surface of my feelings for Jules has finally been allowed to reach maximum capacity. Coursing through each and every vein beneath my skin. Pulsing at her touch, shooting embers from behind my eyes. As if something inside me has been lying dormant my whole life, waiting for this exact moment when she decides that it's us.

I forget that we're standing in the middle of a sidewalk in Italy.

Forget why we're even here.

All I can think about is her arms wrapped around me, her lips pressed into mine.

I don't want to feel anything else in this moment but her. Like she's the only thing keeping me grounded in a hurricane.

Breathlessly, she backs up from me again, this time stooping down to grab the two lemons she dropped a moment ago.

"I–I can't forget the lemons," she says, picking them up, nearly laughing, like she doesn't know what else to say.

She holds them up between us, blinking, but her face shifts into something new. She's grinning, looking at me in the way I've always been too afraid to imagine.

It makes me laugh — knowing that my face must look the exact same way as hers.

"No, I wouldn't want you to forget those," I tell her, grinning too, taking another step toward this most beautiful woman in the world.

She drops the lemons to her sides and we each take another step. It's neither her nor I closing the gap alone, but both of us doing it together, and our lips entwine again.

The lemons must be back on the ground because suddenly her hands are everywhere. Pushing against my chest, wrapped around the back of my neck, pulling me closer to her, fingertips raking over my scalp, sending waves of yearning all the way down through my legs, bouncing off the pavement, and racing back up my body again. She can't hold still.

Leaning against me, then arching her back, fisting my collar and yanking me to her, as if I will never be close enough.

She steps back but pulls me with her, until her back is up against the stone-wall path we've been following toward the hotel.

"Oomph." She giggles and I love the feeling of her lips turning upward, smiling against my mouth.

I press against the wall, testing the strength of it before I lift her onto it, sliding her knees open just enough for my hips to fit between them. She squeezes them around me, pressing herself forward so we fit together just like we should.

"I've never wanted you to have a driver waiting so bad in my entire life," she says, breathlessly.

"I swear to God I'll have him here in the next three minutes. I'll get a chopper. I'll fucking teleport us to that hotel right now if you want me to."

She looks around, as if trying to decide if the street is dark enough to take this a step further.

"How far is it?"

"Too far," I say, grabbing her face between my hands. Knowing damn well that she might change her mind if we have to break this spell apart in order to get ourselves all the way back to a room. We came straight from the airport to Nonna Lisi's so we haven't actually checked in yet.

"There," I tell her, pointing to what looks like a tiny Bed and Breakfast just a half a block away on the other side of the street. It's not the Ritz, not even close. One of the lights is flickering under a dank, striped awning but I couldn't care less.

"That's our hotel?" she asks.

"It is now," I say, grabbing her hand to pull her across the street toward it.

She plants her feet, holding me back, laughing.

"We can make it back to our bags, to the original hotel where our reservation is," she says, looking amused.

"But—"

She turns me around slowly, rubbing her thumbs across my jaw. Her eyes dart between mine, and for one gut-wrenching moment, I think she's going to tell me that everything about this is a mistake. That the spell has been broken. That the walk here was just long enough to bring her back to her senses.

I'm about to apologize for following her lead, forever thinking that this could be something and that *we* could be more.

But I don't say a word. If all I have to remember her by is this kiss on a dark cobblestone street in Amalfi — then it will always be enough.

It will have to be, even though it never will.

"Jules, listen—" I start to say, hating myself before I can even get the words out.

"I'm not going to change my mind," she says firmly, reading my mind.

"Are you sure?" I ask, still unsure whether I heard her correctly.

"I'm not changing my mind, and you better not either. I need you, Si. I think I need you as much as you need me. Another few blocks isn't going to change that."

I wrap my arms around her back and hold her, closing my eyes, feeling her heart beat wildly against my chest. Knowing with everything in me that I've never loved her more.

We somehow make it the rest of the way to our hotel another few blocks down the road. Stopping every half block or so to kiss each other some more on the pavement, or up against a tattered stone wall, each time using more and more self-control to break ourselves apart before breathlessly speeding through another half a block down the road toward the solace of our hotel.

By the time we arrive at the front desk, her lips are pink and swollen. She places the two lemons we somehow managed not to forget on top of the counter.

"I believe my crew may have already checked us into the suite earlier and had our bags taken up. There should be a key waiting for us," I tell the man behind the desk, keeping my eyes glued to Jules.

"Name?" the hotel attendant asks.

I hope this momentary blip in the momentum we had cruising down the sidewalk isn't enough to break whatever is happening between us right now.

"Juliet Hart and Silas Davenport," I say, trying to keep the impatient edge out of my voice. I grin over at her and place our passports down. She looks like the most gorgeously disheveled mess I've ever seen.

"Oh, yes. Here are your keys," the man says, placing two key cards onto the counter. "And here's the letter that was to be delivered to Ms. Hart upon arrival."

CHAPTER 40

Juliet

The letter.
How could I have forgotten the letter that would be waiting?
We'd gone straight to Nonna Lisi's house from the airport. I hadn't even thought about the letter that was waiting for me at the hotel all afternoon. A cold wave of guilt crashes through me, like ice rushing to my core.

"Thank you," I stammer, then grab Grant's letter off the counter, suddenly avoiding Silas' gaze.

He's frozen beside me.

I lick my bottom lip before biting down, staring at the envelope in my hands.

My mind's blank, like a dank fluorescent light that's about to go out, buzzing loudly, ringing harshly in both ears. I feel stupid and embarrassed and angry with myself that just the sight of Grant's letter makes me feel like I'm gasping in the dark beneath the weight of it.

Silas quickly swipes the keys off the counter. We somehow make it to the nearby elevator and begin riding up in silence.

We should have stopped at that Bed and Breakfast.

We should have allowed ourselves to just live in that moment, consequences be damned. To be simply two people with no past and no future, making one uncomplicated memory on a sidewalk in Italy together.

If only it were that easy.

I pretend to stare down at my feet the whole way up to our suite, but instead, I'm watching his hand hang empty by his side and I scream at myself to just grab it.

Hold it.

Hold on to *him* before he retreats back into himself, too.

Nothing has changed from just a moment ago. I still want him. And I hope he still wants me. But I don't move.

The elevator door chirps cheerfully when it slides open, directly leading into our penthouse suite on the top floor.

He clears his throat and holds out his arm, to let me out first. I walk a few feet into the suite, then close my eyes before planting my feet, not going another step further.

All the way back to the hotel, I'd kissed Grant's best friend while his next letter was waiting for me behind the counter here.

Three hundred and seventy-some days now, just waiting for me to pick it up.

What kind of woman am I?

The kind of woman that's chosen to go on, a light voice answers back in my head.

Nonna Lisi's words echo next.

You find the best things in the most messy parts of your life.

The elevator door slides shut behind us.

Heavy silence fills the room.

Without a word, Silas walks toward the gilded bar in the corner near a pile of our luggage to pour himself a nightcap. He looks stressed, exhausted, like just seeing that letter has torn him up just as much as it has me.

"Want one?"

He holds up a glass, but doesn't wait for an answer. Grabbing a crystal decanter filled with some type of alcohol, he splashes a good amount inside, then offers it to me.

"No," I tell him, firmly.

He takes a gulp, puffing his cheeks out before swallowing, closing his eyes as it likely burns down his throat.

I shake my head, realizing I do want some. "Shit, I mean, yes."

He throws me a faint smile, then pours another splash into the same glass and holds it out to me.

I try to take the glass from him but my hand envelops his instead. Our fingers overlap, draped over the tumbler, and I pause, waiting for him to give up the glass, but he doesn't let it go.

I study him, his eyes, which at this moment are saying far more than either of us are willing to say out loud.

He takes a step closer, his lips twitching at the sides in that familiar way they always do, like he knows something I don't. A secret he isn't willing to share, but one he loves to keep for himself. Then he blinks and a thousand memories flood in. Memories of us that never belonged to just the two of us, and I realize we're both haunted by a ghost that'll never stand here between us again.

Not anymore.

Not ever.

And it doesn't seem fair to pretend we're all here when there will only be two of us from now on.

He turns. "I'll head to bed for the night," he says, suddenly relinquishing the glass to me. Sliding his fingers out from mine. "Give you time to read that alone."

He taps the letter in my hand, then kisses me lightly on the cheek before walking toward one of the two bedroom doors.

"No."

Between the two of us, I'm probably more startled to hear my own voice come out before any of my thoughts are fully formed. But I won't stop. Not now. If I live the rest of my life in a space stemming from pure logic, formed only from my past, then I'm going to get to the end with a drawer full of regret.

He turns to face me.

"I don't want to read it tonight, Si. I don't want—" My voice cracks as I drop the letter onto the coffee table, taking a step away from it before shifting my eyes up to meet his. "I was feeling so happy after tonight. Hopeful, really, for the first time in forever. I don't want to risk that going away if I read it right now."

I swallow hard and Silas takes one small step away from his room.

"Jules, I don't want you to do something you might regret in the morning. This is too important. *You* are too important to get caught up in something we might not be ready for."

I step away from the letter, still sealed, knowing that I'm more sure now than ever.

"I know why Grant sent us on this trip. I know why he pushed us back into each other's lives. He knew that I'd need you, as much as you needed me. I guarantee that, as crazy as it sounds, he saw all this unfolding exactly like this." I shake my head, knowing in my heart that I'm right. "You should see his letters, Si. They're all about *you*. They aren't just love letters to me. They're love letters to *us*. The us from *before*. It's all about your friendship with him, and mine with you. If you'd read them, you'd understand why there's no doubt in my mind that this was always the way it was meant to be. He wanted me to know that you'd be there for me. That you were always going to be there for me."

I close the gap between us and he grabs me the second I get to him, holding my face between his hands, kissing me more desperately than he had out on the sidewalk and all the way here. I shove his jacket off and it falls to the floor, then kick my shoes onto the carpet without breaking the connection between us.

"Jules," he pants, pulling me back by the elbows. Concern and hunger fill his eyes. "Are you sure you want this?"

"Yes," I tell him. My face morphs into a grin. Then I pull him toward me. "Less talking," I whisper.

I don't want to talk.
I don't want to think.
I just want to get completely lost in this exact moment with this exact man. The one that feels more like home than anything else in the whole world. The man that somehow brought me back to myself.

It isn't just the familiarity I've felt with him since the first second I sat in his car outside my house in Boston. Free to be angry and tired and moody and finally — after every other emotion fizzled out — free to be *alive*.

It's the way he's made me feel every step of this crazy journey we've been on. Like something in his eyes helps me remember that I'm beautiful, and adventurous, and always enough. I love how his eyes always make their way back to mine, whether we're in the middle of the Spanish sea, or standing across the flour-covered counter at Nonna Lisi's, or during each takeoff and landing across the aisle between us while Andy pretends not to see the way he watches me. I love the look he gave me in the seconds before I rolled from the plane at thirteen thousand feet, screaming above the turquoise lakes of Interlaken.

We've been all over the map, but we've always found each other's eyes in everything from chaos to joy to arguments to gut-wrenching moments, and everything in between. Silas is my home away from home, and the friend I've missed so, so much.

He's not who he was. Now, different from the man I loved as my friend back then, before everything that happened. But somehow, he's better. Better now than he ever was before.

And, thanks to Grant's letters, I know that he's always been the man who, unbeknownst to me, would stay up all night just to fan a fire if he knew it'd keep me safe.

He's always been the guy cast behind the scenes, but never stolen the show. Never allowed himself to overstep the invisible boundary following whatever ridiculous coin toss they had over me a decade ago.

I want *Silas*. *This* Silas. *All* of Silas.

And I don't want whatever is in that letter to get in the way of this moment any more than it already has.

"I know you wanted a chance with me back when you flipped that coin with Grant," I whisper. Then I press my lips against his. "And I know it was forever ago. And maybe you changed your mind about wanting me. But I want you." I watch his eyes flicker, hoping for any fragment of an answer to flash behind them. "This might be messy. But if Nonna Lisi was right, then messy can end up being okay. It can end up being more than okay. Right?"

The green pools of his eyes dart back and forth, studying mine, making sure this is everything it should be before kissing me again. The sheer intensity of his self-control is making me lose mine all over again.

"I've never wanted anything more in my life," he tells me. "But I can't forget that—"

I interrupt him before he can finish. "Then just think of me as another girl — begging you to take her," I whisper. I don't want either one of us to say his name right now. Not tonight. Not when I'm feeling so desperate to be right here. Fully present, and not in the past.

I try to kiss him again, but his lips brush against mine as he answers. "You have never been *just* another girl," he says in a way that makes my knees go weak. "You have only ever been *the* girl. The only one I ever wanted."

He rubs the warm pad of his thumb across my lips, and I bite down gently, catching one of his thumbs between my teeth before releasing it back to him with a smile.

"I have wanted you since the day I met you," he says, still holding on. Then he presses his forehead against mine and kisses me softly. So gently that stars begin spinning behind my eyes. "And believe me when I say that you will never, ever be *just another girl*."

CHAPTER 41

Juliet

Silas swings me around by the waist and I walk backward until my spine is up against the wall behind us, the length of his body pressing me into it. His teeth drag across my bottom lip, tugging it gently, before devouring my lips all over again. I can feel him growing hard between my legs, and I widen my stance to let him push against me. I let out a groan when he grabs me tighter, leaving no space for anything to get between us.

Silas knows how to take what he wants — and what he wants right now is me.

"To the bed," I manage to say.

"Not yet."

He releases my waist and presses both of his palms into the wall above my head, staring down at me, intensely. His eyes darken to a shade I've never seen and he tips my chin up.

"I'm going to take my time with you," he says, leaning in. "Make you forget your own name. Make you forget which continent you're on."

My stomach twists, hoping he's serious. Knowing how much I want him to do exactly that.

I feel dizzy with my back against the wall, grateful I have the support to stay standing.

He tilts my chin higher and my eyes roll to the back of my head when his lips find that sensitive spot just beneath my ear. This time he doesn't hold back. I have to fight my legs from turning into liquid as he works his way down my neck. My wrists held firmly above, totally at his mercy.

He presses his hips to mine and links both my wrists in one hand, then runs the other hand down my arm, cupping my body, as the heat from his palm sinks into my skin.

Then he steps back to yank my dress open, each button flying off the front before it slides off my shoulders and falls to the floor.

"Silas!" I exclaim, not mad but laughing.

"Promise I'll have two more delivered first thing tomorrow," he growls into my neck. "One to keep, and one to do the same thing with again."

I laugh until he finds that spot under my jaw and my laughter fades into a moan.

Then he hoists me up against him and I wrap my legs around his waist while he buries his face into my chest, kissing the heaving flesh he's just exposed above my bra, before bringing his face to mine. His eyes lose their humor when he finds the clasp halfway up my back. I feel the band tighten as he holds both sides between his fingers.

I grin at him, signing the silent permission slip with a look.

"I dare you," I tell him.

My heart thumps in my chest while I wait for his response. His face curls. "Atta girl," he growls, releasing the fabric with a tug.

The bra falls to the floor and I take it as my cue to rip open his shirt, like he did to my dress. The buttons fly across the floor. I want the feel of his skin against mine.

Instead of looking angry, a wicked grin comes screaming across his face. I love it.

"Only fair," I remind him, raising a brow, then add, "I'll have two more delivered for you tomorrow. Both of them so I can do that again. Twice."

This makes him laugh until his eyes wander lower on my chest, my breasts now on full display near eye level while I'm pressed against the wall.

He groans, then grabs the flesh between his lips, tightening his teeth around the hardened bud. My mouth opens as my eyes roll back, pushing the fullness of my chest deeper into his mouth, and he groans again. I grab a fistful of his hair when he switches to the other side, already feeling myself grow more and more ready for him.

When I can't take it anymore, I gently yank his hair back, tilting his mouth up, and he draws his tongue against mine. Silas is, without a doubt, the best kisser I've ever had. Rough and playful, but somehow leaving me wanting more each time he stops to look at me.

"To the bed," I moan again.

"Not yet," he repeats, setting me down, dragging his hands to the rim of my panties, the only thing left on my body.

"Too . . . many . . . clothes," he says, running his fingertips along the waistline.

"And you?" I ask, grabbing ahold of his torn shirt. I push it aside and grip the waistline of his pants. "You're one to talk."

My eyes stay on his as I turn my fingers downward, pressing my palm against that spot between his washboard abs and the V I haven't been able to stop thinking about since seeing him half-naked on the plane.

He licks his bottom lip and bites down, an arrogant smirk playing across his features, daring me to go lower.

But I pause, just above his waist, my hand pressed to his skin, eyes burning into his.

"I want to see your face when I touch you. I want to see what a man like you does when he's nearly brought to his knees."

His face curls, tortured, like he's ready for the air to evaporate from his lungs at my touch. He leans in and bites my bottom lip, releasing it as quickly as he does.

"You might like it when I'm on my knees," he whispers. His breath mixes with mine.

He grasps my hips and slowly lowers his knees to the floor in front of me, kissing me just once between my legs. The fabric presses between his lips when he presses them to me, and I can feel the heat of his breath through the thin material.

My knees buckle and I steady myself against him, reveling in his breath while it travels back up my body as he rises again to his feet.

The tease of just one kiss planted right there has me panting.

I slide my hand under the fabric of his boxer briefs to feel the tightness of his skin.

His breath hitches when I reach lower, and I don't dare blink. Not wanting to miss one second of his reaction. He licks his bottom lip again, glancing down at my hips, and I can tell he wants to kiss me while I feel him for the first time, but I don't.

Instead, I cup my palm around him, the full length of what he's working with, while I watch his eyes dilate from just my touch alone. His jaw clenches slightly.

I kiss him once, watch his eyes when I drag my hand up and down so lightly that I wonder if he can even feel me teasing him.

"Jules," he growls, restraint simmering just below the surface, nearly closing his eyes. "I wanted to take my time with you but with you touching me like that . . ."

I grin menacingly, then shove his pants to the floor. His briefs follow.

Then as slowly as I can, I pull my own panties down, letting them fall in a small heap over my toes while I keep my eyes tied to his.

Silas' breath grows ragged.

He takes a step back, biting his fist, opening the space between us where his eyes can dance freely over my body, my skin.

I suddenly feel the years of familiarity between us flare, afraid he's not going to like what he sees. That the fantasy of me and the realness of me aren't even on the same page in his mind.

I turn, shifting my hips to the side, clasping my hands over my chest, laughing out of sheer nerves, now that we've gotten to this point. Even in the dimness of the room, I can feel my cheeks flush red. To go from friends to enemies to nearly lovers — it's almost like there's nowhere left for me to hide. He's seen everything I have to give, been on the receiving end of it all. All but *this*.

"Don't," he commands. "Don't hide anything from me."

"You've been with some of the most beautiful women in the world," I remind him.

"And not one of them compares to you," he says, but it's not the words, it's the way he says them that makes me suddenly believe him. And the look in his eyes that makes me feel as if my whole world belongs to him now.

I turn my hips back to him and release my chest.

He takes my hand.

"Let me see you," he says in a gravelly voice, one I've never heard come out of him before. Then his gaze travels over my skin, drinking me in. Like it's the first time he's seen a woman stand naked before him, every hill and valley a work of art in his eyes. "You are everything I never knew I could have," he says, not moving his eyes away from me. "Bed. Now."

He suddenly snatches me up in a kiss, walking us both backward toward the bed. I reach out a finger to turn the light off completely, but he stops me, grabbing my hand, bringing my fingertips up to his mouth.

"On," he says, kissing the tip of the finger I nearly used on the switch before slipping the whole thing into his mouth, nipping the end as it slips out again. I swallow, wondering what else he's capable of doing to me with that mouth. "There's no way I'm missing one second of you in the dark."

"On," I agree. I want to see him too. The look in his eyes right now is intoxicating. "But what exactly do you want to see?" I ask.

He lifts my hand overhead and spins me around slowly in front of him.

"If we stopped right here, I'd die a desperate man," he says. He slides his fingertips down the curve of my breasts and torso, until his fingers land at the lower curve of my hip. I suck in a tight breath at the feel of him grazing me there. "But seeing you . . ." He trails off, making a sound in the back of his throat. I wish I could hear his thoughts, experience whatever it is that's making him look at me the way he is. "Seeing *all* of you like this? Jules, I could spend the rest of my life with the view I have right now and I'd *still* die a desperate man. It'll never be enough. I'd always want just one more second with you."

His words, his gaze, all of it is making me breathless.

But I want to be *more* breathless.

I take his hand and drag it lower until he's cupping the softest part of me. He groans against my lips, tucking one finger up inside.

"You are perfection," he murmurs before kissing me again and I moan into his mouth, desperate to show him how much he means to me, too.

CHAPTER 42

Silas

My cock throbs each time I push my finger back into her, the walls of her body clenching around me, like a silent prayer to take her.

This moment. The woman of my actual dreams is like putty in my hands for the very first time. Her breath, the way her every move fills me with need, the soft curves of her body being controlled by the motion of my fingers inside her, on her, wrapping desperately around her.

Her lips part, but she keeps her eyes on mine. A line of teeth barely visible behind the soft pillows of her lips.

She is more beautiful than anything I could have ever imagined.

The way she looks at me like that, desire filling her eyes with nothing left to clothe her but the softest light of this room.

I reach for her again but she side-steps away from me, suddenly turning around. The line of her back draws my eyes in, swaying back and forth as she moves toward the mattress, arching her back, then bending over as she lifts one knee up to climb onto the bed. Once there, she looks back over her shoulder and grins, giving me the most incredible view before tipping onto her side and patting the space right beside her.

"You know exactly what you're doing to me," I tell her. "I need to grab a condom from my bag."

After grabbing one, I crawl onto the bed, positioning myself over her, taking in the sight of her lying beneath me. A thousand times I've wanted to experience this, but never thought it right. For the next moment, we gaze at each other. Jules grins up at me, looking as incredulous about everything as I feel. Both of us unsure of how we got here, but charged with the same level of unexpected desire anyway.

"Is this real?" I ask, pushing the hair back from her face. She flushes, light shades of pink and red spreading across her cheeks, bringing out a sexy glow. "If not, it sure as hell beats the dreams I've been having about you."

She bites back a laugh.

"Did you see it coming?" she asks.

"I never let myself imagine any of this," I tell her, tracing the line of her collarbone with my fingers, unable to keep my eyes off her skin, or the way her hair falls onto the bed right beside me. "But the real thing might be better than anything I could have imagined. Like these eyes," I tell her, lightly kissing each eyelid as she closes them for me. "And how they're looking at me right now." She smiles again, so sweetly, that I nearly dissolve into the bed. "And don't even get me started on your smile." I kiss her again. "The best songs in the world are all written about this smile."

Her eyes shine at mine.

"Silas." She grins, blushing, then tilts her head back, laughing. "Please tell me these lines are not the same ones you've used before."

"You wouldn't even recognize me with another woman," I tell her, gruffly. "No one has ever made me feel the way you do. Not even close."

I kiss her neck and she lifts her jaw higher, giving me space to reach the soft spot beneath her jaw while goosebumps prickle up across her skin. She moans softly as I kiss and nip my way across her.

"And this," I say, kissing her neck. "This has always been a tease." I run my tongue the length of her collarbone where my fingertips traced a moment ago.

"A tease?"

"Always making me wonder what lies just south of it," I tell her as I travel down toward her perfect breasts. I gently push against her shoulder until she's lying flat against the mattress, each nipple standing at attention. "And these," I say, tucking each into my mouth, one by one, kneading the heavy flesh as it fills my palm. "There are no words for these."

She laughs, dipping her head back into the pillows behind us, arching her back each time I swirl my tongue around the centers.

"Go on, then" she says, breathlessly, challenging me to go lower. "What else?"

I trace one finger lightly between her breasts, pressing gently when I reach the dip of her bellybutton.

"And then there's this, which if I remember correctly, used to be pierced back in college."

She laughs again, pressing her hand over the tiny scar to cover it.

"God, you have a good memory," she says, then laces her fingers through mine.

"Believe it or not, I remember everything," I tell her, kissing her hand covering mine.

She draws in a sharp breath as I shift our hands and use my tongue to circle her belly button, leaving a trail of soft kisses against the skin leading down to her hip bones.

"You have no idea how good my memory is when it comes to you," I say, flicking my tongue over the curve of her hip before pressing another kiss into her skin.

She moans, but lets me keep her fingers laced in mine as I move further south.

"But the rest of you," I say, eyeing below her hips. "The rest of you is new to me. Never before seen. It might actually turn out to be my most favorite part of all."

She immediately sobers when she catches me traveling further down her body, taking her all in. She inhales a quick breath through her teeth when I press a kiss into the space between her thighs. Then I keep my eyes on hers, our fingers still intertwined, as I drag my tongue down the final folds of her skin, pulling her apart with my fingertips before flicking her with my tongue.

"This is the part I think I must be dreaming about now," I tell her, positioning myself to finally bring her into my mouth, squeezing her hand in mine. "Because you are absolute perfection," I tell her when her eyes roll back.

Then I lie between her legs, my cock pressing into the mattress, pulsing sharply at the very first taste of her.

"Then please don't ever stop," she moans. And that's all the permission I need to go on.

CHAPTER 43

Juliet

Within moments, Silas has one hand holding me apart while the other is still firmly on my hand. His tongue finds each sensitive apex, expertly moving between them, circling me slowly before following down the line. Bringing everything in me twisting right up to the edge before backing off again.

As if in my dream, I spread my knees wider, an invitation to dive deeper into every part of me, grabbing a pillow to stifle my moans.

He slips a finger inside, then pushes one of mine in too, sliding past each other, while his tongue holds me captive from the outside. I'm completely lost in the moment, not just beneath his control, but under mine too. Showing him exactly how I like to be touched and where. And although I don't think Silas would ever need any sort of lesson in how to touch a woman, I love that he wants me to show him exactly what I want.

I flip around, wanting to taste him the same way, and position myself so he's just within reach of my mouth. Then I lick my lips and push him inside, letting him fill my mouth while his tongue presses into me, too.

The soft hardness of him between my lips, while I'm lost under his control, nearly has me careening off the edge.

"I need you," I tell him, sliding his cock between my fist. "Now."

He flips around on the bed and pushes himself into me, easily sliding in despite his size.

"Silas," I groan into his ear as we start moving together, so slowly at first, while his breath hitches in his throat as he watches me come closer, not letting me come yet.

I push my hips into him, lifting and reaching for more of him to fill me with every push, as if I can't get enough of him buried between my legs.

"Jules," he groans.

"Si," I moan back, my voice higher. "Don't stop. Don't ever fucking stop."

"I've wanted you so long," he tells me.

"Don't. Stop," I repeat in a jilted whisper, clasping his back and burying my face into his shoulder.

I can't hang on another second and come first, moaning out his name, biting into his shoulder to stop myself.

"Fuck," he moans into the crook of my neck, then kisses me hard as he comes too, letting everything go, shuddering back onto the mattress beside me, holding me tightly like he won't let me go again. I kiss him, lighter this time, while we both spiral back down to earth from the high we've just ridden together.

He bites my neck gently, all fire dying down into a hazy smolder, nipping softly beneath my ear, sending another shiver of pleasure rocketing down my body, still pulsing with an orgasm so memorable that it's going to be hard not to want this again in the next five minutes.

He kisses my shoulder, and finally my lips, like he can't pull himself away, even though the climax has already taken place.

"Oh my God," I tell him, closing my eyes. "We just—"

"Unless I'm dreaming," he says weakly, as if all his energy has dissolved.

"This is what I dreamed about," I tell him, in my hazy, post-sex glow, throwing one arm over my eyes and laughing. "When we were leaving Spain."

He laughs, then turns to me. "Was it better than what we just did?"

"I don't know if anything could be better than what we just did," I tell him.

"I want to hear every detail of what your dream entailed," he fires back, as he grabs a pillow to prop our heads up on. "Don't leave anything out."

"Tomorrow," I murmur, suddenly feeling drowsy. "First thing in the morning." I roll onto my side so Silas can wrap around me from behind. I don't even want to open my eyes yet, but I'm not ready to exist outside this moment. I fight the sleep that threatens to come, threatens to finish everything that's transpired here tonight into a new day. At some point, I fall asleep like that, with me feeling more safe, secure, and cherished than I have in a very long time.

***

At three a.m. I wake up needing a glass of water. I make my way into the attached suite, happy to have found that the crew must have unpacked our belongings when they checked us into this enormous suite together, or at least set out Silas' toiletry kit on the counter, with a robe and his pajamas hung up neatly in the corner of the sizable bathroom.

While washing my hands, I notice the white envelope that the attendant from the front desk had given me, tucked underneath the corner of Silas' toiletry kit on the counter. Just the sight of it wakes me up out of my half-asleep stupor with a jolt, reminding me that I never read it last night when we got back to the room. A smaller wave of guilt rises up in me, but I squash it back down, reminding myself that Grant curated this trip for me to move on. Silas must have woken up and brought it inside the bathroom for me to see and read it whenever I got up. He's incredibly thoughtful. Always thinking of my needs, even before I can sometimes.

Grabbing the letter, I smile to myself, thankful to have him looking out for me.

I'm still unsure of whether I should read it now or wait until morning, but deep down I know that I won't be able to sleep after being reminded of its existence just a few yards away. Better to get through it now in the dead of night and then sleep off the residual emotional hangover instead of tossing and turning the rest of the night — only to start with fresh heartache first thing in the morning if I wait.

I pull the letter out from inside the envelope.

It's filled with the same handwriting as all my letters before, but it's not my name I see at the top.

It's addressed to Silas.

I flip the envelope over. Although I thought it was, this isn't the one I'd retrieved from the front desk last night. It has Silas' name written across it, not mine.

Startled, I begin folding the letter back up but catch my name written throughout it over and over again. The exaggerated J of Jules — almost as recognizable as Grant's laugh or his signature — repeated time and time again throughout the whole thing.

I drop the letter from view, forcing myself to look away.

This isn't yours to read, my mind begins to scream.

Then my gut joins in the fight.

Stop now — before you see something you can't un-see.

But I can't force myself to stop. I pick it back up and scan the page all the way to the end.

Jules.

Fiancé.

Jules.

I'm not just a quick mention here and there. This entire letter is about *me*.

I scold myself harshly for scanning something so personal that isn't meant for my eyes, and nearly toss it away from myself. But before I can force myself to stick the letter back in the envelope and leave it be, curiosity kills the best part of me.

I very well might hate myself in the morning, but instead of doing what I should, I carefully sit down on the edge of the bathtub and read the entire thing.

CHAPTER 44

Grant
One year ago

> *Silas,*
>
> *I want to thank you for agreeing to take Jules on the trip. I know you've been reluctant about the whole thing, and I know there are probably other ways you'd like to spend your time than racing around the world with my fiancé, but you need to know that this plan with Jules means everything to me. You've never been one to turn me down in the past, for anything, really, so I appreciate you humoring me by changing your mind.*
>
> *Considering how you feel, this is all far-fetched, I know, but I hope it works out better in real life than you're thinking it will.*
>
> *I'm glad you're giving Jules a chance to prove to you that she's changed. That she's not the same person she was to you so soon after your father passed. There's a chance that after Jules loses me, she'll understand what you went through, and how much it changed you afterward. I understand that you two had your differences, but I hope this trip will give you both a*

chance to reconcile all that, because I need you to take care of her, whether you want to or not.

If that's the case, and you and Jules are truly able to forgive each other for your errors of the past, then I have one more request of you: Do whatever it takes to take care of her. I don't want her to live the rest of her life missing out or never fully living again.

Nothing about this is easy, so I'm going to say it as quickly and as clearly as I can, because the fact that I'm asking this of you still blows my mind. Like a bad dream I can't escape from. But the truth is, you're someone who I know Jules would be happy with. We both know you've loved her ever since that stupid day we flipped the coin ten years ago. Believe me, I've wrestled with that fact, and maybe even encouraged her to dislike you more after your father died, back when you were throwing yourself off the cliff a bit. But there was a secret part of me that always felt like maybe there was a chance Jules would wise up and choose the better man between the two of us. So when she saw you faltering, I didn't exactly persuade her to give you the grace you deserved.

I'm sorry for the part I played in that. Or at least for the fact that I didn't discourage her from acting despondent to the changes we saw you go through back then. Try not to hold it against her. Try to do right by her. No matter how upset you might be.

Life, loss, and friendship are messy. Even more so when there's love mixed up in the middle of it all, too.

So, here it is in black and white, Si . . .

I'm asking you to love her.

Love Jules.

There it is: the proverbial green light you've always dreamed of having. The one that gives you permission to show her that you've always loved her — maybe even build a life with her next, if she'll let you. Make her fall in love with you. Or try. It's the very least you can do, and you'll have the chance to try while you're together on this trip.

I truly believe that, if you're both willing to set your past differences aside, you could have the most amazing life. You'll be a good life partner to whoever you choose one day. I know because I got to live a lifetime as your best friend, and it was everything. You were the brother I wanted. The one I chose.

With the hole I'm going to leave behind in both of your lives, I need you to choose Jules to fill it. Not just because I know that deep down you have always loved her, but because I think she could love you too, if the right moment presented itself. We all make mistakes. But missing out on this second chance with her would be the worst mistake of your life.

Sure, try for me, but at the end of the day, try for Jules. And for you, too.

As much as it hurts to imagine. That's it. My final request.

And no matter what happens, thank you for giving it your all.

For this lifetime and the next,
Grant

CHAPTER 45

Juliet

I'm shaking by the time I fold the letter back up and stand to toss it on the counter next to the envelope, feeling like I've stepped out of my body and am having a moment separate from reality.

My heart races, pulsing in my ears with every beat like a drum.

I sit back down on the edge of the tub before growing restless and pacing all over the room, from wall to tub, over and over, unsure of where else to go. My mind pulls apart what I've just read. I never should have read it in the first place since it wasn't addressed to me, but I hate every word of it anyway.

How could I have been so stupid?

How could I have thought that Silas had changed? That there wasn't some backward plot to what's just unfolded between us?

He was asked to make me fall in love with him. Just like all the women he's been with before me. And I can't believe I fell for it. For whatever this was — Silas fucking me to fulfill some final request of my late fiancé. Just to say he's done what he could, and that he did his best to get me to fall for him, before probably turning back into who he's been all along when he finally fulfills the request.

The man I've always known to be an egotistical womanizer somehow managed to play me, too. *How could I be so stupid?*

And worst of all, I can't un-see the fact that Grant was the instigator of this horrible prank. The one I managed to fall prey to.

My stomach churns and I feel like I'm going to be sick.

I close my eyes to steady myself, but I find myself replaying every minute Silas and I have spent together since he picked me up outside of my house.

The way he seemed to be at my beck and call every moment of every day, tirelessly listening to each word I said. Even turning away those two women at the bar back in Spain by pointing me out like I was actually someone special to him. The way the color drained from his cheeks when I accused him of playing a deadly part in Grant's passing — probably because he saw the promise he'd made to Grant going up in flames.

But he'd pushed through every uncomfortable moment between us, each harrowing adventure, all with a smile on his face. And in the end, he'd succeeded at what he set out to do.

He got me.

Silas succeeded at getting me into his bed last night in order to come through on this promise. The one that he apparently made to Grant. To, at the very least, *try* to get me to fall in love with him while probably trying to force old feelings he used to have back up to the surface. Feelings he probably hasn't had about me in years.

According to that letter, Silas didn't even want to go on this trip with me in the first place. Grant had to convince him to take me with him using some end-of-life guilt trip he'd apparently laid on pretty thick.

I should have never gotten in Silas' car that first day back in Boston. Should have never trusted that he'd changed or accepted the eight bags full of gear he had Ryan drop off — which I now know was just his first step at buttering me up. Making me think that he cared.

I want to tear that letter up and flush its remains down the toilet. Pretend it never existed in the first place. But even if the physical letter ceased to exist, I could never forget what it said.

How could Silas do this to me?

I don't know how I fell for it, but I know one thing for certain: I won't fall for it again.

And I certainly won't be here when he wakes up. Won't give him the satisfaction of trying to explain whatever the hell this charade is all about.

He's too good with his words, and his eyes. If I let him try to explain in person, I'll fail to stay away from him. I have to go.

I tiptoe out of the bathroom, then fight the urge to take a shower to strip the grime of our lovemaking session off me in favor of throwing on a quick outfit so I can walk out of this hotel and Silas' life without waking him up. This time, forever.

CHAPTER 46

Silas

I throw my arm over to her side of the bed without opening my eyes. Still in disbelief that I'm waking up next to her in what I hope will be many future mornings wrapped up in bed together. I've already made up my mind to take the next few weeks off work to focus on whatever this is growing between us. I want my every day to be full of her, nothing but her.

My arm lands on a cold pillow instead of her warm body and I crack my eyes open.

The spot beside me is empty and cold, like no one has been in it for hours. I pat around the mattress, feeling for a warm spot in the sheets to indicate that she was only just here a moment ago, but my stomach sinks steadily as my brain catches up.

She's not here. And she hasn't been for a while.

I hop out of bed and walk toward the bathroom, straining to hear a shower running or see a light coming from under the crack of the door.

It's not locked but I knock and wait, then push the door open. The room is empty but the first thing I notice is Grant's letter, the one I've carried with me ever since we left Boston.

It's sitting prominently on the counter *out* of the envelope it's been stored in.

Fuck.

My letter. The one and only letter Grant addressed to me. The somber words that arrived at my office just a few days after his passing, handed to me by the same courier that dropped Jules' first letter off at her door a whole year later to kick off this wild idea we've been working our way through.

No, no, no.

The flight crew must have placed the letter from Grant that I had in my belongings on the counter for some reason when they brought our luggage up to the suite yesterday. It probably fell out of my jacket pocket or something, and they put it there so I would see it.

I bet Jules thought it was hers from last night and opened it up before realizing it was mine.

I close my eyes to imagine her sitting in here in the dead of the night, just minutes to hours after we made love, reading the words that were never meant for her to see. Knowing how harsh they'd be without explanation.

I grab my phone off the nightstand, hoping to see a text or missed call from her, but there isn't one. Only work texts and emails coming in one after another, just like they do every day without end.

I throw on a pair of pants from last night and half-run through the suite of rooms.

They're all empty and the other bed is untouched.

While I know there are plenty of explanations of where she might be — the restaurant downstairs, out for a morning jog to clear her head after last night, grabbing coffee from a nearby café — something inside me tells me that she's gone. Truly gone. She read that letter and didn't want to stay here another second.

I just know it.

I look for the other letter — the one addressed to her that she tossed on the coffee table last night — but that's gone too.

Just like her luggage. More confirmation I don't need. How could I have slept so soundly as she wheeled everything out the door with her?

Three glasses of wine and the fuck of a lifetime, that's how.

I grab my phone off the nightstand to call her, but the phone rings until her voicemail greeting picks up. The happy tone of her recording forms a pit in my stomach and I can't bring myself to leave a message. I call two more times, then send her a text asking her to call me back.

Where are you? At least tell me that you're okay.

I stare at the phone screen, hoping to see those three little dots appear that say she's at least considering writing me back, even if it's only to type a scathing reply. I wait, and wait, until I accept there's nothing coming in.

I call Andy next.

It sounds like I've just woken him up.

"Have you or anyone else from the crew heard from Jules this morning?" I ask.

"Sorry, sir, no." He yawns sleepily into the phone before I can practically hear the meaning behind my call register, and he startles, sounding instantly alert. "Wait, why? Don't tell me she left on her own."

"I'm not sure where she is yet, but if you hear from her, tell me right away. Even if she asks you not to."

"Of course."

I hang up and call Ryan next.

"I need you to look up the location of Juliet's phone."

"Sure," he says, like it's the most casual request in the world. I'm thankful he doesn't ask why.

A few moments later, he tells me that he has her location, but that it doesn't make any sense.

"I thought you were in Amalfi today?" he asks, sounding confused.

"I am." I quickly correct myself. "*We* are."

"The GPS shows her in Paris," he answers, reluctantly.

"Paris? What the—" I look at the clock. It's nearly ten a.m. here. If she boarded one of the earliest flights to Paris, she'd definitely be there by now.

Jesus Christ.

"Change of plans. Get the flight crew ready to fly there. Now," I bark at him.

"Sir?"

"Now," I nearly shout into the phone. "And see if you can get her to answer her phone before we go. She's not answering my calls."

"Right away," he says before hanging up.

I send Juliet another text.

Stay where you are. I'm coming to Paris.

This time, the three little dots appear for only a mere second or two before disappearing. I wait another moment, hoping they reappear, but no such luck. At least it means she's okay. She might be fuming mad at me, but at least she's safe enough to read a text and nearly send a reply.

I start throwing whatever the crew had unpacked yesterday back into my luggage, while pausing to pull a T-shirt over my head. I need to get to Paris before she takes off again.

Then I get an idea that makes my insides twist. It's awful, but it may be worth a shot.

"Ryan." I call him back as soon as the questionable plan enters my mind. "Call my connection at the embassy in Paris. We need to ask them a favor."

I explain my asinine plan.

"Sir?" He doesn't have to say the words for me to know how confused he is. Or, more likely, how disappointed. "I'd like to confirm this is the route you want me to take. Grounding her in a foreign country might not—"

"Just do it," I interrupt before I can change my mind. "And do it now, please."

Then I practically sprint out to the car that I know will be waiting in front of the hotel to get me to the airport as fast as I can.

CHAPTER 47

Juliet

"What do you mean my passport isn't registering?" I ask the ticket agent behind the counter. I wish my French was better, but I've resorted to English to try and get my point across with the help of Google Translate in between.

I can't think straight while I want to murder Silas.

"I'm sorry, Miss, but I cannot sell you a ticket."

I drop my head into my hands.

Unbelievable.

He's going to use a power play to force me to talk to him. *This* is the side of Silas that I was afraid would come back. *Arrogant prick.*

"Please try again. Maybe it was just an issue in the system."

"It is not unclear on my behalf, Miss. I'm sorry, but—"

"Thank you. I'll just try another airline." I sigh, grabbing my passport and license off the counter.

"You won't be able to fly out with any of them," she tells me, apologetically. Then she leans in closer to add more quietly, "It's system-wide. You won't even be able to board a ship or train to anywhere outside France."

"Are you serious?" I ask, widening my eyes at her.

"I'm so sorry," she says, frowning. She's trying to look apologetic, but there's an unmistakable suspicion behind her eyes. I can't blame her for looking at me like that. I'm sure this type of thing doesn't happen every day.

I glance behind me at the line of impatient travelers waiting to speak with her next. I don't want to attract more attention to myself if I don't have to.

"Thanks anyway," I tell her, forcing a smile. It's not this agent's fault that I fell for Silas biggest-asshole-of-all-time Davenport.

I step out of line and drag my bags behind me to a quieter part of the airport, one buckled to the next so I can handle them all myself, then pull my phone out to call Silas. There's no getting around it. We have to talk.

Annoyed, I listen to his phone ring until the voicemail cue picks up. I stare down at the phone in shock. So much for urgently sitting beside it, waiting for me to call.

I call Ryan next. If anyone will have a handle on Silas' state of mind and his whereabouts, it'll be him. Plus, he's called me enough times for me to know he's concerned, too.

"Juliet!" Ryan sounds a bit breathless after picking up on the first half-ring. "How are—"

"Where is he, Ryan?" I interrupt, anger filling my voice. We're a little past pleasantries at this point. "And please tell me why the hell I'm grounded in Paris?"

"He's on his way to see you. They're all in the air right now, which is why you can't get ahold of him, if you tried." A fresh wave of guilt sloshes around the walls of my stomach. The crew must have had to scramble everything together to change their flights around today, just to follow me here sooner than planned.

It didn't have to be like this, I remind myself. Silas didn't have to call whatever connection he has here in France to corner me.

He also didn't have to fuck me in order to make good on a promise either, but here we are.

"Will you release my passport, then?" I ask, not bothering to check whether or not it was Silas who made that call. Of course it was. No normal, everyday human has the power to ground a civilian passport in another country, but Silas has friends and associates in every corner of the globe with power and authority over things that someone like me — someone who has zero power — could only dream of.

"Where are you? I can direct the crew over to—"

"Oh no, I don't want you directing anyone to me. I want you to make the call to release my travel restrictions. Now, please. This isn't a normal thing to do when two people are having a disagreement and you know it, so just make the call, Ryan."

A heavy silence follows and I know I'm not going to win this.

I lean my head back and fight the tears from coming.

"He's just worried about you," he answers, quietly.

I imagine Silas waking up to an empty hotel suite, instantly panicking when he saw the letter I left out for him on the bathroom counter. Realizing all my luggage was gone too.

"I get that. But when I'm worried about someone, I don't usually confine them to a foreign country just so I can go have a conversation with them. He hasn't changed at all."

Silence again.

"Are you at the airport?" he finally asks.

"Yes." I sigh, angrily. There's no getting around this. "But I'm not sticking around here, just waiting for him to swoop in and convince me that he's sorry. If he wants to have a conversation with me, he can come and find me himself. Clearly, he's very good at that."

My blood is boiling. I hang up the phone and walk outside to call a taxi or Uber or whatever it is that's available as quickly as possible. Then I double-check the text I received back from Monica after asking for the name of the hotel where my final letter from Grant is waiting. Paris was supposed to be our final stop together. I was going to book a later flight, retrieve the letter, and hop back on a plane to fly back home tonight, but now I just need to get that letter and apparently find a new way out of here, if at all possible. If not, we'll have to talk here, but at least I can try.

Le Petite Fleur.

"Le Petite Fleur," I tell the taxi driver when he pulls over. I throw my bags in the trunk, not bothering to wait for him to assist me. "Accéléré, s'il te plaît," I add, calling upon the three years of high school French I'd taken over a decade ago. *Please hurry.*

"Tu l'as eu," he says, behind the wheel. *You got it.*

I've never been here, but I take in as much of the city as I can while we pull away from the curb to start the drive. Tall buildings and tiny cafés roll past the backseat window of the black sedan while I try to keep the blurry edges of my eyesight from spilling over to ruin the view racing by. I never imagined that my first time seeing this *city of love* would be while running from two unimaginable heartaches.

When I arrive at the hotel, I have to convince the staff to hand Grant's final letter over to me without Silas present, but I've come prepared.

"He's been in an accident," I tell the three people gathered behind the counter, forcing a deeply troubled look into my eyes. It helps that I already look like I've been crying. One of the staffers is a manager who's been called over on my insistence. "He'll be here eventually to sign for it, but you'll see that it's my name on the envelope." I hand them my Massachusetts state driver's license, hoping they don't ask to see my passport too, just in case they're connected to the same system as the airport somehow, which would only add to their budding hesitation.

Reluctantly, and after a bit more arguing, they finally hand it over.

Feeling like a fugitive on the run, I grab my keycard off the counter, along with the last unopened letter before they can change their minds. Then I race off to my suite, glancing over my shoulder like I've just managed to rob a bank. Between the forced grounding in Paris, and now this, my heart is pounding, even though I've done nothing wrong.

Except trust a man you never should have trusted.

It's only a matter of time until Silas finds me here. Monica probably already let him know that I asked about the name of the hotel so I could pick up the last letter here without him. When he does arrive, we can have whatever conversation he wants to have so I can get out of here and back to Boston. Even if it means flying separately. Something I'd prefer to do at this point anyway.

I shut the door behind me and push my back against it, slowly sinking onto the cold tile floor.

I'm relieved to be in my own space again, if only for an hour or two before he arrives. I need time to collect my thoughts and wade through everything that's happened since leaving Nonna Lisi's cozy stone cottage near the water last night.

Last night.

God, it feels like a lifetime ago.

I force the memory away and hold the envelope out in front of me with both hands, tracing the letters of my name on the front with my finger.

It's the last one.

My final piece of him. Unread words I have yet to feel before it's truly over, before I head back home without any more letters to look forward to. I read Grant's letter from Italy on the flight over here and it nearly broke me in half. It was everything I wanted to hear before last night, which only made me regret reading Silas' letter even more.

I don't know whether to rip this one open, or to cherish this bittersweet moment of suspense that I know I'll never feel again. At least when it comes to him. To *us*. Grant always loved to write me letters and little notes, old-fashioned and romantic until the bitter end. I've probably held a hundred or so unopened letters in my hands from him — each providing a moment of anticipation that no phone call or text could ever compare to.

It's bitter, but not yet sweet, knowing this is the last time I'll ever hold one again.

I close my eyes, allowing my thoughts to dance with the butterflies now filling my stomach. Even after I retire this final letter to the memory box I have back home filled with all the letters and ticket stubs and programs and photos of us smiling like two people who never knew the end was drawing so near, I know I'll still think back on this moment.

The moment I had to open it.

The last memory of just him and me.

I hug it to my chest. Wishing it was more than just a piece of parchment filled with words that used to pour from someone who was still very much alive.

Then I trace my name one more time before flipping the envelope over, unsealing it with the swipe of my finger against the sticky strip that held it in place over the past year. Pulling the familiar paper out, I unfold it in front of me, sucking one last breath in before reading my love's final goodbye.

CHAPTER 48

Grant
A year ago

Jules,
    Welcome to Paris, sweetheart. The birthplace of love, the City of Light. The most romantic setting in the world!
    Have you opened your window yet? Monica promised to get you the room with the view of that tiny little tower you always hoped to see one day. The one that'll sparkle with a thousand lights later tonight once the city has dimmed enough to let her shine. I hope you pop the bottle of champagne I arranged to have delivered to your room so that you can have a celebratory glass before heading out to your reservations inside the tower tonight. And I hope that you wear the gold dress I'm having delivered to your suite when you go. I can see it in my mind, and I already know that the whole effect — you, the glittering tower, the gorgeous dress, the long champagne flute in your hand — it's all stunning. Imagining it is almost as good as getting to be there with you when it happens.
    Almost.
    And when you're sitting in that tower, looking as beautiful as ever, with Silas by your side, I want you to think about

what it is that I'm about to tell you. Let it all sink in before you react, or do something rash, because if you still can't stand him by the time you're reading this, then what I'm about to say is going to come as a rather unwelcome surprise. Or maybe, by this point, it won't shock you at all. You might even be happy to hear it and welcome him even more openly than before.

If that's the case, then I want you to know that it's okay.

Silas is in love with you, Jules. That man has always tried to hide it from us both, and I want you to know that he never acted on it, or even uttered the words out loud to me. He's too good of a friend to act on anything like that, but I think you've always been his kryptonite, whether he'd ever admit that to anyone or not.

But I know my best friend. And I know that he's loved you since the first moment that I did too. Ever since you asked for that pen in class and we flipped that stupid coin before I lost and chucked it in the river anyway. You were always his one that got away. If he hasn't yet told you that, or tried to show you in his own ridiculous Silas type of way, then let me be the one to break the news. I wouldn't say that it's my pleasure to do so, but rather, my last, gut-wrenching gift to you.

The last time Silas and I talked while I was in the hospital, you were out with your mother for her birthday (remember, I insisted you go?) so Silas and I had time to discuss this trip alone over the phone. It was one of the hardest conversations we've ever had.

When I told him about this plan, about this trip, he shocked me at first by saying no. Absolutely not, were his actual words, and I about fell over if it weren't for all the rails and cords keeping me in the bed. I thought I'd be giving him permission to have the trip of a lifetime with the woman I knew he secretly pined after.

But when I asked him why, at first he putted around the answer, making jokes that weren't all that funny like "She'll never want to spend that much time with me" or "You know I hate flying." But I'd grown serious and insisted that he give me one good reason why he was saying no to all this.

"Because she deserves better." He finally sobered up enough to say it. *"She deserves someone like you. Not someone like me."*

Now, I'd always envisioned Silas as the guy who had everything. The kid walking in wearing the cut-off tank with the coolest shoes, who didn't give a fuck about the dress code. The one who always knew how to keep one foot in the game without ever taking anything too seriously. In so many ways, from such a young age, he was my idol, not just my friend. The guy who taught me how and when to grow up. How to exit my sheltered childhood and become a man that was worthy of someone like you loving me. I owe all that to him. So, to be told that he felt like he didn't deserve you shocked me.

"I've already screwed things up with her. Irreparably, I think. There's no way she'll want to spend that time with me. It'll be torture for her."

I told him that, given the chance, you might find yourself missing him as much as he missed you. And that the two of you could learn to trust each other again because you'll both need each other.

But, most of all, I asked him to try to repair things with you. None of us are perfect, but we all make the most perfect mistakes that lead us to the life we were meant to have.

He eventually agreed to go and try. His reluctance wasn't because he didn't want to, but because he didn't think YOU would want to. He didn't want to put you through any of this.

So whether the two of you find it in yourselves to be strictly friends because it's just too bizarre to cross that invisible boundary placed between you a decade ago by a silly little coin toss — or maybe you've found yourselves to be closer than you ever have — I want you to know that wherever I am, whether six feet under or looking down from above, I'll be smiling if the two of you have found each other again. Because the friends who choose to be family are what I already miss the most.

So, go feel unbelievably beautiful tonight, then return to Boston with a friend, or perhaps, more than that by your side.

Keep having the most incredible adventures and don't stop. Feel the wind in your hair, the spray of the ocean in your face. Laugh in stone houses overlooking breathtaking views, and tonight, fall in love in a city that demands it.

You were the love of my life, sweetheart. But I hope there's room for more than just one in yours.

I love you more than I ever thought possible. So, once again, I'm reminding you of my final, most annoyingly ever-persistent request: Live this one-and-only life you have. Love ferociously. Fall freely. Be exactly who you are now, without one single regret. Trade the mundane for messy, and be irreverent. Take it all in until there's nothing left missing at the very end. And that goes for love, too.

Most importantly, from the very bottom of my heart, thank you, always, for letting me love you,
Grant

CHAPTER 49

Juliet

I'm wiping away a fresh slew of tears by the time I'm finished reading it and have to get up to grab a tissue from the table nearby. On the way, I drag open the curtains near the black marble fireplace on the wall, gasping when I see what's right outside the glass.

There she is.

The view Grant promised in his letter.

The Eiffel Tower stands practically up alongside me, almost close enough to touch, but far enough out that I can see the whole thing glistening from top to bottom just outside the floor-to-ceiling balcony of our suite. I stand there for a moment to take it all in, grateful to have made it here to my final destination, the letter still clutched in my hand.

On a small table beside the window, there's a bottle of champagne on ice, and beside it, a long white box. I lift the lid and stare down at what's inside.

Grant's very last words to me fade from view as new tears fill my eyes.

Unsure how to feel, I leave the box and settle into the nearest couch, pulling a heavy blanket over my lap to read the last letter again, before tucking it into the envelope where I know it'll stay until we arrive back home. I glance at my phone screen to check the time, wondering how long I have until Silas bursts through that door, suddenly missing him all over again.

But instead of Silas' name, there are over a dozen missed calls and a few texts from Andy.

My stomach cinches in a tight little knot the moment I get the first text to open, then I quickly scan the rest, now aware of why none of the new messages or missed calls are from Silas himself.

I pull up Andy's phone number to call him as fast as I can.

"Jules." Andy sounds panicked when he picks up the phone on the second ring. "Did you get my messages?"

I nod silently at the phone, unable to form any words yet, feeling the weight of what his texts just revealed. The events of the last twenty-four hours now threatening to crush me.

"There's been an accident, honey. They — they didn't see him crossing the street outside the airport. I've sent a car over to you. It should already be downstairs—"

I don't hear the rest of what Andy's saying because I'm already racing toward the elevator to go join him.

***

Hours later, Silas and I slowly make our way into the suite at *Le Petite Fleur*. Andy is behind us, carting Silas' luggage down the hall toward our room. He insisted on staying with us to help me get Silas into bed, but I assume it's also to make sure that I don't bolt on him again.

It's only a fractured elbow, and a nasty cut above his eye, but it was enough to give me quite the scare. Even worse for Andy, who was right beside him when the bike came out of nowhere. He saw the whole thing happen and I can tell that he isn't too keen on leaving Silas' side just yet. Especially since, just a few hours ago, I wasn't even civil enough to take any of Silas' calls. I don't blame Andy for wanting to keep an eye on him personally, given the events of today.

"Promise me you'll stay with him this time, honey. No running off to Amsterdam or Machu Picchu or somewhere else the first opportunity you get. It was hard enough to keep up with you this time," he says, after we've tucked Silas into his bed.

The view of the Eiffel Tower outside all the windows in the suite is exactly as Grant described it to me, now lit from top to bottom against the black night sky. It's stunning, and I wish we were all in a more jovial mood to enjoy it.

"I'm not going anywhere," I promise, somberly. Then add, "I don't even know if my passport would allow it, to be honest."

He chuckles.

"Well, no point in checking that out right now," he says, stifling a smile. "He's going to need you here the next couple days at least. But if you do need to go anywhere, please call so he's not stranded here all alone. I'll come just the second you need me."

"I'm not leaving him, Andy," I repeat, touching his arm. "I promise."

"And I'm not deaf or mute, you two," Silas pipes up from the bed. "I'm perfectly capable of hearing."

Andy raises his brows at me, then places Silas' phone within his reach on the nightstand.

"I'm calling you every other hour to make sure *this one* is still here," Andy says to Silas, eyeballing me.

"No need, Andy," I assure him, smiling. "But you're welcome to call Silas repeatedly if that'll make you feel better. However, if we don't answer, it's not because I'm not here."

I smile wider at him, wishing I had handled things more civilly instead of trying to disappear, throwing everyone into a frenzy. I already feel guilty, like this never would have happened to Si if I'd just given him the chance to explain everything the way Grant's letter did for me.

"Well, in that case, maybe I'll start the calls tomorrow then," he says, a nosy smile playing on his lips. "Give you two a chance to get reacquainted tonight without me interrupting, I suppose. Go easy on him though."

I grin and start pushing him toward the hallway. "I can't promise that."

I shut the door behind Andy, thankful he was there with Silas when it happened.

When we're finally alone, I walk toward the open doorway of his bedroom to get him a glass of water so he can take the pain medicine the doctor sent him away with. I pause at the entrance, studying him more carefully while he watches the glittering view outside our window. His arm is in a cast, slung up around his shoulder with a sling. The cut above his eye has been stitched up, but it's still swollen, casting a dark bruise over his brow that makes him look more exhausted than he already is. Thankfully, the bump on the back of his head is hidden by his hair.

I could have lost him today. The doctor who stitched him up said he got very lucky that the biker who hit him only got a side-swipe in, but he was going fast enough to have done some real damage if Silas had been hit straight on. I shudder to think of what could have happened, and how he could have been hurt badly, or worse, all while thinking I was never going to speak to him again. The thought of it nearly brings me to my knees, as I recall every word of Grant's letter, and how this should have all ended so differently. I've already learned how quickly you can lose someone you love.

Silas has only ever looked out for me, even when I couldn't look out for myself. And yet, I'd left him today at the first sign of a conflict.

It's *me* who doesn't deserve *him*.

"Hey, stranger," he says, smiling at me as I stand in the doorway. Even though his face is marred by the gash, he's still more handsome than any man in Paris. Possibly the world.

"Hey." I force a smile, to stop any more tears from falling, unsure if I have any left in me after today. "How are you feeling? Do you need more pain meds? I was going to get you a glass of water. More pillows from the desk downstairs maybe?"

"I'm feeling a lot better after whatever they gave me at the hospital." He grins, looking a bit loopy from the pain meds. "I think whatever they have here must be better than whatever they give people back in the States. I don't feel one ounce of pain at this point."

I chuckle, grateful he's feeling better, then make my way over to sit beside him on the bed. We both look out at the Eiffel Tower for a few moments, the silence oddly comfortable between us, considering everything that's happened.

Eventually, I turn to him, ready to apologize for running. Between the endless stream of doctors, nurses, and Andy who refused to leave his side, it's the first time we've been truly alone since I got to the hospital.

"I'm so sorry," I tell him, my voice cracking. "I'm sorry I left like that. I shouldn't have disappeared. I should have stayed and talked it through. I'm sure you figured it out, but I need to tell you that I read your letter. The one Grant wrote you. I shouldn't have done that in the first place. It was a huge invasion of your privacy and I apologize." He turns toward me, smiling faintly. I narrow my eyes, trying not to laugh at the look on his face. "Maybe we should wait to talk about all this when you're not so hopped up on pain meds?"

"Nah, pain meds or not, it won't change how I feel. I knew you probably thought that letter was the one you'd gotten from the front desk that night. The crew put it on the bathroom counter for me when they were unpacking my stuff. You shouldn't have had the chance to confuse it with yours, and they felt pretty bad about it when I asked how it happened. I don't blame you for mixing them up."

"Once I realized it was yours, not mine, I never should have read it."

"But you did."

"Yes, I did." I frown.

"I wish you would have given me a chance to explain everything," he says, resting his eyes. "I planned to show you the letter at some point, but reading something like that without knowing the entire story behind it? It would have left me feeling the same way. I can't imagine what was going through your head, especially right after we—"

He opens his eyes again and raises his eyebrows, recalling what we did last night.

Making love to him feels like it happened weeks ago, considering everything we've been through since.

I nod. "You're right. It was too easy to take everything out of context. But then I got Grant's letter at the desk this morning."

He narrows his eyes. "How did you get them to give it to you without me?"

I swallow miserably. "I told them that you had an accident and couldn't be here to sign for it."

He erupts in laughter, then winces. "God, Jules, the irony of that."

A tear spills out the side of my eye and he wipes it away. "I know. I'm so sorry, it's like I vocalized your fate before it happened. You have no idea how guilty I felt when I found out."

He laughs even more, and I'm glad he's not mad.

"No wonder no one looked surprised when I walked through the lobby looking like this," he says.

"I'm the worst, I know," I tell him, biting back a smile. "When will I learn?"

"Jules, I grounded your passport. *I'm* technically the worst," he says, tapering off a laugh. "I'm sorry I did that, too. Trust takes time to build, and we're both working it back up, I guess."

I grin. "You should have seen my face at the airport when the poor woman had to tell me."

"I bet Grant never saw the trip ending like this," he says, his eyes suddenly more tired than they were just a moment ago.

"Actually, I'd just finished reading his last letter when I got all of Andy's messages. Right before I rushed to see you at the hospital."

He takes a deep breath and settles deeper into the pillows we propped up behind him.

"So Grant guessed that I'd be nearly run over after grounding your passport in Paris, eh? Boy, he did see us coming a mile away."

I laugh. "No, but I can show it to you if you want. His letter sort of explained everything I needed to hear after accidentally reading your letter — how you initially said no to doing all this, and why."

He exhales deeply, nodding. The room is dark except for the gas fireplace that has been turned on as part of the hotel's turndown service and the illuminated view of the tower outside the window.

"What did it say?"

"That we need each other," I tell him, quietly. "That neither one of us is perfect. That maybe I need you as much as you need me. That once upon a time, we were each other's chosen family." I pause before adding, "And that maybe we can be again."

He reaches his uninjured hand to clasp mine, dwarfing my palm in his, lacing his fingers through each one of mine. I squeeze back, remembering what it felt like to get the call that he'd been in an accident today, and move a little closer to him on the bed.

"Grant was always so good with his words." He stares at the fire, remembering. "Wise and mature past his years."

I smile, remembering all the times Grant had given Silas or me advice that felt spot on. Various times his words made more sense than whatever chaos I'd created around myself on so many occasions. And now, knowing that these letters were Grant's final collection of wisdom — nudging us back toward one another, his final gift to both of us months after he's been gone — when he knew we could finally be in a place to receive it. He saw something that neither of us could see, that what we each needed could transpire long after he was laid to rest. Sitting here now, I know deep down that he was right.

"He said one more thing," I add, inching closer to rest my head against his chest on the side of him that doesn't have the sling. He wraps his good arm around me, shifting to make me more comfortable against him.

"What else?" he asks, as we stare at the view out the window.

"He said no matter what happened between us, whether we end as friends—" I pause — "or more, he'd be glad that we'd made our way back to each other again."

Silas' chest rises but doesn't fall, holding his breath for a beat before letting it out in a long sigh.

"He was a better man than I will ever be," he says into my hair. Then he kisses the top of my head. "I don't think I could ever imagine you being with anyone else but me if something were to happen. Pretty sure if I was in Grant's position, my letters would have been full of threats about me haunting you from beyond the grave, and coming up with creative ways to scare anyone else away from you."

I burst out laughing, knowing he's telling the truth.

"Same," I admit, truthfully. "I can't imagine the strength it must have taken for him to imagine this scenario — not just two people he loved the most living out their lives without him but also doing so together."

"That was Grant. He taught me more, even after losing him, than he'll ever know."

"Funny, he said the same thing about you." I smile, nestling into his chest again. Then I listen to him breathe for a few more moments, reveling in the fact that our day could have ended so differently from this. "Are you sure I can't get you anything else? More pain meds? A snack? What do you need?"

He tightens his arm around me, planting another kiss on the top of my head, and I lean up on my elbow to face him. I push my cheek into his palm, loving the warmth of it.

"I have everything I need right here," he says.

I lean in to kiss him, gently.

"I don't want to hurt you," I whisper, pulling back. "I already feel like all this was my fault. We'd be dining in there" — I point out the window — "without a broken elbow instead of lying in here, if I hadn't run off."

"Jules, I would have been hit by a bus instead of a bike if it meant getting to have this moment with you by the end of today," he says. The serious tone of his voice makes me laugh, the sound of it ringing through the room, but when I open my eyes to look up at him, there's more written on his face than could ever be conveyed with words. "So much had to happen for us to get here. I'm not sure I'll ever stop feeling like you deserve so much more than me. But if every mistake we've made has brought us right here to this moment, then I would make every stupid mistake over and over to get back here to you. I'll do everything I can to make it up to you. To take care of you."

I need to ask the question I've had in my mind ever since last night. "And not just because he requested that of you?" I ask, afraid he might stumble or stutter through his answer, leaving me to question it, always.

He pulls me back so I can see his eyes more clearly. "I could never try to fake feelings like this, if that's what you're asking," he says, his voice deep. "That letter you read last night made it sound like everything that's happened between us was simply me fulfilling a promise to Grant. But that letter was also written by someone who took a wild guess at how I felt about you. I would have never told Grant while he was alive that you were always it for me. That no woman I've ever dated or spent time with has ever compared to you. I have loved you since the moment I laid eyes on you, Jules. From the first time you smiled at us, asking for a pen, when I swear I saw a few sitting in your bag just before. I loved you that night we spent on the beach after graduation. And I loved you when I pulled up at your house before we even started this crazy trip. I loved you when you were pushing me out of your foyer, so fucking mad, and I've even loved you in my dreams. I never wanted to love you, Jules. But I've also never been able to stop."

My face flushes, held steady by his hand. "He suspected it," I tell him, quietly, "and I think he sent us here on this trip *because* he knew."

"Yes, Grant had it figured out. I never, ever admitted it to him, but I didn't have to."

I take a long, cleansing breath, feeling more sure now than ever when I tell him what I've already known deep down. "I love you, too, Si," I say. And just hearing how sure I sound makes me smile. "I've always loved you. First as my friend, and even when I thought I hated you, I still loved you. And now, after today, I know I never want to lose you again."

CHAPTER 50

Silas

I don't know which is better: hearing Jules say she loves me, or the way her lips find mine in the near-dark while the Eiffel Tower springs to life, sparkling like a thousand camera flashes outside the enormous window at our feet. The tower glitters like this every hour, perfectly timed to echo the fluttering now inside my chest.

This isn't how today was supposed to go. We're supposed to be dining in that tower right now, but this is somehow, even with my arm in a cast, so much better.

"Wait!" Jules pulls back from my lips long before I'm ready. "I have something for you to see."

She slips out from under my arm. I watch her leave the room, wishing whatever it was could wait. Then I hear some paper rustling around, and the clinking of glasses. A moment later, she reappears wearing a short gold dress. It's covered in tiny sequins, and she sparkles like the Eiffel Tower with every micromovement she makes. She's holding two glasses and a longneck bottle of champagne. The sight of her standing in the dark, lit only by the glittering tower and firelight takes my breath away. I wish I wasn't laid up in bed with half of one arm rendered useless.

"What's this?" I ask, grinning.

"We were supposed to be having dinner over there," she says, nodding toward the window. "This champagne was to pop open beforehand. I think it's meant to be a little celebration for making it all the way through our trip without killing each other."

She smiles.

"And that dress?" I ask, eyeing her up and down. She's barefoot, which I think I prefer to any heels she would have chosen to go with it. Her long blonde hair is down, cascading across her shoulders, while she's barely got any makeup left from the tears she shed beside me.

Jules is stunning. Always.

"A little something I was supposed to wear to dinner tonight, I guess," she says, smiling. "The note that came with it only had three words attached."

I widen my eyes, wondering what could possibly be written to make sense of a dress like that.

"For starting over," she tells me, smiling.

"Wow," I say, feeling speechless.

"I finally feel like I'm . . . I don't know how to describe it."

"At peace?" I ask her, knowing the feeling deep down in myself. This might have been a journey to help Jules to move on from the love of her life, but I feel like I've also taken myself on the same journey. To say goodbye to someone I, too, never hoped to live without.

"I guess," she admits. "But also like I'm ready, in a really good way."

She takes a step toward me, holding up the two glasses.

"Stop right there," I tell her, letting my eyes slowly wander down the length of her, all the way down to her bare toes and back up again to meet her eyes.

"What? What's wrong?" Her eyes search mine.

"I want to remember you exactly like this," I tell her. "You in that dress, the Eiffel Tower outside our window. That look on your face."

"This look?" she asks, taking another step toward me, beaming.

"That and the one you're about to have next . . ." I say gruffly. "Now, get over here."

She laughs and walks across the room back to me.

"Can you even have this?" she asks, holding a glass out to me. "With all the pain meds in your system?"

"Absolutely," I tell her, clinking the bubbling glass against hers.

"To new beginnings," she says.

"To you," I add.

"And to him," she whispers, leaning in to kiss me. "For the foresight he had to create a trip like this, knowing how it might end."

We smile at each other, but before I can get a tiny sip down, Jules takes the glass from my hand and sets it on the nightstand beside me.

"I think I know what will help you feel even better than that," she says, raising a brow.

Then she leans in to kiss me. My body springs to life at her touch as she runs her hands down my chest. I wince when she accidentally grazes my elbow.

"Oh my gosh. Did that hurt?" she asks, looking panicked.

"No," I tell her. "At least not the part where you were touching my chest. My elbow is a little tender though."

She pats my leg apologetically. "Let me see if I can help you forget the pain." She smirks up from under her lashes, then leans in again, this time careful to stay back from the side with the cast. "How about here?" she asks, brushing her lips against mine.

"Mmm, that definitely helps," I murmur into her kiss.

"And here?" she asks, tracing her lips down toward my jaw. She finds that sensitive spot just under my ear and nips it, before biting down on my earlobe, tasting it between her teeth, sending a shiver down my body.

"That's even better," I tell her, tilting my jaw up to give her more space to do whatever she wants.

"I think I remember the doctor saying something about this helping, too," she says, caressing the growing bulge of my pants. She looks up to watch my face while slowly unzipping them, then slips one hand under the fabric of my boxers. "This doesn't hurt, does it?" she asks, dragging a gentle fist up and down, barely skimming the surface like a tease. I'm already hard in her hand.

"Not even a little," I groan, pressing my head back into the mound of pillows behind me. I may be laid up in bed for a few days, but I don't mind if this is how we end up spending the time.

"Let me see if I can help you out even more then," she says, pulling my shaft out of my boxers. She hikes her dress up, positioning herself right above it, teasing me with anticipation.

I push my hips up, as she sinks down.

"God, you are incredible," I murmur. The sparkling tower lights up the window behind her, but I only have eyes for Jules.

"Is this okay?" she asks, kneeling on either side of my hips.

"You're not going to hurt me." I breathe the words out like a prayer, hoping she's not afraid to keep going, and she lowers herself onto me again, filling her body with the entire length of me until I disappear inside her again. "You're going to have to do the work for me this time, baby," I tell her, wishing I could take a more active role in everything that's unfolding if it weren't for this stupid cast on my arm. But I love getting to watch her take charge right now.

"You're welcome to pretend that sling is just a pair of handcuffs if it makes it more sexy for you." She laughs, giving me a playful look. Then she leans forward and presses my lips into hers, gently leading me up and down as she begins to move. "And until that thing comes off, I'm just going to have to own every inch of your body exactly the way I want it."

She circles her hips, slowly at first, before a desperate need takes over and she starts moving faster, pulling her dress up over her head and dropping it to the floor, freeing her breasts and the rest of her body from the material. Her skin, now on full display, the fullness of her chest bouncing against her ribcage as she arches her back in front of me, giving me an unforgettable view. A moan escapes her lips as she tips her chin back, letting her long hair cascade down her back while grazing her shoulders. Then she rakes it back, grasping onto her crown of hair with one hand while her other hand holds onto my shoulder, steadying herself against me while she gets lost in the ride.

The restraint of not being able to fully embrace each other feels maddening, and I'm tempted to ignore the pain and wrap her up in my arms anyway. She leans toward me, suddenly grasping my face between her hands so gently. Her kisses draw out long and tender as her lovemaking turns from desperate to soft and sweet. Showing me what she's already told me — that she loves me.

She pauses the movement of her hips, then brings her face into mine, clasping the edges of my jaw, kissing me slowly until the feeling of her lips tasting mine sends shooting stars out from the darkness. Her hips come to life again, slowly and deliberately moving against me, bringing me close to the edge all over again. I feel as everything in her starts to clench around me. Her body feels magnetic, pulling me right to the edge with her.

Jules opens her eyes and her lips hover an inch from mine. She watches my face as she takes us both into the oblivion. The release like a cannon going off within me, her lips parting just so as a gasp escapes them, and for one incredible moment, the world stops on its axis. She begins rocking against me again as the waves of pleasure course through her, sending me over the edge one more time along with her.

When we're finally breathless, with tiny beads of sweat forming along her hairline, she leans her forehead against mine, like she can't muster up the strength to tumble off me just yet.

"I can't imagine doing this with anyone else ever again, Si," she whispers.

"Then don't," I tell her. "It can be that easy."

She laughs and her breath tastes sweet against my tongue.

"I can't believe I've fallen in love with you," she says, almost too softly for me to hear. As if she truly only meant for herself to hear it.

"And I can't believe I ever thought that I could live without you," I answer.

The tower begins flashing outside again and a thousand different light bulbs blink at our feet. She rolls to my side and I wrap my good arm around her, knowing that as close as we can get to one another will never be close enough. Unable to believe that every moment between us — between *all* of us — has finally led us right here. To a view I'll always remember, and a night I'll never want to forget.

CHAPTER 51

Juliet

Silas passes me the bottle and I take a sip, careful to lower it slowly so the delicate champagne bubbles don't rocket back out the neck of the bottle and up my nose like it did all those years ago.

We're sitting on the edge of the Seine River, our feet dangling above the water running lazily at our feet. A few couples and groups of French teens are scattered on the banks around us, each watching the evening dinner boats pass by on their way to view the lights of the city from the water. Some of the passengers wave and smile as they do. Others laugh at stories and jokes being shared across the water in French, most of which I don't understand.

Silas and I stopped at a market street full of shops on the way here, grabbing strawberries and cheese, a baguette, and macaroons. All selected at a handful of shops that sell only the items they have an expertise in, including the incredible champagne Silas picked at the wine store around the corner. We forgot to ask for a few glasses to take with us, so we've been passing the bottle between us while we, too, watch the boats drift by on the water. I might even prefer drinking it like this.

It's our last night here and although Monica was able to reschedule dinner reservations at the Eiffel Tower if we wanted, we opted to make our way down here instead. Our makeshift picnic now spread on either side of us while we lean back and enjoy the perfect early summer evening.

This wasn't on Grant's itinerary, but somehow that makes it feel just right. It's a step down a new path, one that will always have the memory of him behind it, but only us to move forward.

"I can't believe I forgot the glasses," Si says, watching me slowly tip the bottle back down from my lips, thankfully not spilling a drop.

I grin.

"I can," I say before passing the bottle back to him. He sets it down on the pavement beside us and wraps his uninjured arm around my shoulders.

"Are you sure you don't want to move here instead of Italy one day?" he asks, pulling me closer. "I like how this place feels with you in it."

A boat slowly drives by, this one with a singer on board belting out a French version of "Ave Maria" that makes my eyes tingle with tears. Not because I'm sad, but because everything about this moment is unbelievable. Paris has hit me square in the soul. I love it here.

"I promise nothing will change, no matter where we are," I tell him, loving the way his eyes seem to glisten ever so slightly at the sights and sounds of where we are, too.

"Do Andy and Carl know how busy they're about to get?" I ask, wondering if Silas has already shared our travel plans for the next few weeks. We're starting with a stop back at Nonna Lisi's so we can show her that she was right. Si has promised to take the next few weeks off work, while I already let my clients know I'll handle all my sessions with them when I get back.

"Andy was ecstatic about it. I think his exact words were that he can't wait to tell you a certain little phrase the second we're back on ol' Gloria." He nudges me closer.

"Ah, let me guess. Does that certain little phrase sound something like *I told you so*?" I ask.

Silas' chest erupts in laughter. My favorite sound, as it turns out. "We'll just let Andy handle that one when you see him next."

I snuggle into him, wishing this moment would never have to end. We chose a spot on the river where the Notre Dame Cathedral is peeking out across from us. It's nearly done being rebuilt from the fire that destroyed some of its architecture a few years ago.

"I feel a little bit like that church," I tell him, nodding toward it.

"A fucking work of art?" he asks, and I can hear the smile in his voice. It makes me grin.

"No. Healing. A little scarred, but lucky to be here," I tell him, pausing to watch another boat drift by.

"You forgot to add utterly breathtaking," he says, kissing the crown of my head.

I smile and rib him with my elbow, careful not to hit the other side of his body. His other arm is still carefully tucked into a sling. He has a few specialist appointments lined up for when we get back to Boston, all of them promising he'll be good as new after a few months.

"I love you," he whispers. "And I have never loved anything more."

I smile. He always adds that second part, but this time the words open something deep inside me because I *have* loved before, which possibly makes loving someone again even sweeter.

Not because I love Silas *more*.

But because I love him differently.

This time I know how fleeting a love can be. How quickly it can disappear when you least expect it, and how the swift loss of that love can change you.

Fiercely. Unrecognizably. Irrevocably.

Because no matter how long ago those footprints were left, they leave a mark. Shifting our shape, the very essence of who we are, until we are never, ever the same again. And maybe it's because we aren't supposed to be.

I know that this time, loving this man, I won't take a single moment of it for granted.

I have Grant to thank for that. That piece of his legacy was the best gift of all: a reminder to live our days to the fullest extent that we can. Without regrets, and without second-guessing what a life could and should look like based on the past.

Silas slowly picks up the bottle and holds it out in front of him, not taking a sip quite yet.

He winks at me.

"So, where do you see yourself in five years, Jules?" he asks.

I inhale sharply, but the memory of the three of us playing this game rolls through me, bringing only good feelings this time.

I smile back at him.

"Happy," I tell him. "And with you."

He kisses me, still holding the bottle out between us.

"I couldn't have said it any better myself," he agrees before adding, "Until then."

EPILOGUE

Jules
Five years later

Nonna Lisi pushes Emmy's tiny hands into the puff of dough that's nearly as big as she is. The two of them scrunch their faces at each other, just a few inches apart, then burst into laughter at the very same time. Emmy turns to me and holds her hands up, completely covered in a sticky mess of flour and egg. Her eyes glow up at Nonna Lisi when I snap a photo of them. The view of the sea glitters out the open window behind her.

They continue working the dough together, Nonna Lisi tutting over the way Emmy's already *quite the natural* when I realize that Emmy's melodic giggle has become my very favorite sound in the whole world, tied only with her twin brother's giggle, too. *And* their dad's.

I turn to watch Si, who's on the other side of the worn, wooden counter, doing the same thing with our sweet little boy, Emmy's twin, Grant. The two have flour almost exclusively covering their chests with an additional swipe of dough on Si's cheek from Grant's chubby finger. Si must feel me watching because he turns to look at me and mouths, "I love you" as our eyes meet across the sunbathed kitchen.

I jump when Nonna Lisi's voice echoes across the little stone kitchen, startling me out of the moment.

"I knew it!" she cries out, her curled, doughy finger pointed up toward the sky, grinning so wide that her eyes look like tiny blue crescents of light. She turns to our daughter and whispers, "I knew your mamma and papá were in love. Even before they did."

Emmy points to me, repeating her new favorite word, "Mamma!"

I laugh. "You were right, Nonna," I tell her, even though she already knows she was right. We tell her every time we come back for a visit. "We just hadn't admitted it to ourselves that night. Not for another twenty minutes or so at least," I add, smiling at Si.

"I know. You were too busy up here," she says, tapping her head, "when you should have been busy in here." She moves her finger to tap her heart.

Si chuckles, just as little Grant blows a puff of flour across the counter at his shirt, which is already covered in a thick layer. Silas closes his eyes when the cloud of flour hits his face, and we all laugh.

We've tried coming back to visit almost every year since moving to Milan a few summers ago, but it's been harder since the twins were born a little over a year ago. This is her first time meeting the kids, and they both took to her immediately, just like Silas and I knew they would. It's impossible not to. She immediately approved of our son's name, adding, "I loved him the moment I saw him, too."

I haven't stepped foot in this kitchen since before I found out I was pregnant and it's taking me back to the night Silas and I first arrived in Italy, ending our evening with a decision that would completely change the course of our lives.

I smile to myself, thinking back on the memory which now seems like something out of a dream.

It wasn't until I'd boarded the plane to Paris, alone and angry the next morning, that I'd pulled out the letter from Grant I'd gotten at the hotel the night before. I don't know if I was looking for validation that leaving Silas was the right thing to do, when I had, in fact, found the exact opposite in Grant's words as I began to read.

Now, years later, here I am. I'm watching what he wanted for me — for *us* — playing out in front of me.

I replay the words I've read so many times that I've practically memorized them at this point. Although Grant's letters have been tucked in a box and hidden away in our closet for a few years now, I can almost recite every one of them from memory. His letter from Italy begins playing softly through my mind:

Jules,

My love, you're never going to believe what you're doing next.

Alright, I'll tell you . . .

I'm giving you a break from crash courses in adrenaline by sending you to do something a little more your speed. You and Si (if you haven't parted ways and have managed to make it this far together) are heading to a pasta-making lesson in a tiny little stone house. I have no idea how Monica found this woman, but you're going to love her. Nonna Lisi is her name, and she insisted that she have a call with me before she'd agree to the lesson since she only does a few of these each year for people somehow connected to her.

So, while you were out of the hospital room earlier today, this sweet woman put me on Facetime, right there in her perfect, stone-wall kitchen surrounded in ancient bowls with the coastline shimmering out these huge stone windows behind her. She's perfect, Jules. She's exactly the type of person you might always dream of making pasta with while in Italy. And the second her face lit up my screen, I knew that she was exactly what you'd need in your life right about now.

Why pasta making in Italy, other than it just being utterly awesome and something you mentioned wanting to try? Because Italy is all about a good meal surrounded by family and friends, Jules, and finding the heart of your life in something that lives outside of yourself. When I saw the warmth this woman and her tiny kitchen were exuding, even through a phone screen, I knew I had to send you there.

You've always wanted to have a family. It's one of the things we dreamed about together, and if I'm being honest, it's one of the things I already miss the most without ever having gotten the opportunity to experience it. Leaving the world without a scrap of evidence that I was ever in it may be in the cards for me, but it doesn't have to happen for you, too.

When you're standing in the heart of her home, hopefully with a mess of dough in front of you, I want you to remember something: You deserve to feel love. Whether your future includes kids or not, or maybe it's a hand-selected chosen family made of the people you'd give the world for because, when you're with them, you feel so damn loved and at ease that you always leave their company feeling perfectly whole again.

However you get there, just get there. Fill your life with people and places as warm and loving as the home you'll be standing in.

And please go easy on Si while you're there. He needs the exact same thing you do. You might not know this yet, or maybe he told you while you two were sailing on Vivi *in Spain, but I went to visit him there after his dad passed. It was while you were on that wedding prep weekend with your friends and I flew to see him with the sole purpose of bringing him home. You and I were about to close on our townhouse in Boston to move into together, while he buried his dad and had nothing left to ground him.*

I boarded the boat he didn't know his dad owned or had named after his mother, and I can see why he didn't want to come home. The whole experience of sailing out there was beautiful. All of it. The glowing blue water, the sails billowing, the raw edge of slicing through the sea like butter.

I couldn't believe he had all that and more at his fingertips. I told him he was crazy for risking his future like that, threatening to not come home. But he'd looked right at me and said, "I'd give it all back for a chance to have the shit that matters more. Family that loves you. A future that means something to somebody other than yourself. Someone waiting up for you at the end of the day."

His words hit me square in the gut. It didn't matter that he could have probably bought the whole coastline of properties in Cádiz that day if he wanted without a second thought. What he really wanted was the one thing his money could never buy. A family. Love. In his words, the shit that matters.

I want to give you both this experience at Nonna Lisi's house. You, to remind you of what you have right in front of you, and Si, to remind him that what he's always wanted is right there. Remember that you're exactly what you both need right now: two people that have always felt like home to each other. Don't let a few dumb mistakes in the past make it impossible to feel that way again. Even if it's only for one night spent around a glowing kitchen in an ancient house that somehow feels like you've been there before.

Just take him with you.

Treat him like the family he's always been for you, which I hope you now realize, and maybe you two can find your way back there again someday.

Tell Nonna Lisi I said hello. She promises to remind you that the worst messes can sometimes turn into something worth loving.

And more than anything, sweetheart — thank you, always, for letting me love you,
Grant

Looking around the kitchen now, with all the loves of my life giggling while they play in piles of flour on all sides of me, I can feel his presence here, too.

The very first love of my life.

And I know that he was right. Silas was always meant to be a part of our family, of *my* family. I just needed a little nudge to find my way back to him again.

THE END

ACKNOWLEDGMENTS

When I told my husband the idea behind Silas and Jules' story, I said, "I have to write it, even if no one wants to publish it. It needs to be taken off my chest and put onto a page."

Of course, he responded, "Then write it!" So, I did.

The Best Wild Idea was exactly that before any words were put on paper — just a wild idea that became a labor of love. I plotted Silas and Jules' story and their lives, but ultimately, at some point as I was typing out their most messy layers, the characters themselves began to pave their own way and I fell head over heels in love right along with them.

Each book in my *Off-Limits* series features a woman who is somehow standing in her own way, staring down the face of whatever feels off-limits to her, even if deep down she knows it's what she really wants. Or, even more so, what she deserves.

It's a common feeling for so many of us, I think, so much so that just the act of writing Olivia, Abby, and Jules' stories felt a bit freeing — to write about women brave enough to get out of their own way on their road to happiness. Even if it means making a mess of things as they go and finding themself in the most unlikely places. The experience has been nothing short of cathartic.

Thank you for picking up a book from an author you didn't previously know before my debut series came out. Thank you for coming on this journey with me as I've unleashed my books into the wild — into your hands, and into the hands of anyone who's ever looked for the perfect life in all the wrong places. You, the readers, are why I do what I do! And why I pinch myself that I get to do any of this at all.

Thank you to my friend and editor, Becky Slorach. I won the lottery getting to work with you, and love that we can chat through edits just as easily as the weather. You make everything about this process feel comfortable and limitless. Plus a huge thanks to the entire UK team at Joffe Books and Choc Lit for being the most passionate blend of cheerleaders, genius creators, and industry leaders. You have exceeded every expectation I had while publishing this series, and I can't thank you enough.

To every friend, family member, and fellow author who has talked me off a figurative ledge or celebrated the tiniest wins with a round of oysters, a fizzy bottle of champagne, the most intense charcuterie spread, or just a strong collection of celebratory emojis and messages in all caps: I love you. I love having you in my life, and I know how incredibly lucky I am to have such a strong foundation to support me.

Last but never least, to my husband for showing me how simple it can be to cherish someone throughout a lifetime of wild ideas. You never fail to let me be perfectly imperfect. And I want to thank you, always, for letting me love you.

THE CHOC LIT STORY

Established in 2009, Choc Lit is an independent, award-winning publisher dedicated to creating a delicious selection of quality women's fiction.

We have won 18 awards, including Publisher of the Year and the Romantic Novel of the Year, and have been shortlisted for countless others. In 2023, we were shortlisted for Publisher of the Year by the Romantic Novelists' Association.

All our novels are selected by genuine readers. We are proud to publish talented first-time authors, as well as established writers whose books we love introducing to a new generation of readers.

In 2023, we became a Joffe Books company. Best known for publishing a wide range of commercial fiction, Joffe Books has its roots in women's fiction. Today it is one of the largest independent publishers in the UK.

We love to hear from you, so please email us about absolutely anything bookish at choc-lit@joffebooks.com.

If you want to receive free books every Friday and hear about all our new releases, join our mailing list here: www.joffebooks.com/freebooks.

www.ingramcontent.com/pod-product-compliance
Lightning Source LLC
Chambersburg PA
CBHW011351290925
33306CB00021B/1079